THE WIDOW OF DARTMOOR

by

Warwick Downing

Paperback ISBN 978-1-78092-601-8
ePub ISBN 978-1-78092-602-5
PDF ISBN 978-1-78092-603-2

Use of the Sherlock Holmes characters created by Sir Arthur Conan Doyle by permission of Conan Doyle Estate Ltd.,
www.conandoyleestate.co.uk

Published in the UK by MX Publishing
335 Princess Park Manor, Royal Drive, London, N11 3GX. United Kingdon
www.mxpublishing.com

Cover by www.staunch.com

2

To Shirley, whose smile can light up a dark room

To Steve Cribari, with the soul and

uncompromising honesty of a poet

And to an odd group of fellows in the Colonies

called

Dr. Watson's Neglected Patients

Chapter 1

Allow me, if it please you. I am Edward Greech, solicitor, getting along in life--but unlike other aging fellows, with no desire to write my memoirs. They would be dull indeed. Yet I would tell you of the legal adventures of one whose memoirs would be far from dull. He was a barrister, who called himself Jeremy Holmes. It was widely assumed that his uncle was Sherlock Holmes, the famous--some would say, notorious--consulting detective.

Jeremy's gifts were not those of his uncle, however. He could not absorb the scene of a crime in all its detail in a glance, or read the story of one's life from his appearance. Yet his talents admirably suited him for what he was. When he examined a witness at the Old Bailey, his questions pierced the hide, as do spears. If the fellow wore a mask, Jeremy would peel it off his face. Should he falsify the truth, Jeremy would use the fellow's words to reveal the falsehood. It was as though the witness was being examined by God.

As did Sherlock, Jeremy hungered for justice. But where Sherlock perceived an evil puppeteer, a Moriarty if you will, pulling the strings of puppets that slashed and burned a wide swathe of misery through an otherwise well-order British society, Jeremy had a different view of the matter. He saw that well-ordered British society as the villain. Was it not the soil out of which had grown those institutions that allowed the evil puppeteers to flourish? And what of the grandest institution of all: the common law?

Virtually all of those in our profession--and I include myself--saw the common law as a bastion of freedom. It was a fortress that checked the arbitrary exercise of power, built from the bodies of the heroes who had fallen while tearing those rights of freedom from tyrants who would not give them up. Yet Jeremy regarded the common law as a "glorious cesspool." He fancied it had the foul odor of human excrement, that it was a depository of human waste. Adept at wielding it as a sword to arrive at his vision of justice, he had contempt for those who used it as a fortress to protect the institutions he loathed. He wept at the cruel infliction of punishments, and raged at the power of the righteous, to oppress.

Jeremy had experienced the power of the righteous to oppress. He was a bastard, defined in law at the time of which I write as the product of the illicit lust of a lewd mother. As a bastard, he had no right to the surname of his father, or right of inheritance. Perhaps because of the stigma that the law had fixed upon him, he battled such institutionalized righteousness with the devotion of Cyrano de Bergerac, who had dueled against the hypocrisies of his day. And though many of the barristers treated Jeremy as they would a leper, he was revered by those with a true knowledge of his worth: the criminals of London.

It is of Jeremy Holmes and his battles in the courtrooms of England that I would write.

#

The turnkey at the quadrangle for women, Newgate, led me down a dark passage. We were in the ward maintained by the gaolers for the titled and the wealthy. 'I am Caroline, Mr Greech,' the massive woman said, 'after our Queen of the big bosoms, God rest her soul. Lady Russell sent for you, sir.'

'Lady Russell sent for me?' I asked. 'By name?'

'No sir,' she said, stopping in front of a door. 'She asked for The Bastard. 'Twas me as sent for you, knowing as I do that you would bring to 'im her brief.' Opening the door with a key, she motioned me in. 'Please wait here, sir.' She left the room, closing the door behind her and locking it.

The small space was furnished with a table, two chairs, and a bench with leg-irons bolted to its posts. In spite of its tortured cast, the crudely-furnished room was well-lighted by gas lamps on opposite walls. Sitting at the table, I sweetened my breath with Irish whisky and tried not to breathe the rancid air. Though the wards for the prisoners who could afford them were luxuriously appointed, the stench from the tap room was quite enough to destroy the illusion of gentle living they might otherwise entertain.

I reflected on the turnkey's remark. Solicitors were not known by the barristers to whom they would bring their briefs. Yet I brought mine to Jeremy Holmes with such regularity that I was known to the gaolers of London as the solicitor who carried the brief for The Bastard. It was a badge I had come to appreciate. It earned me their respect, and I shamelessly warmed myself in its glow. It mattered not that I had done nothing to deserve it. I was a man of means, but had not lifted a finger to earn the fortune off of which I lived. Ancestors of mine had amassed it in the slave trade, and I lived quite comfortably on the income from a trust fund. Capping my flask--emblazoned with the Greech coat of arms--I returned it to its nest in my coat.

When the door opened, I struggled quickly to my feet, quite taken by the woman whom Caroline of the big bosoms brought in. 'Please take the proper care of me mistress, Sir Edward,' Caroline said, promoting me to knighthood. 'I be in the 'all, Lady Russell, should you require me.'

I had been prepared by the *Times* for a woman of beauty, yet I was staggered by her comeliness. Perhaps thirty years of age, she radiated the allure of her sex. The hair that covered her shoulders was of a vibrant blackness that glistened blue. It electrified the room. The complexion of her neck and face breathed with the luxury of life. The thought of that soft, firm loveliness blackened and broken by the hangman's noose was quite shattering.

Yet the Crown had charged her with murder, and all of London thought her execution inevitable. According to the charge, on the 28 September, 1891--not yet two days ago-- "Lady Beryl Russell did murder Christian Vandeleur, a person in being under the Queen's peace."

Sitting across from me, she seemed as serenely composed as a statue at Trafalgar Square. 'Are you The Bastard, sir?' she asked, in a wonderfully melodic voice. Her dark eyes searched my countenance for signs of brilliance. Finding none, they were dimmed with a quiet despair.

'I am not, Lady Russell,' I said. 'I am Edward Greech, a solicitor. Mr Holmes is a barrister. He can not engage in the business of taking a brief, although I as a solicitor can do so. As a barrister--assuming I take the brief to him, and he accepts the cause--he would appear in court, on your behalf. Barristers alone are heard in Her Majesty's courts.'

'Would you give him the brief?'

'It would be improper for me to promise you that I will do so. But let me assure you that there is little likelihood I would take it to another.'

The light returned to her eyes. 'He is the nephew of Sherlock Holmes, is he not?'

'So it is said. However, that relationship is one that neither Mr Holmes, nor Dr Watson, has acknowledged.'

'I am not a wealthy woman, Mr Greech, even though I have done rather well as a dress-maker. Yet my situation is desperate.' She smiled at that, as though perhaps her desperate situation would amuse me. 'I am willing to pay whatever is asked, to hire The Bastard.'

She made no mention of Peter, Lord Russell, her husband and a man of great wealth. Would not he pay for her defence? Or had the circumstances of the crime estranged them? It mattered little to me. Her modest assertion that she had 'done rather well as a dress-maker' was an understatement. Her *boutique* on Marylebone Lane was the envy of the industry. It drew ladies of fashion away from the finest stores on Oxford Street.

There was a reason for her success. Before her marriage to the dashing Peter, Lord Russell, she had been married to Jack Stapleton, a scoundrel known to all of London. He owed his notoriety to the gripping account, by Dr John Watson, of *The Hound of the Baskervilles*. When the *Times* revealed that *Fashions Sabor Brazilenos* was owned by the woman whom Sherlock Holmes revealed to be the wife of Stapleton, she was dubbed by the paper as The Widow of Dartmoor. In an odd twist of fate, her *boutique* was rescued from obscurity--and once discovered by the women of London, it became a place of rare fashion. 'Lady Russell,' I replied, 'although The Bastard is not opposed to compensation, he is not moved by the size of the fee. He is not for hire.'

With the suddenness of a candle snuffed out in a dark room, the light vanished from her being. With her head down and her shoulders drawn in, she collapsed onto the table, her body shaking with an unquenchable terror. 'Forgive me, Mr Greech,' she managed, a few moments later. 'I am terrified by the prospect of the gallows. Will he not help me?'

Although I should like to have comforted her, I could not. The report in the *Times* of the crime would hardly permit anything other than her execution. She had been caught dragging the body of Professor Christian Vandeleur into the alleyway behind her establishment, at two o'clock in the morning. He had been stabbed in the neck with a cutting shears, and the crime was done in one of the fitting rooms. According to the *Times*, Professor Vandeleur had been an instructor in the natural sciences at a college for women in East Sussex. But he and Lady Russell had been seen at lunch in intimate conversation, and the paper suggested they were lovers. Lady Russell's statement to Scotland Yard had not helped her cause. She claimed, to her astonishment, to have found the man in a back room of her business, bleeding to death from the stab-wound in his neck. To avoid embarrassment to her husband, she determined to cover the matter up! Her intention had been to load the body into her carriage and leave it on the grounds of the Toxopholite Society at Regent's Park, in the belief that when found, it would appear that Professor Vandeleur had been struck in the throat by a wayward arrow!

'Lady Russell,' I said, 'Mr Holmes cannot be manipulated by tears. If they are the basis of your appeal for his help, I would suggest that you allow me to take the brief to another barrister.'

'I have not the ability to turn my tears on and off, Mr Greech. They come without my bidding. I appeal to him because I am innocent, and need his help.'

She spoke with conviction. But I found her words most difficult to believe. 'I shall give him your message,' I said.

She looked at me through eyes that had no room in them for artifice. They were filled with terror. One could imagine those lustrous eyes staring in horror at the cold approach of death.

Chapter 2

The Bastriche Club, where I met Jeremy that evening, was as exclusive as any club in London. But it differed from most, in that it did not pretend to pursue some laudable purpose. Rather it spoofed the pretensions of other clubs. Membership was restricted to men who were either actual bastards, as was Jeremy, or honorary bastards, as was I. Of rituals, we had none, and our "laudable purpose"--emblazoned on our coat of arms--was to provide "A Sanctuary for Bastards."

The comfortable stone-walled building was north of Fleet Street, between the Old Bailey and the Royal Courts of Justice. It was a short walk to both of the above, as well as to all of the Inns of Court. Jeremy had a small flat on an upper floor. My rooms were two stories below his, above the hall.

Jeremy was seated in the smoke room above the hall, near a window that looked down on a small green square below. There was a sketch-pad on his knee. He was so keenly involved in his drawings that his body seemed actually to hum with the intensity of his concentration. 'Old sot,' he said, on my approach.

It had been remarkably clear during the day. Though there was light enough to see, the sun had settled below the horizon. 'Can you draw in this dimness?' I asked, standing behind him and looking at his work.

'Oh yes,' he said, as though he could not possibly want more. 'Even in London, the light can caress with wonder. It is as though the City is touched with the breath of the Great Spirit.'

I had become accustomed to his nonsense--or so I characterized many of his observations, then. But I was not accustomed to the magic of his work. It astonished me.

Small scenes were scattered around the edges of his pad. They were of those who lounged below us, in the green. One of them depicted the approach of a stout gentleman with a cane, who stalked--or was stalked by--a girl of questionable virtue. Two unkempt women haggled near a fruit vendor's wagon in another scene, and a gang of urchins leaned against a wall in a third one. Jeremy worked rapidly--eagerly--over the center-piece: a portrait of one of the urchins. With his cap at a careless angle, and with hard, brittle eyes that were not evenly placed along the sides of his nose, his thin mouth slanted in a line from cheek bone to jaw.

'Brutal looking fellow,' I said, as I compared the drawing with the model, below. The sketch suggested the force of an inner ugliness in him that I had not seen, without the drawing.

'How old is he, would you say?' Jeremy asked.

'Not yet twenty,' I ventured.

'His left eye is sightless, and the fellow is consumed with hate. He derives pleasure through the infliction of pain.' He put his pencil down. 'A pity. He has an original mind, and is possessed of a rare, single-minded focus.' Jeremy's expressive eyes softened as he spoke of the young brute. 'Destined for the gallows. Or great wealth.'

Allow me to indulge in what can only be regarded as a monument to effrontery. I would compare myself to Dr Watson, and Jeremy to Sherlock Holmes. No one--certainly not I--will ever write with the clarity of Dr Watson, or better portray the genius of one such as Sherlock Holmes. But I stood in the same relation to Jeremy, as did Watson to Sherlock. And I was as awed by the brilliance of the barrister, as was Watson by the genius of the master detective.

But where Watson attributed the genius of Sherlock to

11

what some would call an unyielding, even a terrifying sanity, I was not able to regard the genius of Jeremy as the product of a sane mind. I confess that in the early days of our association, I considered my young friend mad. Sherlock could articulate his conclusions, and show precisely how he reached them, step by step. But Jeremy rarely bothered with an explanation, and when he saw fit to provide one, as often as not, it made no sense.

I could not refrain from casting aspersions on the conclusions Jeremy had articulated, after sketching the young brute below. 'Jeremy, you can not *know* that the young animal down there gets a boost of some sort by hurting others. Nor can you *know* that he has an original mind, and single-minded focus. Admit to me that you *assume* he has those characteristics.'

'Forgive my conceit then, but I will admit to you no such thing. I assume nothing, regarding his characteristics. When I do a sketch--not in all cases, but in this one--I become the subject I draw. His pulse beats within me, and I feel his hates and fears. It is all here, Edward.' He pointed at his work. 'Surely you see it, too.'

'I only see the portrait of a boy who repels, yet fascinates me.'

'Perhaps you should learn to paint then.' He put the pad away. 'It might help you to see the obvious. What brings you here?'

Jeremy bore a striking resemblance to Sherlock, though no one of decency would remark on it. One might easily believe that their jaw lines, their deep-set eyes, and their prominent foreheads had been cast from the same mold. Their complexions were made from different mixtures, however, and their hair came from opposite poles. Sherlock was the darker of the two, and his straight hair was black as ink. Jeremy had been browned by the sun, but was fair-skinned, and the mound of wavy hair--which he must hide under his barrister wig--was golden, as was the sun. And though Jeremy was not as tall or thin as his uncle, his presence was as arresting. Broad, muscled shoulders swayed with masculine grace above his thin waist, and he had the torso of an acrobat.

Yet where Sherlock's countenance reflected boredom on those occasions when he was without a crime to occupy his mind, the expression worn by Jeremy was always curious. He seemed perpetually in awe of his surroundings.

I opened my leather case and pulled out a file. 'I have a brief for you.'

'Give it to another,' he said. 'I have too many.'

'You will want to see this one, I think. I've been to see Lady Beryl Russell.'

He frowned. 'The Widow of Dartmoor?'

'She asked for The Bastard.'

'What have you then?'

'A report on Professor Christian Vandeleur, the victim. The statement of Lady Russell to Inspector Lestrade of Scotland Yard. The statement of Constable Firstson, the bobby who caught her dragging Vandeleur's body into the alleyway. And a report of which the press knows nothing. Shortly after the marriage of The Widow to Lord Russell, both the victim and Lady Russell were followed by detectives. The report shows quite conclusively that they met on several occasions before the murder.'

'Lord Russell had them followed?'

'So it would seem. It is rumoured that he suspected them of being lovers.'

When Jeremy opened the brief, it was as though his

eyes would swallow it. His eyes transformed the type-written pages into scenes, or so he would have me believe. Though I thought his comment to be more of his nonsense, I marvelled at his powers of concentration. An earthquake would not have shaken him.

Rather than read words arranged into sentences, he claimed he could see the pictures that they painted. Some pages were absorbed at a glance, as are photographs, printed in a magazine. He understood the words and paragraphs on those pages as quickly as he could turn them. Others were as paintings in a museum, requiring thought to comprehend. Uncapping my flask, I wondered at the images that the dry reports of Scotland Yard would generate in his mind.

The report on Professor Vandeleur described the victim as an entomologist who had published a paper in 1887 with the British Museum, on the moths of Yorkshire. One such moth had born his name. In April of 1891--the year of which I write--an article of his had appeared in *New Review*, a magazine devoted to the natural sciences. It had documented the evolutionary changes of a species of African moth and, though not without detractors, the article had excited many in the scientific community. It supported the rather fanciful work of Charles Darwin on the evolution of monkeys into men.

Most recently, Professor Vandeleur had been engaged at Queenland College for Women in Essex, as a visiting lecturer from South African College, in Cape Town, South Africa. The headmistress at Queenland had viewed his body and had positively identified the deceased as Christian Vandeleur.

The statement of Lady Russell to Inspector Lestrade expanded on the newspaper accounts, subtracting therefrom the innuendo. She identified herself as Lady Beryl Russell, married on 6 July of the present year to Peter, Lord Russell. He had allowed her to continue as the owner and operator of *Fashions Sabor Brazilenos*, on Marylebone Lane in London. She had become attached to her employees, and for many of them, was their sole support.

It was her habit to personally close the business in the evening, attending to details that she alone must deal with. Usually such matters took the better part of an hour, after which her chauffeur would take her to her home in Kensington. But that night she would stay in the rooms above the *boutique*, to prepare for a fashion show in Paris she was scheduled to attend. She would travel to Paris the next day. Her chauffeur had stabled the carriage at the Portland Hotel with instructions to come for her at seven, the following morning.

To her surprise, at shortly after seven o'clock that evening, Professor Vandeleur appeared in her office. The doors were locked, and she had not let him in. She begged him to leave, which he refused to do. He attempted to take her into his arms. His unwelcome advances were interrupted by a knock on the front door, the familiar rap of her husband. Vandeleur released her and she hurried to the door, imploring Vandeleur to leave through the back exit.

Her husband stepped inside, wished her well on her venture to Paris, and informed her that he would stay at his club in London until her return. Should she wire him, would she be so kind as to send it to the club? Then he embraced her and took his leave.

Believing Vandeleur had gone, she returned to her office to compose herself--when she heard a noise in the fitting room. Fearfully, she approached the door, which was slightly ajar.

She heard a gurgling sound. Upon entering the room, she found Vandeleur on the floor, his hands gripping his throat as blood gorged from his neck.

Horrified, she went to his assistance. Finding strips of cloth on a work-table, she wrapped one around his neck in a desperate attempt to stem the flow of blood. While so engaged, a pair of cutting shears clattered on the floor beside her, and the back door to the room slammed shut. She caught the briefest glimpse of a figure wearing a dark cape, who she assumed was a man.

When Professor Vandeleur expired, his head was in her lap. She willingly admitted that she was shaken by his death. It saddened her.

But not for long. How would the matter appear to her husband, whom she had only recently married? Or to a public that thrived on scandal? Terrified, she knew not what to do. To complicate matters in her mind, it was her husband who had introduced her to the professor. He had thought highly of the man. What conclusions would he draw from the situation that presented itself now?

Better, she decided in a moment of dreadful weakness, that the entire incident be concealed.

In her rooms above the *boutique* she found a blanket, which she brought down to the fitting room. She rolled the body onto it, wrapping it up and dragging it out of the way. Thus able to concentrate on her task, she thoroughly cleaned the room, and herself.

At some point during her grisly mop-up, it occurred to her that there was a society of archers, the Toxopholite Society, with grounds at the south end of Regent's Park. She knew of it because Lord Russell belonged to the society, and excelled in the sport. The grounds were but a short distance from Marylebone Lane. If the body were found there, might not the authorities believe a terrible accident had occurred?

She waited until two in the morning, then pulled the body of the poor professor into the alleyway behind her business. He was wrapped in the blanket, which had been secured with strips of cloth. Her ill-considered plan was to fetch her carriage from its near-by stable at the Portland Hotel, put the body inside, then drive to Regent's Park and drop it near the grounds of the Toxopholite Society. After which she would return the carriage to the stable, return to her apartment at *Fashions Sabor Brazilenos*, then go to Paris as though nothing had happened.

It was not a well-conceived plan, she readily admitted, for she would have had to steal her carriage from the stable at the hotel, drive it to the alleyway, then lift the body of Vandeleur into the carriage without help. Constable Firstson saved her from her own madness. On that note, she concluded her statement.

Thoughtfully, Jeremy turned to the statement of Constable Manfred Firstson, of the Metropolitan Police.

Firstson had seen the glow from a light in *Fashions Sabor Brazilenos* in the early morning hours, which roused his suspicions. He thought perhaps that if he waited in the alleyway behind, he would surprise a burglar emerging from the rear door. Thus, he was in a position to watch Lady Russell pull her burden through the doorway of her *boutique*, and onto the bricked alleyway.

He did not know what she was dragging, until the wrapping at the back end of the longish object opened up. The booted foot of a man was exposed, and he knew she dragged the body of a man. Following the protocols of his office, he detained Lady Russell, secured the location, and summoned a team of inspectors from Scotland Yard. He remained at the scene of the crime, and was there when Lady Russell was taken for questioning to the Yard.

The final report summarized the diaries of two detectives, one who had followed Lady Russell and the other Professor Vandeleur. Their assignment had been to ascertain if they were lovers. Of the Fleet Street Detective Agency, the detectives were not named. Neither was the principal who had requested the investigation.

Lady Russell and Professor Vandeleur had met for lunch in August and September, though the locations were not released. On two occasions, both in the evening after the store was closed, they had met at *Fashions Sabor Brazilenos*. Alone. The last such occasion was the evening before the crime.

Closing the file, Jeremy stared out the window. 'What is your impression of Lady Russell?' he asked me.

'Most striking, even after her ordeal,' I said. 'She would make an excellent witness. You will be challenged by her beauty, if you do her portrait.'

'She does not justify the crime. Rather, she claims innocence. Do you believe her?'

'Of course not,' I said. 'Clearly terrified, she will say anything. She would have the Yard believe that Vandeleur was an insolent intruder, but it is perfectly obvious that he was her lover. Perhaps the fellow threatened to expose her.'

'What of him?' Jeremy asked.

'A man of science, I am told. As susceptible to lust as a sailor, though from all accounts, he was possessed of a remarkably brilliant and original mind.'

'What would you have me do?'

'Take the brief, by all means,' I said. 'Perhaps you can portray Vandeleur as a mad scientist, and Lady Russell as his victim. I should say you have more than enough of the fare of a story-teller, to build a suitable defence.'

18

Chapter 3

At ten the following day, Caroline of the big bosoms admitted Jeremy and me into the cage at Newgate where one conducts interviews with prisoners. Though the stench from the tap-room had soaked into the stone walls, Lady Russell seemed impervious to it. She was seated in a chair, exuding the wonder of her person. After greetings were exchanged and Caroline had taken her post outside, I explained to Lady Russell the purpose of our visit. 'Mr Holmes has read the brief and is aware of your need for a barrister, but is not altogether certain he is the right man for you. He wished to see you, the better to assess his concern. Do you mind terribly?'

Jeremy had taken a chair in a corner of the small room with a note-pad on his knee. He was quite taken by her dark loveliness, it seemed to me. Without watching the pad, his right hand stroked the paper, as though caressing it.

'Indeed,' Lady Russell said to Jeremy. Though her mood was despairing, she forced a smile. 'I had not thought that obtaining the services of a barrister would require an interview.'

'Forgive me, Lady Russell,' Jeremy said. That odd electricity he generated on occasion was enough to start a fire, and she was warmed by it. 'You have proclaimed your innocense, and in this particular case, I believe that to be a circumstance of great weight. Quite frankly, I would form my own impression as to your intention.'

'"Intention"?' she asked. 'What an odd choice of words.'

'Perhaps "veracity" would be more to the point,' he said.

'Is that something you can do in a gaol room?'

He glanced at the emerging picture of her, then nodded,

as he continued to draw her likeness. 'Let me assure you that, upon being in your presence, any hesitation I might have had has vanished. I would welcome the opportunity to represent you.'

Quite becomingly, she blushed. 'Thank you, Mr Holmes.' But her eyes looked down. 'Unfortunately, I find that I am no longer seeking your services.' Her smile as she spoke was not from her heart. Rather, it was the reluctant expression of one compelled by the laws of her class to do her duty. 'My husband, Lord Russell, has retained a barrister for me.' She shrugged. 'As the lord of the manor, I have no choice but to do his bidding.'

'Dear me,' I said, and began the struggle I engage in to stand.

'What is the name of your barrister?' Jeremy asked. 'Perhaps I know him.'

'Sir Percival Jersey.'

Jeremy motioned at me with his head, signaling me to resume my chair. Then nodding at her, he changed pencils. 'Sir Percival does not frequent the Old Bailey, though he is highly regarded at the Royal Courts of Justice. Perhaps he can be persuaded to associate me in your cause.'

The pursuit of the matter by Jeremy was highly improper, and I was appalled by it. Our proper course, upon learning of her representation by another, was to leave immediately. My expression conveyed my sentiments to Jeremy more clearly than words. 'Old fellow,' he said to me, 'it seems you have some misgivings about our remaining with Lady Russell.'

'I do indeed,' I said. 'I should not like either of us to be barred from the Inns of Court.'

The door opened abruptly. 'What is the meaning of

this?' said a large silver-haired man with the florid face of one who enjoyed rich sauces.

Jeremy shrugged his shoulders at me. 'How do, Sir Percival,' he said, rising and extending his hand. 'We had not known Lord Russell had engaged you, Sir, until a moment ago.' His hand was ignored. 'We are here because Lady Russell had sent for me.'

'She shall not have a bastard in her corner, Mr Holmes. Lord Russell would never allow it.'

Jeremy responded with a remarkable calm. 'Sir Percival,' he said, in the mildest of tones, 'I had believed your family had more charity in their hearts than you display at this moment.' The tone belied the volcano I knew boiled within him. 'Allow me to finish, Sir.'

The renowned civil litigator had opened his mouth, as though to interrupt, but Jeremy could be quite intimidating. His mild voice resonated with power, and a raised hand evidenced a willingness to engage.

'Let me suggest, Sir, that I might be of assistance to you at the Old Bailey,' Jeremy continued. 'It is not your court of choice, as it is mine. Lord Russell's sense of propriety is admirable perhaps, but permit me to suggest that Lady Russell's neck is more important than maintaining a socially acceptable sense of appearance.'

The florid face of Sir Percival drained of color. 'Please remove yourself from my presence and the presence of my client,' he said, with great civility. 'Do not, under any circumstances, engage in conversation with her again.'

Slowly and carefully, Jeremy picked up his writing pad, then reached for Lady Russell's hand. Taking it, he raised it to his lips. 'Lady Russell,' he said, 'my very best wishes. Edward?'

I nodded at Lady Russell, but could not look at Sir

Percival Jersey, Q C. 'Sir Percival,' I managed, brushing past him.

'Mr 'Olmes,' the massive turnkey remarked as she led us down the dark hallway, 'you are not the bastard here sir, beggin' yer pardon.' Embarrassed by her own boldness, she stopped.

Smiling at her, Jeremy touched her arm. 'Most kind of you,' he said.

Upon reaching the heavy metal door that would let us out of the women's quadrangle, she opened it with a large key. 'Mr Greech,' she said to me, 'another time?'

'I beg your pardon,' I replied, surprised and incensed by her effrontery. Surely she knew that I, as a solicitor, would not associate with gaolers.

It was but a short distance from Newgate to the Bastriche Club. Jeremy breathed deeply as we walked, no doubt discharging the volcanic rage that seethed inside him-- when his eyes seemed to catch on a cloud. He watched it with absorbing interest. 'See how it changes its shape, Edward,' he said. 'From lobster, it is transformed into scorpion.' It was as though he had become enveloped in a sense of gratitude. 'Of course, it is neither. The cloud owes its shape to the forces of nature, to which I bring my imagination. Rather wondrous, wouldn't you say, old fellow?'

'"Wondrous"?' I asked, ever the cynic. 'Ordinary, I would say. What do you suppose the turnkey meant at the last, Jeremy?' I did not grace my reference to Caroline of the big bosoms, with her name. 'When she spoke to me with such uncalled-for familiarity?'

'"Mr Greech, another time?"' It was a perfect imitation of her pattern of speech, and her manner. 'She has a message for you.'

Of course. I should have known that she wanted only to tell me something. I did not ask Jeremy how he came to his understanding of what the woman meant. His explanation would no doubt have subjected me to more of his nonsense.

Inside the club, we found our corner in the smoke room where Jeremy set up his stand, then propped a sketch pad on it. The writing pad on which he had drawn the broad outlines of the facial features of Lady Russell rested on a table, for reference. He began to draw. 'She'll hang, of course,' he said as though her execution was a foregone conclusion. 'But not until Sir Percival, in the finest tradition of British justice, has pleaded for mercy. He will attend her hanging too, ever mindful of his duty. Then with impeccable loyalty, will remain with her to the end, and provide a suitable escort for her remains. And for his service, he shall be paid an enormous fee.' His voice vibrated with raw intensity, as the pencil in his hand brushed back and forth across the paper. 'A rare woman, Edward,' he said. 'What a hideous waste.'

I would have none of it. 'A waste?' I asked. 'She is a murderess. What of Professor Vandeleur, the man she stabbed? A man of remarkable scientific ability, by all accounts. Was he a waste?'

'She stabbed no one,' Jeremy said, leaving no room for doubt.

'Dear fellow. Are you mad?'

He shrugged. 'Perhaps. But my madness does not prevent me from seeing what is there to see, for I have drawn her.'

I refrained from the sarcasms that wanted to rain on his pronouncement. From the facts gathered by Scotland Yard, one could reach but one conclusion. Yet, even though Jeremy was a barrister and acquainted with the laws of logic, he was not persuaded by reason. He had told me that his search for truth was through his art! To draw an object was to absorb it; to know it in the way of those ancient hunters who painted vivid images of their prey on the walls of caves. In the act of drawing the creatures, he had said to me in all seriousness, the hunters became the animals they hunted. Thus, they knew where to find them!

What nonsense, I had thought at the time. Jeremy knew nothing of those ancient paintings. He did not even know whether the cave painters were hunters. I told no one of his delusions as to his art, because of his genius as a barrister. Yet I confess that his madness had disturbed me. 'Surely you do not believe her,' I said.

'Old fellow, your tone is that of a teacher who cannot believe the idiocy of his pupil.'

'Jeremy, how can you possibly believe that Lady Russell told Inspector Lestrade the truth? She is a wonderfully imaginative woman, I will grant you that. Not many of her sex would have the brazen impudence to dream up that Toxopholite Society business.'

'Quite a lovely touch. I agree with you.'

'But dear fellow, her mind refuses to stay within the bounds of reality! How could anyone--other than you, perhaps--persuade themselves that the police would mistake a stab wound from cutting shears with the piercing of an arrow?'

'The mind is a wondrous thing,' he said.

'Professor Vandeleur was her lover, Jeremy. Surely you at least you will acknowledge that much. The passionate nature of women will often overflow the banks. Is that aspect of her character in your drawing?'

He carefully inspected his picture. 'She has secrets,' he said, 'but that is not one of them.'

'"Secrets"?' I asked. 'What are they then? Surely you know them through your art.'

'No, old fellow,' he said, unruffled by my scorn. 'I know only that her secrets are enough to justify the wearing of a mask. Of many masks. But infidelity is not something she could ever have allowed of herself. And it would have been quite impossible for her to murder.'

'You cannot *know* that, Jeremy,' I said. 'Is there something blazoned on her forehead that says, "I am innocent"?'

'There is not,' he said, then showed me his drawing. 'There are no words written on her face, or on her heart. But it is there to see, for anyone whose eyes are not ruled by the obvious.' I stared at the drawing. 'She has never intentionally killed a living thing in her life, Edward. She is not capable of it, even to defend herself.'

How had he drawn her with such perfection? It did not seem possible to me that pencils on paper could portray the soul of a woman, through a sketch. But I fancied that I could see a soul of incredible loveliness, though it peered at me through many veils. The vision of her was made even more appealing to my male sensibility by the rays of terror that stabbed outward at me, from her eyes.

Yet I saw nothing that changed my mind. A magnificent woman indeed, but only a woman. 'What do you see, Jeremy?' I asked.

'Beauty. Purity. Innocense,' Jeremy said. 'A woman who has not allowed herself to be twisted and molded into something unlovely, by the pretensions of life.' Once again, I could hear his body hum with rage. It frightened me. 'A Joan of Arc, whose goodness the righteous cannot accept. A sacrifice, to that rigid sense of righteousness.'

Chapter 4

When Jeremy was proposed for membership in the Bastriche Club, there was no dissent. His qualifications were impeccable. Though the man who sired him had not been publicly identified, Jeremy was known to be a well-born bastard. In a month after his admission into the club, he resided there.

His habits were singular, but no more so than many of the members. He drank little, went on long walks, and would sketch for hours at a time. Though he frequented the kitchen, he rarely attended meals. It was as though he preferred the company of the staff to his fellow Bastriches.

Even his flat set him apart. Known as the Monk's Room, the small space occupied its own little corner of the building, almost as an after-thought. To reach it, one must climb a narrow and twisted stairway. It was difficult to bring even a trunk up the stairs, into the room. The bed was a pallet on the floor, which was quite enough for Jeremy, who wanted the room for its view. From it, he could see the Thames, and London Bridge.

I first made his acquaintance one summer afternoon at the Old Bailey. Of Lincoln's Inn, Jeremy had recently been called to the bar. That day, he sat at the pew for barristers with a sketch-pad on his knee. Glancing in my direction, he recognized me as a Bastriche, and nodded. I regarded the gesture as an invitation to take him by the arm, at the close of proceedings for the day.

He accepted my familiarity with good grace, and agreed to go to the King's Tavern. The pint he ordered was little consumed. 'Are you drawn to the dark side of the law, Mr Holmes?' I asked him.

'I am.'

'Perhaps I can bring you a brief then.'

There was little chance of that, but it wakened his interest. In the hope of exchanging histories, I told him of the Greech coat of arms, and that I was descended of slave traders. That, together with my propensity for Irish whiskey, had gained my membership in the club as an honorary bastard. I offered as well that I had mentored with a barrister, but had not been called to the bar, for which I suffered relief, rather than disappointment. 'As a solicitor, I have all that I require out of life. '

'What is it that you require, Mr Greech?' he had asked.

'The appearance of respectability,' I replied. 'Nothing more.'

His response to my maneuvre was unexpected. It did not draw him out, as I had hoped it would. 'May I draw you, Mr Greech?' he asked. And that was when I first heard his body hum.

It startled me. Can one's body actually hum? He appeared in the dim light to be relaxed, not afire with the intensity one must certainly experience for such a phenomenon to occur. I reminded myself that I was a solicitor, trained in the reality of the law, and not subject to the illusions which were visited upon the uneducated. 'You would draw my picture?' I asked.

'I would.'

I had no objection. There was a sketch-pad in his brief-case, which he lifted out. With a pencil in on hand, and the leather case for support, he rested them on his knee and seemed actually to embrace me with his expression. Sitting across from him in our dark booth, with one lamp from an overhead chandelier servicing the entire pub, I held myself still.

'No need to pose, sir,' he said. 'May I assume you have an interest in my heritage?'

A blunt question indeed, I thought. 'Why do you ask me that?'

'Ah. That is better.' He smiled, continuing with his sketch. 'An impression I formed, when you told me of yours,' he said, exposing my maneuvre with the same bluntness.

'You are something of a mystery, Mr Holmes,' I said. 'I confess I should like to know more about you.'

'What have you heard, Mr Greech?'

What a charming fellow, I thought. 'That you are a bastard, sir.'

He nodded, and smiled. 'I am indeed. Is that all?'

'There are those in the club who believe your mother is of the house of Wendelton, and it is rumoured that your uncle is Sherlock Holmes.'

'You would have me confirm the gossip? Or correct it?' he asked, watching me with great interest, his hand rapidly moving over the pad.

'I would have you . . .' No. I stood up, pulled out my flask, and uncapped it. 'To your health, sir. I am done with you.'

'Please stay, Mr Greech,' he said. 'And I would ask you to overlook my rudeness. I see you now.'

What a curious man, I thought. Had he provoked me to bring blood into my face? My hesitation was my downfall.

'We will work well together, Mr Greech,' he said. 'You shall provide me with cases to try, and I will do wonders with them.' He smiled at me with impudence. 'Sit? Allow me to tell you what I know of myself, which is precious little.' I sat down. 'But I must have your word that you will speak to no one of what I would tell you, without my permission.'

'If that is your wish.'

Do I now break my word to him? He has yet to give me his permission. But how can I tell of him otherwise? And his story must be told.

His birth mother, of whom he had little memory, was indeed of the house of Wendleton. 'Her name was Cecilia, and she was fifteen years old when I was conceived.' As he spoke, his eyes continued to probe me, and the pencil in his hand to dance. 'Her father, the Duke of Wendleton, took her to America where I was born. I first saw the light of day in a Western territory during their War between the States. And, though my mother was fond of me I have been told, I was a source of embarrassment to the Duke. As a consequence, I was to remain in America and my mother would go back to England with him, free of her burden, and wiser.' The intensity of his gaze momentarily touched my shoulder, jolting it. 'He would have her re-claim her life, but she died unexpectedly on the voyage to her home.'

'Who brought you up then? Her father, the Duke?'

'I had been given over to an Indian woman, who brought me up as a Cheyenne Indian.' I could not keep from registering my surprise. 'Ah!' he said, as though I had done him a kindness. 'Her name is Rose Thorn,' he continued, 'a name of her own choosing, which is not uncommon there. They have little in the way of records, and take whatever name suits them. She still lives in America, though no longer as a member of her tribe. She is the wife of a lawyer.'

'Is that how you were drawn to law?'

'I knew nothing of law until coming to England at the age of thirteen.' He was done with his sketch and closed up his pad. 'You are a good man, Mr Greech. Shall we go?'

'Mr Holmes,' I said. 'Will you not show me your work?'

There was reluctance on his part. 'Of course,' he said,

and handed me his pad.

The man he had drawn was not me. The eyes of the man in the sketch were vacant, until they descended into a deep pool of sadness. From the depths of the pool, they seemed to comprehend the incomprehensible. And though his features were mine, they were on the shoulders of an Indian brave! Two ropes of hair hung in front of his ears.

Though not offended by the work, I was puzzled by it. 'Am I a savage in your eyes?'

'I tried to show your heart,' he said.

'Your drawing is not complete then,' I said. 'It needs a bottle.'

The other drawings in his pad were of more interest, I thought, glancing at them. They were of persons we'd seen that day at the Old Bailey, though not drawn as I would have done, had I the ability. The peelers, villains, prostitutes and judges on display were portrayed with sympathy. 'What is it that you see in a person when you draw him, Mr Holmes?' I asked, giving him the pad.

'Their promise,' he said. 'Their magnificent promise as human beings.' He put the pad away. 'Quite often, all that is left of it is a reflection, which one can see in their features, their posture and mannerisms. But so often, the wonder of that promise has been warped into a grotesque cartoon by their lives as Englishman. Shall we go?'

'You have not told me who your father is,' I said.

'Sherrinford Holmes,' he said.

'Who is he?'

'The oldest of the brothers Holmes,' Jeremy said, standing. 'There are three. Sherrinford, now a country squire in Yorkshire, is the oldest. Then there is Mycroft, in the service of our Queen. Sherlock is the youngest.'

We left the pub. It was lovely out, and we walked along a busy street of well-dressed gentlemen with ladies on their arms, in the soft light of a warm London evening--when a small urchin darted from a doorway and yanked the purse off the shoulder of a woman. 'Hold this, please,' Jeremy said, handing me his case. His eyes burned with mischief . . .

And he was off, amidst a growing hue and cry. The urchin darted into a labyrinth of alleyways and I followed as well as I was able, to find Holmes with a grip on the boy. Three older toughs had them surrounded. The young lad held the purse away from Jeremy. 'Toss it to me, Benny,' one of the toughs said, and the boy flung it at him. But in a display of remarkable athleticism, Jeremy reached out and caught it by the strap. He pulled the strap over his head, and let the boy go.

'I'll have that, guv,' the largest of the toughs said to Jeremy, a knife with quite a long blade in his hand.

'Run, man,' Jeremy said. 'Off with you.'

The third tough, also with a knife in his hand, swung it at Jeremy's back. Dodging the strike with the grace of a Spanish bullfighter, Jeremy knocked the weapon out of the fellow's grip and slammed an elbow into his head. The tough went down.

The woman arrived on the scene, in the company of an older gentleman. He spotted the young thief and caught him in the crook of his arm. Another of the toughs swung a plank of wood at Jeremy, who easily stepped out of its arc. As it thudded to the ground, the sound of a policeman's whistle froze the young hoodlums. A crowd menaced their front. Galvanized into flight, they were gone through a narrow passage, leaving the waif.

'Young thief!' the silver-haired gentleman stormed angrily, tightening his arms around the boy's neck.

'Ow--ee-ow!' he cried out, desperate for breath.

'Put him down, sir,' Jeremy said, as he pulled the purse off his back and handed it to the woman. 'You are suffocating him.'

'I caught the thief!' he stormed, angrily. 'I shall hold him for the police!'

'Sir, you are choking him.' Jeremy gripped the man's arm with such force that his hold on the boy went limp.

A bobby appeared. 'Wot. Benny,' he said, taking the boy by the wrist. 'You disappoint, lad.'

'I needs to eat,' the waif said, through tears.

'You shall hang!' the man said. 'Before you grow into manhood, you shall hang!'

'Let me have him,' Jeremy said.

'You sir?' the officer asked. 'And who are you?'

'A barrister,' Jeremy said. 'This is Mr Edward Greech, a solicitor. We can use a boy of obvious enterprise.'

Some of the gentlemen and ladies gathered there appeared to approve of Jeremy's action. There was a smattering of applause, and the bobby came to a sudden decision. 'Take him then,' he said.

'The devil!' the older gentleman said. 'I should like . . .'

Holding the boy by the hand, Jeremy motioned to me and abruptly, we left the scene. When we had gone round a corner, out of sound and sight, Jeremy let go of the lad--who clearly considered running off, but did not.

Jeremy kneeled down, so that their eyes were at the same level. 'Just as I thought,' he said. He reached into his pocket and pulled out a sovereign and three shillings. 'You are better than to be a thief.' He pressed the coins into the boy's hand. 'Do you know Lincoln's Inn?'

'No sir.'

'Find it then, and ask for The Bastard.'

Chapter 5

'Upstand!' proclaimed the usher, to a virtually empty hearing room at the Royal Courts of Justice. 'Upstand all!' Jeremy had been summoned to appear before Lord Reginald Arlington, by Sir Percival Jersey. 'All persons with business before my lady the Queen's Justice of Special Proceedings for the Royal Courts of Justice, draw near and give your attendance. God save the Queen!'

Lord Reginald Arlington swept into the small chamber. Wigged and robed, as were Jeremy and Sir Percival, I watched His Lordship stuff a bit of snuff up his nose as he sat at his bench, in front of the table for the barristers. 'Sir Percival,' he said, greeting the silver-haired barrister whose cheeks bloomed like ripe tomatoes with easy familiarity.

'My Lord,' Sir Percival said with a nod and a smile. He stood behind the table for barristers, next to Jeremy.

'Mr Holmes,' Lord Arlington said to Jeremy, without warmth. 'And you, my good man?' he asked of me.

I stood in front of a pew behind the bar. 'Edward Greech, My Lord,' I said. 'I am a solicitor, here at the request of Mr Holmes.'

He nodded. 'Be seated, gentlemen.' He waited until we were in our chairs. 'Sir Percival, you requested this hearing. Be so kind as to inform me of its purpose?'

Sir Percival stood up with grave dignity. 'My Lord, it is to charge my learned colleague, Mr Jeremy Holmes, with conduct quite unbecoming of one who has been called to the bar. I have chosen to do so formally, rather than in chambers, to impress the serious nature of the matter on one who has little more than a year on this side of the bar.'

'Very well,' Lord Arlington said. 'Proceed.'

'Allow me to recite the circumstances of the case. I believe the facts will speak for themselves.' He moved away from Jeremy. 'A week ago, I was requested by Peter, Lord Russell, to undertake the defence of his wife for the murder of Christian Vandeleur. Perhaps Your Lordship is familiar with the cause?'

'Of course,' His Lordship said. 'It is much in the news. A most unpleasant business.'

'Following an inquiry by the magistrate, Lady Russell was charged with murder and taken to Newgate Prison, where she remains, pending her trial. It will be called in the December Sessions at the Old Bailey, hence, some urgency.'

'I should say there is,' Lord Arlington said. 'You have only two months.'

'Such was Lord Russell's concern for his wife that he requested me to go to Newgate,' Sir Percival said, 'to assure her that she was not alone. I did this before receiving the brief from his solicitor, who was in Bristol on other business. Though unusual, it seemed the proper course, under the circumstances, out of respect for her gender. Who should I find, in her company, at Newgate?' A flowery gesture introduced the culprit. 'Mr Jeremy Holmes.'

His pronouncement of Jeremy's name dripped with malice. 'I regard his conduct as most inappropriate, and quite beyond the boundaries of our profession. After being requested by me to leave, he did so. But not without ingratiating his way into the distraught woman's favor, by taking her hand in his, raising it to his lips, and kissing it.'

Lord Arlington frowned at Jeremy, who--armed with a sketch-pad rather than a legal tablet--was drawing the features of Sir Percival. 'Is there more?' Lord Arlington inquired.

'Indeed there is, My Lord. Mr Holmes is a man of much

charm, a fact that can be attested to by many of the unfortunates who have appeared in the criminal courts of London, as well as those who have served as jurors in cases he has tried. The influence he exerted over Lady Russell in the short time he was in her company persists. It is as though he cast a spell over the unfortunate woman, who continues in her misguided efforts to persuade me to associate him.'

Jeremy was far more interested in his sketch, than the comments of Sir Percival. When Sir Percival realized what Jeremy was doing, he was at first annoyed. But after, it seemed, he struck a series of poses.

'As Your Lordship is aware, I am a barrister of some experience. My instructing solicitor tried to reason with Lady Russell, who now refuses to see him. If the choice were hers to make, she would discharge me and replace me with this younger man of far less experience. Fortunately the choice is not hers. She must yield to the dominant reasoning power of her husband.'

'As it should be,' Lord Arlington said. 'What is the relief you seek?'

'I beg you to direct Mr Holmes to accompany me to Newgate, there and in my presence to confer with Lady Russell. I would ask that Mr Holmes be directed to advise my client in the strongest terms to comply with the wishes of her husband. Lord Russell is a man of principle who has no desire to allow someone such as Mr Holmes to taint her cause in any way. If Your Lordship will be so kind as to direct this young . . . man . . . to explain to her that she has no alternative other than to abide by the wishes of her husband, I am confident that she will listen to my advice. I should then be able to prepare her cause.'

'A perfectly reasonable request, Sir Percival. I am sure Mr Holmes is aware of the consequences that would follow, should he refuse to comply with a judicial directive.' He both smiled and frowned at Jeremy. 'Mr Holmes, what have you to say?'

Jeremy placed his sketch pad face down on the table, then rose to his feet. 'My Lord. Allow me to observe that this is the first I had heard of Sir Percival's difficulties with Lady Russell. My esteemed colleague has not seen fit to acquaint me with his problem, nor to request my help in remedying it.' Jeremy spoke with the calm assurance of one who was not in the least intimidated by the proceeding. 'Allow me to state further that two days ago, my instructing solicitor--Mr Edward Greech--acquired some information that is of great concern to Lady Russell's cause. I attempted to see Sir Percival for the purpose of conveying it to him, but he refused to admit me into his chambers.'

'Mr Holmes, I suggest to you that perhaps Sir Percival is from the old school,' Lord Arlington said. 'It is not easy for him to open the door of his chamber to everyone.'

I could not believe my ears. The reference to the bastardy of Jeremy was unmistakable.

'Surely you can understand his reluctance,' Lord Arlington said.

'I do not understand it at all,' Jeremy replied, sharply. 'I am a bastard, My Lord. I am not a leper. What I have is a status, conferred upon me by our laws. I do not have a communicable disease.' He continued in a softer voice. 'If it please you, My Lord, may I have your permission to address Sir Percival here, in this courtroom, in which I am permitted to stand next to him, though he will not invite me into his chamber? Perhaps I may do so, as though he were a witness.'

'Would you have me put him under oath?' Lord Arlington asked.

'Of course not, My Lord,' Jeremy said. 'All England knows Sir Percival to be an honourable man.' Although he spoke without a trace of irony, Sir Percival--judging by his expression--was not flattered.

'What would you ask of him, Mr Holmes?' Lord Arlington inquired.

'I would have two questions of him. As Your Lordship has observed, this cause is much in the news. And rumours abound, especially in the Inns of Court. One such rumour has it that Sir Percival would have Lady Russell admit her guilt. Then he would present evidence to the jury of her fine character, after which he would implore those good men to recommend to our gracious Queen that she grant mercy. The strategy is frequently attempted, though rarely with success. I would ask Sir Percival if the rumour is true.'

'The second question?'

'I would ask him, again, to associate me in Lady Russell's defence.'

'Why would you ask him that?' Lord Arlington inquired. 'Has not your name been featured enough of late, in the *Times*?'

Jeremy did not flinch at the provocation. 'My Lord, I truly believe that I can be of assistance.'

Lord Arlington pursed his lips. 'I see,' he said. 'How would you respond to the questions of the learned young barrister, Sir Percival?' he asked, smiling at him. 'Or would you rather not respond to them at all?'

Sir Percival had not the slightest bit of hesitation. 'I have no wish to offend my young colleague,' he said, 'but I regard the questions as impertinent. I care nothing for rumour, and have little patience with it. As to his suggestion that I would profit from his assistance, that is intolerable. Such would be my response.'

'Quite so,' Lord Arlington said, then leaned toward Jeremy. 'Mr. Holmes. I am directing you to arrange a suitable time with Sir Percival to go to Newgate, there to urge Lady Russell to abide by the wishes of her husband. I further direct you to inform her that under no circumstance will you entertain any misguided effort on her part, to associate you with Sir Percival. Do you have any questions?'

'My Lord, before you make a ruling, may I be so bold as to request an opportunity to reply?'

Lord Arlington and Sir Percival exchanged glances that eloquently spoke to the colossal impertinence he would subject them to. 'That is your right.'

'With your leave, My Lord, allow me to call a witness.'

'An appalling suggestion,' Sir Percival said, quite improperly interjecting himself into the colloquy between the court, and counsel. Lord Arlington should never have allowed it. 'This is a special proceeding,' Sir Percival continued, 'most commonly conducted in chambers. It has been conducted openly in order to impress my learned young colleague with its importance. But there is not even a reporter here, to make a record. It would be quite improper to call a witness.'

'Mr Holmes,' Lord Arlington said, 'the matter involves your conduct with the client of another barrister. What possible benefit is there in enlarging this proceeding into that which is need not be?'

'Her testimony would speak for itself, My Lord. Allow me to advise you of what she would say.' He continued, without receiving the permission of the court. 'Her name is Mrs Laura Lyons, a woman with whom Mr Greech has talked at some length. I am informed, and believe, she would testify that Professor Christian Vandeleur, the man whom Lady Russell is accused of having murdered, was not the true name of the

39

victim. It was an alias that had been adopted by the victim to shield his true name from the public.'

'Nonsense!' Sir Percival said, standing. 'Impossible! Professor Vandeleur was a man of stature in the scientific community, and quite well-known. He was positively identified by the headmistress of Queenland College for Women, where he was employed as a professor.'

Jeremy held Lord Arlington with the strength of his gaze. 'It is true that the headmistress of Queenland College hired a man whom she believed to be Professor Christian Vandeleur, to teach there. His employment began in mid-July,' Jeremy said. 'However, ...'

'My learned young colleague,' Sir Percival said, addressing Jeremy! 'Do you suggest that the Crown is mistaken? Before his employment at Queenland, he had been in South Africa, at a college there. That employment has been verified by Scotland Yard. An article of his appeared in *New Review*, a prestigious journal for scientists, on eighteen February of this year. He had also published a paper for the British Museum in 1887. Yet you suggest he was an impostor?'

'If I may finish ...'

'When I am done,' Sir Percival said, imperiously. 'Let us assume this distinguished entomologist chose an alias for some unimaginable reason. What possible difference could it make? It is perfectly clear that Lady Russell has been charged with murdering the man, no matter his name.'

I had never before witnessed a proceeding in a Queen's Court, conducted in such a manner. Jeremy alone retained his dignity. He faced Sir Percival in the manner of one who would save another of further embarrassment. 'Sir Percival, the man's true identity is of a rather inflammatory nature,' he said. 'I had hoped to talk the matter over privately with you before publicly divulging it, even to the Crown.'

'A moment, Mr Holmes,' Lord Arlington said. 'Who is Laura Lyons? I have heard the name.'

'As has anyone familiar with the account of Dr John Watson, known to the public as *The Hound of the Baskervilles*,' Jeremy said to him. 'It tells of the murder in 1889, of Sir Charles Baskerville. According to Dr Watson, Mrs Lyons operated a secretarial service in Coombe Tracey, which was a hamlet in Dartmoor near Baskerville Hall.'

'My Lord, the woman is also the secretary for Lady Russell,' Sir Percival said. 'My instructing solicitor has informed me that Mrs Lyons has re-opened the business of Lady Russell, that dress-making business. For Mr Holmes to have actively engaged in this matter, as though he and not I were the barrister for Lady Russell, goes well beyond what I had supposed.' He breathed deeply, through his nose. Rather surprisingly, there was no fire. 'He has actively involved himself in a cause assigned to another.'

'My Lord,' Jeremy said, addressing Lord Arlington, 'were Mrs Lyons called to testify, she would tell us that the victim was not Christian Vandeleur. Mrs Lyons had known him in Dartmoor as Jack Stapleton.'

Sir Percival, QC, had quite lost his composure. Again, he interjected himself into the colloquy between Lord Arlington and Jeremy, heaping scorn on the observation of Jeremy. 'Of course,' he said, addressing Jeremy. 'Dr Watson simply misinformed his readers when he told them that Jack Stapleton was dead. He wanted merely to tease his public by informing them that Stapleton had been swallowed up in the Grimpen Mire.'

Jeremy smiled. At complete ease, he addressed Lord Arlington, as though Sir Percival was not there. 'Though some might suggest that Dr Watson would not mislead the public by informing it that Jack Stapleton had been swallowed up in the Grimpen Mire, it should be observed that in the account of that adventure by Dr Watson, the body of Mr Stapleton was not found,' Jeremy said. 'His death was assumed.'

'Are you certain of that?' Lord Arlington asked, in great surprise.

'Quite certain, My Lord,' Jeremy said. 'Mr Greech has a copy of the account, if you wish to see it.'

Oh dear I thought. Though Jeremy had asked me to bring it, I had forgotten.

'I remember it now,' Lord Arlington said. 'I recall wondering, when I first read it, if perhaps Stapleton might appear in another adventure.' He actually smiled at Jeremy. 'I should say that the disclosure will surely embarrass the Crown, but I fail to understand how it alters the issue here. Lady Russell remains the client of Sir Percival, does she not? Why should not the remedy I have prescribed remain in place?'

'My Lord, if the identity of the victim is Jack Stapleton, then the issue . . .'

'The issue was and is your unseemly and unprofessional interference,' Sir Percival said loudly, as though he would drown any attempt by Jeremy to defend his conduct in a torrent of verbosity. 'This proceeding may have brought to light a fact which the Crown would undoubtedly have learned. But it has also established behavior on your part that has gone beyond even what I could have imagined.' Were sparks at last coming out of his nose? 'I intend to instruct my solicitor to file an appropriate grievance procedure against you, Mr Holmes. I am outraged.'

At last, Lord Arlington gave a sign of impatience toward Sir Percival. He frowned at him.

'My Lord,' Jeremy said, 'there is the suggestion of interference on my part, in the defence of Lady Russell, who is being defended by the esteemed Sir Percival Jersey, QC. Yet Sir Percival has stated here today that Lady Russell would rather have me. May I ask, by what right does Sir Percival go against her wish?'

Lord Arlington immediately recognized the point Jeremy raised. But Sir Percival could not mask his anger. 'How far will you go, Mr Holmes, to see your name in print?' he demanded.

Jeremy continued to address Lord Arlington. 'I do not make up the facts, My Lord,' he said, mildly. 'If the victim was in fact Jack Stapleton, then the woman charged with his murder was a married woman in July of this year, when she married Lord Russell.'

What would have been painfully obvious to Sir Percival, had he not been so keen on embarrassing Jeremy, dawned on him. He sat down.

Jeremy continued, addressing Lord Arlington. 'Her marriage to Lord Russell was void *ab initio*,' he said. 'From the beginning. It never occurred. From the moment that her husband, Jack Stapleton, was dead and continuing until this moment in time, she has been a single woman, answerable to no man. She is under no obligation to conform her wishes to a man to whom she was never married.'

'Why was I not informed?' Sir Percival asked, of himself.

Jeremy looked down at him. Then he turned his sketch-pad over, peeled off his drawing, and folded it up. He held it in his hand. 'I venture to say,' he said to Lord Arlington, 'that Peter, Lord Russell, as a man of honour, might wish to be relieved of his responsibility for Lady Russell. Or should I say, Mrs Stapleton. Lord Russell is under no obligation to shield and protect a bigamist.'

Chapter 6

'Well done, Mr Holmes,' Lord Arlington said, after we were adjourned. 'Perhaps you won't mind waiting a moment before discussing the matter further with Sir Percival? I am confident that between you, any points of difference will be resolved. But first, I would visit in private with my old friend.' He put his arm on Sir Percival's shoulder.

The soup of cordiality of which British barristers partake had thickened. Even Sir Percival managed to smile at Jeremy, though he could not look at him. Jeremy was invited to remain in the hearing room, to which Sir Percival would return after the "old friends" had had a moment together in the chamber of Lord Arlington.

'You were going to show your drawing to Sir Percival, were you not?' I asked when they had gone.

'Yes.' He opened it up. 'I had not the heart.'

'You felt sympathy for him?' I asked, looking at the sketch, then laughing. 'Not your best effort, Jeremy,' I said, 'but quite good.' He had drawn the striking figure of a man with flowing hair, a protruding jaw, and an air of great dignity and determination. The fellow sat on an over-stuffed chair, inside a box. 'I would have portrayed him as a bully on the playground. I would have showed his savage nature.'

'Those are echoes,' Jeremy said. 'They are not his voice. But I think you are beginning to see.' High praise indeed, I thought. 'May I suggest that you find our witness and tell her what has happened? We can meet later in my chamber at Lincoln's Inn.'

'Of course,' I said, gathering up my brief-case and hurrying into the hall.

Mrs Laura Lyons was seated on a bench, outside the

hearing room. When first we met, she had presented herself to me as an attractive woman, blessed with a modest charm. But that was not her manner at that moment. She stood up when she saw me, with a hand over her mouth, as though in fright. 'It is over,' I said, approaching her and extending my hand. 'You will not need to testify. If what you tell me is true, then all will be well.'

Her relief was palpable. 'Thank God,' she said, gripping my hand with both of hers. 'Then you will get her brief and take it to The Bastard?'

'Not immediately,' I said, aware of the warmth of her hands. 'Are you certain that the victim was Stapleton, and not Vandeleur?'

'Beryl is quite adamant on the subject,' Mrs Lyons said, releasing her hold on me. 'Who would know better than she?'

'Why has she said nothing until now?'

'Months ago, she told me,' Mrs Lyons said. 'But then she seemed to have changed her mind.' She opened those lovely hands of hers, expressing mystification. 'Even after the murder, when I first came to see her, she said nothing about it. But after conferences with Lord Russell, and his solicitor, and Sir Percival, she returned to the subject. Though she told no one else about it, she told me. Then she asked . . . I should say, begged . . . me to get a message to you.' She smiled. 'Carolyn, her gaoler, is such a dear.'

'Then she has told no one but you?'

'She has not,' she said. 'Most certainly, she has said nothing about it to Lord Russell, his solicitor, or Sir Percival.'

'Is there any possibility of mistake?' I asked. 'Could the victim in fact be Christian Vandeleur, and not Jack Stapleton?'

'There is always that possibility, I suppose,' she said. 'But cannot the body be exhumed? There are many who can identify it. Even Sherlock Holmes.'

I would love to have taken her hand again, although it would have been most unprofessional of me. 'Will you see The Widow today?' I asked.

'I shall go to her at once, and tell her . . . what? Sir Percival is not at all to her liking. Will she have The Bastard?'

'I am confident that in good time, she will be able to choose him. Do you see her often?'

'Every day, Mr Greech. My Lady continues to occupy herself with the business, which I am confident she will do as long as she lives.' Her hand flew to her mouth, distressed over her choice of words. Quietly, she continued. 'The doors to *Fashions* have re-opened, and all of us continue in her employment.'

'What of customers?' I asked. 'Have you any?'

She shrugged. 'Many of the women of society, and most of those with titles, have disappeared. But there are a surprising number of women of fashion in London, and not a few from Europe and America, who know our artistry. *Fashions Sabor Brazilenos* will continue until . . .' Again, her eyes closed in contemplation of the unspeakable. 'Will you let us know how we may assist?'

'Of course,' I said. 'And if legal advice is needed in your venture, I should be most happy to provide it.'

Most generous of me I thought, as I watched her walk away. A tall woman, her skirts switched back and forth enticingly, accenting the movements of her hips. I braced myself with drink from my flask, then went to meet Jeremy in his chamber at Lincoln's Inn.

His was more monk-like than most. No larger than a closet, without a window, his small space was furnished with a table, above which three shelves were stacked. There were two chairs, and a lamp. He was not there, but I had not long to wait. 'Sit here, old fellow,' he said when he arrived, yielding to me the comfortable chair in front of the table.

'You have talked with tomatoe-face, I see,' I said, 'and he did not charm you.' Concern had furrowed Jeremy's face. 'The man in the box remains inside his box?'

'Sir Percival was not gracious,' Jeremy said. 'He will not share the brief with us. It will remain his, until it has been established that Stapleton was the victim. He would even deny you access to any of the witnesses, as though you should not begin your own investigation.'

'The word of Lady Russell is not good enough for him?' I asked.

'He attributes it to the spell I have cast over her.'

Jeremy surprised me. There was no exultation, after his triumph. Rather there was a most uncharacteristic uncertainty. 'You are not dancing,' I observed.

'No.'

'Perhaps this will help,' I said, pulling out my flask. 'Trust me, young man. You need a drink.'

Jeremy rarely indulged in anything other than a pint of ale. But he pulled out the stopper and raised the flask to his lips. Swallowing once with a grimace, he took another drink and swallowed it too. With his eyes shut, he returned it to me. 'Thank you.'

'Jeremy, are you certain that you should take this brief?' I asked. His manner was not what one would expect from the nephew of Sherlock Holmes. 'You are not committed to her defence. Think carefully. Is she right for you?'

Perhaps the Irish whiskey had worked its magic. 'I don't know, Edward,' he said. 'Sir Percival would have maintained a suitable distance from her cause. But can I?' In the many briefs I had brought him, I had never seen Jeremy gripped with doubt. I had not thought it possible of him. 'We would have made a good team, once he overcame his distaste of my origins. I wanted to work *with* him, Edward. Now he hopes to see her hang.'

'How can you know that?' I asked. 'Does it show in your drawing of him?'

'He told me.'

'Why would he wish it?'

He shrugged. 'As a tribute to his sagacity.'

'My young friend,' I said. 'Does The Widow mean too much to you?'

'I am not enamoured of her, if that is what you mean. Yet I care for her deeply.'

'How can you care for a woman deeply, without being enamoured of her?' I asked, stating the obvious. 'Surely your feelings for her are not those of a son for his mother.'

'My feelings for her approach reverence.'

'Reverence! Do you *worship* her then?' What did those beautiful eyes of his behold in the creature who, when all was said and done, was just a woman?

'Edward, there is a purity about her, and a goodness, that I have never seen before, in England, or in America. It radiates from her person. For the Crown to hang her, to extinguish that incomparable life . . .'

'I shall take the brief to another,' I said, interrupting him. 'It will never do for you to agonize over her.'

'Perhaps you should,' he said. 'There is a magnificence about her that is holy, and I would indeed agonize over her defence. I do not want the responsibility of the wonder of her life, and of her breath. And of her death.'

I offered him another drink. 'No thank you.'

'That is unfortunate,' I said, taking a long pull. 'There are occasions, my young friend, that demand spiritual guidance. This is one of them. Where would you have me take her brief?'

'I shall have another drink, after all,' he said.

He did so, returning to me only the remnants. I was impressed. 'I believe in my talents as a barrister,' he said, 'as immodest of me as it is to say so. The Widow deserves the best, and I am the best. But her cause would trouble me more than words can express. It goes beyond my belief in her innocence. I see in her a beauty, a wondrous quality that reaches into and enhances the radiance of a clean sky. Does that unsuit me to defend her?'

How could I tell him what I truly believed? It was not in my nature. 'Of course not,' I said.

'I want the truth, Edward.' His eyes wrapped me in their grip.

'Very well. To begin with, you find the possibility of her innocence to be a relevant and important factor.'

He laughed. Perhaps the Irish whiskey had worked its magic. 'Enough,' he said. 'Your arrow has brought down the bird. I am the least qualified of barristers, with such an anchor around my neck.'

A face poked into the doorway. 'Mr Holmes, the black knight!' the fellow boomed. 'The word is you've jousted with Sir Percival, and unseated him. What a thrust that must have been!'

'It was indeed,' Jeremy said with a newly-found gaiety. 'But though I had the privilege of delivering the blow, the victory belongs to her solicitor. Edward Greech.'

'Greech, old fellow!' the man said. His expression became that of a lecher. 'And what of the reward? Is The

50

Widow on the table? And is she on her back? Or does she present herself to you, on all fours?' He roared with approving laughter for himself, and disappeared.

'The Widow will want you to defend her, Jeremy,' I said. 'When Sir Percival lets go of the brief, would you have me bring it to you?'

'I would,' he said, pulling a sketch-pad off the uppermost shelf. He selected three pencils. 'Following that, old man, we put on our armour and ready ourselves for the combat our laws and traditions have blessed us with. That common law ceremony known as trial by jury, in which all good Englishmen indulge, before a hanging.'

Chapter 7

'How does the matter stand?' Jeremy asked me, two weeks later. He stood in the corner we inhabited in the smoking room, engaged in a drawing of Dr James Mortimer from a likeness of the man I had obtained. It was the photograph of a portrait of years ago.

That day, he had been engaged at the Old Bailey with two briefs I had brought him. In the first, a man was charged with stealing his employer's tools, and in the other, a lad of eighteen was accused of murdering his uncle. The tools were shown to have been given to the accused by the employer in lieu of wages, and the case was dismissed. The fellow accused of doing in his uncle had the charge reduced to manslaughter, thus avoiding the noose.

Jeremy's manner in the courtroom had been relaxed and comfortable. With good cheer, he had demolished the cases for the Crown. But I noted that as he worked on his sketch of a witness for The Widow, he was as taut as a sail in a heavy wind. 'Sir Percival has finally acknowledged that The Widow may choose who she wishes,' I told him. 'And that she does not want him. I have her brief,' I said. 'It is in my room.'

He put his pencils on the tray of his easel, and sat on the window-sill. 'His teeth marks are on it, I suppose. What induced him to let go?'

'The body of the man who the Crown had identified as Christian Vandeleur was exhumed early this morning, and viewed by Sir Henry Baskerville and Dr James Mortimer. They declared him to be the man known to them as Jack Stapleton. Your uncle Sherlock is on the continent it seems, and could not attend. But two years ago, he revealed that Jack Stapleton was in fact Rodger Baskerville, a cousin of Sir Henry, and that

Rodger and The Widow were married.' I paused in my recital, long enough to freshen my breath with drink. 'Today, the Crown amended the indictment to reflect her true name, and that of the victim. The charge is no longer against Lady Beryl Russell. Now it is against Mrs Rodger Baskerville. And the person whom she is charged with having killed is Rodger Baskerville.'

'Have you been to her?'

I nodded, nestling in the comforting embrace of cushions on my chair. 'She is most grateful to you. No longer must she withstand the urgings of Sir Percival.'

'Tell me again, old fellow. How would Sir Percival have defended her?' He stood, selected a pencil from the tray of his easel, and continued with his work.

'Sir Percival would have her admit she stabbed him with the shears,' I said. 'He believes her account of the matter to be a fairy-tale, unworthy of belief. He would have her confess her crime to the jurors, then justify the killing by arguing that she was compelled to stab him to keep him from savagely using her a second time.'

'A second time?' he asked. 'When was the first?'

'As you may recall, The Widow and the man whom the Crown at first believed was her lover were followed by detectives.'

'I recall it well,' Jeremy said. 'Last week, someone saw fit to release that tasty bit of gossip to the papers, in spite of the judicial shield raised to prevent it.' His restless eyes switched back and forth, between the portrait on the window-sill, and the pad that stood on the easel. 'Sir Percival has implied that I gave it out. I suspect it was he. What of it?'

'They were seen together on several occasions last summer. One lovely summer night in August, Vandeleur--his name at that time--was seen letting himself into *Fashions Sabor Brazilenos*. With a key. The Widow was known to be inside then, quite alone. Vandeleur did not leave the premises for an hour, after which The Widow did. The gossips would have him leaving with a broad smile on his face, and her with a stiffness of waist, and legs. The matter, of course, has led to much speculation as to how they occupied themselves.'

'It was then?' Jeremy asked.

'So she informed her solicitor,' I told him. 'After questioning her on the subject, her solicitor was satisfied that she would make a credible witness on the point and so informed Sir Percival. Sir Percival was delighted. He would have her tell the jurors that on the night of the murder, Vandeleur broke into her store a second time and forced himself upon her. She stabbed him to prevent the outrage.'

'Does she account for the key?'

'She didn't know how he came to have one. Her inability to explain that point was regarded as a weakness in her defence by Sir Percival, but it should surprise no one now. As Professor Christian Vandeleur, it would have been quite out of character to acquire a key illicitly. But Jack Stapleton was a murderer, a burglar, and a thief, capable of anything.'

Jeremy had professed a determination to detach his feelings for The Widow from the case, and to study it with the objective attitude a scientist brings to his research. But the tension in him was palpable. His pencils on paper were applied with enough force to shred the paper. 'Trust me,' I said, offering him my flask. 'Advice from an old doctor.'

'No,' he said. 'I shall go for a walk tonight. Walking the streets of London clears my mind.'

After one such walk, he had returned to the club with a torn shirt, bruised knuckles, and a nasty cut on his left forearm. 'What possesses you, Jeremy?' I asked, quite impatiently.

'Demons,' he said. 'I have invited some lonely, homeless demons to possess me.' I did not like the look in his eyes. 'One day, perhaps I shall tell you who they are, for each of them has a name. Did The Widow hold back at your questions?' He stood back from his drawing, then let his hands wander over the work with abandon. 'Does she continue to mislead?'

'I cannot tell you, Jeremy,' I confessed. 'We differ on the point. I am still unable to believe her far-fetched explanation.'

'I will meet with her next week, and draw her again,' he said. 'But as I trusted you when you prescribed whiskey for my troubled state of mind, you must trust my knowledge of her soul. She is devoid of the capacity to kill. She simply cannot.'

'A pity,' I said. 'Defending her would be so much simpler if she would admit to having stabbed the fellow. Even if to say so is a lie.'

The smile he offered fell short of good humour. 'Go on.'

'If Vandeleur--rather, Baskerville--did indeed force himself upon her in August as she now claims, perhaps you will allow me to suggest to her that for strategic reasons, the approach of Sir Percival is worthy of consideration. I would further suggest to her that perhaps she did, truly, kill him to prevent further outrage to her person.'

Jeremy thought about it. I was acquainted with the direction of his thought, for I'd listened to his soliloquies on the subject. In order to persuade a jury of twelve British men that the accused was not guilty of murder, after the accused had admitted killing the victim, the barrister must appeal to their sense of justice and fair play. 'And what is that monument of which the British are so proud?' Jeremy would ask, rhetorically. 'I have drawn its likeness. It is a wonderfully convoluted octopus, wearing a crown, who believes in the Divine Right of Kings. This creature has a remarkable mental ability. At one and the same time, he can justify the brutal treatment and enslavement of whole continents filled with human beings, and believe in the Golden Rule!'

Was English "fair play and justice" better, or worse, than the way of the Cheyenne People, in which he had been raised? 'Neither,' he had said. 'We were the Tall People with equally arrogant beliefs in our superiority over the human beings in other tribes we encountered. We would test the courage of captured enemy warriors by torturing them to death.'

'You would have me defend her by admitting that she killed him, then justify her action?' he asked of me.

'I would,' I said. 'I quite agree with Sir Percival on the point. Her explanation of events is a fairy-tale. You should toss it over-board. It is far too dependent on a series of most implausible coincidences.'

The harsh reality of his situation weighed heavily on him. He had little more than a month to construct a defence, and not as a consulting detective would have done. He was not at liberty to put on a disguise and solve the crime. He must accept the situation with which he was presented, knowing that soon he would be engaged in trial, over which loomed the spectre of the verdict. If The Widow were convicted of the charge, there was little likelihood of an appeal. She would hang within three days.

Doubt and uncertainty pulled his shoulders toward one another. 'She would have to lie,' he said.

'How can you be certain of that, Jeremy?' I asked him, playing on his hesitation. 'And what does it matter? Assuming it is a lie, do you think for a moment she would not tell one, to save her pretty neck?'

'We cannot suborn her perjury,' he said. Yet he was clearly torn.

'Is their proof of her innocence? Could you be charged with suborning her perjury, without a clearing showing of that?'

'Quite beside the point,' he said. 'I cannot countenance a betrayal of the ethic of the law.'

'How can you have such principled allegiance to this law which you ridicule?' I asked. He slashed at the drawing, but made no reply. 'Other barristers have no difficulty in offering testimony that is questionable.' I provided him with two examples of recent vintage.

'Would she do it?' he asked.

'Of course, if she thought the suggestion came from you. She trusts you implicitly.'

'That was the tactic of Sir Percival. She will expect more from me than that.'

'Yours will be immeasurably stronger,' I told him. 'You will have the liberty of painting Rodger Baskerville with his true colour, a blackness quite devoid of humanity. A man who would have made a brilliant scientist, but who was afflicted with that aberrant taint of Baskerville blood that first appeared in Hugo, according to the legend, in the 1600s.'

'Demons perhaps?' Jeremy suggested, with a smile.

I found the remark a bit unsettling. 'I trust your demons are not the same as his,' I said. 'My point is that you will be able to contrast his evil with her goodness, that beautiful nature of hers that tortures you so. Yet even a woman of great goodness can be a strong woman. After having suffered one outrage at his hands, she could not endure another.'

With a savage suddenness, he tore his work from the easel and crushed it into a ball. 'I see the artist who made the portrait,' he said. 'Not Dr Mortimer.' At least, the movement straightened his shoulders. They were no longer drawn together with indecision. They were filled with blood, and purpose. With great care, he fitted a blank sheet to his easel and began anew.

'Shall I talk to her then?' I asked. 'Will you permit me to tell her that you have questions on the point, and wonder if perhaps she reacted to another of his unwelcome advances?'

He said nothing to me, but I could hear his body hum. With a renewed vigor, he worked at the drawing, no longer looking at the photograph of his portrait. I stood behind Jeremy and watched as a different Dr Mortimer emerged. The portrait was of a handsome young doctor with a distinctive professional expression, but the drawing of Jeremy invested him with the wrinkles of a unique life. I beheld the picture of a man who appeared to have suffered a psychic wound. Through the force of his will, he had held himself together. 'Curious,' I said. 'Who is he?'

'Guess-work,' Jeremy said. 'No more. The artist who drew Dr Mortimer gave him what he wanted to see. Perhaps-- though I will not know until I see him--I have gone deeper.'

'What is in your sketch of him?'

'A man who has experienced something shameful, and the memory will not leave him alone. He seeks solace now. Perhaps the solace of science.' He turned away from his work. 'The strategy you suggest would fail,' he said.

I returned to my chair. 'Do you have one that is better then?'

'She will make her statement to the jury. And her absolute honesty . . .'

58

'Will be shredded by the Attorney-General, and the judges, and the jurors. The woman has been caught in too many lies.'

'She will radiate the truth, Edward,' he said, 'and someone on the jury may respond to it. But there is a more compelling reason.' He pulled the sketch pad from the easel, and folded it up. 'There is the inescapable fact that Rodger Baskerville was her husband. A jury of twelve British men would never be persuaded that he did not have the right to force himself upon her.'

'But for her to act in anger. . .' My enthusiasm fell by the wayside.

'And stab him in the neck with cutting shears, for doing what he had an absolute right to do?' Jeremy shook his head. 'I would be handing her to the hangman,' he said. 'Her duty quite clearly was to yield to him, to her husband. If she refused, he had every right to force himself upon her. Many would say not only the right, but the obligation.'

Jeremy was right, of course. But at least I had succeeded--for the moment--in pushing him into thinking like a lawyer, rather than as a Knight of The Round Table, with a crystalized vision of the virtue of women. 'What are we to do then?' I asked.

'We need an alternative suspect,' he said. 'An appropriate villain, at whom I can point an accusing finger of guilt. And who knows?' he added, once again at his ease. 'You might be so fortunate as to select the real murderer.'

Chapter 8

Jeremy was most adept, when summing up, at suggesting to the jurors that the evidence pointed in another direction, and that someone other than the person in the dock might as readily have been charged with the crime. Such a person was known, in the parlance of the law, as an "alternative suspect." My task was to find such a person.

The following afternoon, I began my search by calling upon Mrs Lyons at *Fashions Sabor Brazilenos.* My reasons were not entirely professional. She was a charming and attractive female who was not repelled by my whiskey breath. As a married woman who had been abandoned by her husband, I saw no risk of female design or entanglement, although the thought of literal entanglement with her person had entered my mind. Jeremy may have had reverence for The Widow, but I did not entertain such lofty visions when I thought of Mrs Lyons.

Taking a cab from Holborn Circus to Marylebone Lane, I drove by the Ladies Mile on Oxford Street. The bewildering world of women's fashions paraded past me. The women I saw and the mannequins on display had bustles protruding from behind their feminine hips, covered in deliciously-colored skirts. The skirts were made of rustling fabrics and gored with pleats, provocatively plunging down the front. Their arms were in leg-of-mutton sleeves, and the delicate skins of their exposed faces and necks were shaded by elaborate head-dress. Was it thus that the creatures covered the unlovely reality of their bodies?

In the comfort of my cab, I drank to the efforts of women who were so driven by their insatiable desire to attract the opposite sex that they would pour their soft bodies into the curvatures of whale-bone stays. How could Jeremy idealize the creatures, I wondered? And why? Even the smells on Oxford Street were scented of the perfumes of women.

Not so the narrow passage through Marylebone Lane to Wigmore Street. There, droppings of all sorts had been allowed to accumulate, and odors boiled up like clouds. But Marylebone Lane north of Wigmore Street was as cleaned and perfumed as the Ladies Mile on Oxford Street. The shops that lined the cobblestone roadway of Marylebone Lane meandered south to north toward Regent's Park, and they had a most appealing aspect. There was a freshness about them that spoke of the exuberance of the young, rather than the exaggerated elegance of the wealthy, displayed by the shops on the Ladies Mile.

The *boutique* of The Widow had large windows made of small rectangular panes of glass, through which passers-by could see statuesque and life-size Venuses, their adjustable limbs in various poses. The forms were dressed in gowns that hinted of the sensuous mysteries of women, most especially those who dance to the throbbing rhythms of South America. It provided quite a contrast to the garish displays of the Ladies Mile. I pushed open the front door and was pleasantly surprised to find myself greeted by Mrs Lyons herself. 'Do come in, Mr Greech,' she said. 'How nice to see you again.'

What a lovely greeting, for a woman of her endowments, to an old sot.

It was mid-afternoon and I was heartened, unaccountably, to find that the showroom was not devoid of shoppers, even though it did not teem with them. 'Carla, would you take my place at the door?' Mrs Lyons asked of the small, dark-complected woman behind a counter.

Mrs Lyons was tastefully attired in a close-fitting skirt

that showed her trim figure and well-formed ankles to advantage, as though she were strolling through a meadow in the Spanish highlands. Acutely aware of the movement of her hips, it was with delight that I followed her, breathing in the taste of her exotic perfume. She led me past the spacious office that no doubt was that of The Widow, to a smaller one that adjoined it. 'May I offer you some tea?' she asked, when we were seated across from one another.

'I would be most grateful.' You may imagine my delight when she allowed me to sweeten our beverages with spirits.

I reminded her of our previous conversation at the Royal Courts, in which she had advised me of her lady's determination to keep her business open, even though she must manage the operation from gaol. I renewed my offer to provide any legal assistance that might be required. 'That is kind of you,' she said, 'and most fortuitous. Lord Russell has engaged a solicitor to place a lien on the goods and chattels of the store!'

'Has he now,' I said, masking my true thoughts with a generous smile. I had not expected my offer to result in work. 'What is his purpose, do you suppose? She is a single woman.'

'I do not know. Nor do I know by what right. The business does not belong to him!'

'I quite agree with you,' I said. 'Had they been married, he might well have acquired it by operation of law. But they were not married. May I see it?' I asked, referring to the lien.

'We have not been served with papers,' she said. 'Constable Firstson told me to expect them.' She sipped from her cup. 'He also told me something I found scandalous indeed. It too concerns Peter, Lord Russell.' Her tone had twisted, as had her mouth; the former into a dissonant chord, the latter to an unbecoming sneer.

'And what is that?' I asked, adding whiskey to our cups.

'You knew, did you not, that on the evening of this ghastly business, Lord Russell had come by *Fashions*, in his carriage, to see Beryl?'

'Yes.'

Her eyes glowed with indignation. 'He was not alone, Mr Greech. Constable Firstson watched from across the lane.'

'Who was he with?' I asked.

'A woman! A beautiful woman, the constable told me. When Lord Russell was back in his carriage, she raised up from her cushioned seat and threw herself at him!'

'Scandalous indeed,' I said, though it hardly surprised me. The old order of things was not what it had been when barons and dukes had afforded protection to peasants and serfs--then lived in luxury, off their sweat. But Peter, Lord Russell was nevertheless the Baron of a large estate. His blood was as blue as Edward, the Crown Prince of England, which granted him immunity from the conventions that hobbled the rest of us.

'They had not been married three months!' Mrs Lyons continued. 'Lord Russell, with all his estates, is a common philanderer. Beryl is well rid of him.' I refrained from observing that perhaps it were better to be a philanderer, than a bigamist charged with murder.

Soon thereafter I took my leave of her. She promised to notify me when the lien was served, for which I pretended to be most grateful. I took her hand and as I raised it to my lips, she squeezed my fingers and blessed me with her smile.

Later that afternoon I talked to Constable Firstson. He was anxious to help The Widow, he said, and it was obvious he had an affection for her. 'She has been most generous to me, Mr Greech. Christmas Day last was a most happy occasion at the Firstson home, thanks to Lady Russell.'

'In what way, my good man?' I asked.

'She gave me spouse a lovely overcoat, fit for the Queen of Spain.'

The constable assured me I would know immediately if and when the lien was served on The Widow's *boutique*, then walked me through the events he had witnessed at her arrest, affording me and thus Jeremy a thorough understanding of all that had transpired. Though his evidence would be damning to the defence, Jeremy would know he could show that the sympathies of the officer were with The Widow, and not the Crown.

In the days that followed, Jeremy drew sketches of those who would be witnesses. Their characters and their hearts were revealed to him in the act of drawing them, he believed. As to those scenes with which he must be familiar, his method of knowing them was virtually the same. I feared for his sanity.

His uncle would have examined those scenes on his hands and knees, finding what to him were obvious clues available to anyone with a brain in his head. But Jeremy sketched the scenes from various angles, encouraging the drawings to speak to him! Utter nonsense, I thought. Yet perhaps his belief in the delusions of his mind accounted for his success. 'What do they tell you?' I asked.

'The cutting room echoes with rage,' he said. 'Her *boudoir*, of excitement. But not of a sensual nature. Rather, the kind that one might feel when about to embark on a new adventure.'

'Is that all?' I asked.

'I am not able to hear more than that.'

There were also interviews with The Widow, and

sketches of her. Her beauty shined through all of them, even one in which she gripped cutting shears in her hands. But in some inexplicable manner, it was apparent--even to my flinty old soul--that though she could have used the shears to cut cloth with, she could not have thrust them into the throat of a living being. 'Has your knowledge of the inestimable purity and goodness of The Widow changed?' I asked, perhaps unkindly.

'It has deepened,' he said. 'Look closely at what I have drawn. There shines in her the magnificence of womanhood.'

'The *what?*' I blurted.

There was nothing magnificent about womanhood, I should like to have informed him. Women were nothing more than women. The Widow, in all her magnificence, was but a woman. And Mrs Laura Lyons was but a woman. But I held my peace.

On one pretext or another, I managed to be with Laura several times, before the trial. I might need information from her to clarify a statement of The Widow, or her assistance in understanding the operation of the dress-making business. She was possessed of a dark sensuality that perhaps one day she would allow me to taste, and I savoured her nearness with great pleasure. We would meet for dinner, and across a table laden with roasted duck, or a platter of lamb, I would lift my wine glass to her, and she would respond with her smiling eyes. Our knees might meet, out of sight of the other patrons, and there was promise in her eyes, as we talked lightly about all manner of things. But it did not progress beyond that point. She had been endorsed as a witness for both the Crown, and for the defense. For me to be with her at all was highly questionable. To have taken our interest in one another beyond the platonic, was out of the question.

I devoted many of the dwindling days to unearthing provable facts about the character of Lord Russell. At the trial, I was confident that Jeremy could portray him as one who thrived on violent excitement. Lord Russell had been an officer of rank with the 11th Hussars in India. He had soldiered with the legendary joy and recklessness of those in the light brigade. As well, he had become skilled in the dangerous sport of polo. Nor was there the slightest doubt that he could kill a man, if provoked to do so. He had engaged in four duels to the death. In two of these, his adversaries had died, and in the others, been grievously wounded.

I had done my job well. I was satisfied that Lord Russell would make a most engaging alternative suspect. Jeremy elevated him from merely a witness to be called by the Crown, to the mainstay of our strategy.

The remainder of the strategy would flow from the genius of The Bastard. I waited with great anticipation for the trial of The Widow to begin. How would he twist and fashion the evidence at the trial, to suggest that the victim was murdered--not by The Widow--but by Lord Russell?

Chapter 9

It was Thursday, the third day of December, and raw with cold. At nine that morning, I pushed my way through the crowd that had formed in front of the Old Bailey. It steamed with raucous humour and unrestrained expectation, as had the crowds in my youth, when the gallows were up.

The press had been savage in pursuit of The Widow. It had turned on her with the ferocity of a betrayed lover. Such was the clamor to watch her trial that the Lord Mayor of London had restricted the seating. As though to a royal ceremony, entrance to Sessions House--the chamber in the Old Bailey where the drama would be staged--was by invitation only.

There were the inevitable delays. Sessions House had to be cleared of those who had slipped inside the chamber early in the morning, and taken seats. Guards were placed at the entrances, admitting only those with credentials. At eleven o'clock, I took a place in the gallery, reserved for me by special order. It was a front-row seat. With my elbows resting on the railing beside the box that would hold the jurors, I would have an unobstructed view.

Three judges would sit at a large table, centered on a rostrum well above the floor, there to direct the well-mannered struggle that would take place below. On the wall under their table and sticking out like the basket that holds passengers for an air-ship--well within the sight of the judges--was the witness box. Next to it, the court stenographer had his desk, and next to him, the desk for the clerk of the court. The usher, a large fellow in uniform, would sit on a stool near the clerk. A table for exhibits stood a step away from him, located so that he could bring the exhibits to the barristers and witnesses.

Conspicuously, a pair of cutting shears rested on the table's surface.

Across from the table of judges and on the floor of the stage, stood the lengthy table for the barristers. Two pews were stacked behind it. Ordinarily, the pews were filled with barristers with business before the Court, but they were barren of them that day.

To the left of the judges, also above the stage floor, stood the dock: that lonely platform where the wretch on trial must stand or sit. It was illuminated by reflector-panels in the ceiling, above the south wall. They were open to the sky and caught the light of day, aiming the rays of light at the accused: done for the laudable purpose of catching and revealing his every expression to the jurors, who would sit in comfortable chairs across the stage floor from the dock. Thus every nuance of emotion of the accused--or its lack--was displayed, allowing the jurors to better assess his guilt or innocence.

The barristers, wigged and robed, entered through a door under the rostrum and took their chairs at the table for the barristers. Attorney-General Guthrie Featherstone, QC, knighted for his service to the Queen, was engaged in conversation with Mr Roberts, his able assistant. Their chairs were nearest the dock for the accused, and directly across from the rostrum of judges. Jeremy sat alone at the other end of the table, rather near me. He appeared outgunned, a sloop against a Man-o'-War. Even I, as the solicitor for the accused, had been excluded from the stage, but could readily be summoned by Jeremy, if he needed to do so.

A hushed silence filled the large chamber as twelve well-groomed men, warmly-dressed in wool suits, were lead into the chamber by the usher. Good and true subjects of the Queen, they filed into the box beside me, and took their chairs.

The usher took his stool, as the clerk of the court and the stenographer took their seats behind their desks. With a shudder, the dock--with no one on board--slowly began its downward descent, into the dungeon below.

The Sessions House emptied of sound. In absolute silence, the accused and her warder were lifted up from the depths, into the illuminated dock. Wearing a dress that hinted of exotic islands, The Widow literally took one's breath away. A thick woolen shawl was draped over her arm. Her warder was Caroline, of the big bosoms. When the dock was secure, Caroline took the chair at the back. The Widow sat quietly in front.

Three loud knocks echoed through the large chamber, from the door for the judges on the rostrum, behind their table. The usher rose solemnly to his feet and faced the jurors. 'Upstand!' said he, a serjeant commanding his troop. 'Upstand all!' Everyone in the gallery rose to his feet, as well as all those on the floor below.

The judges filed to their places. All were regally dressed in scarlet robes as the silver rings of the locks from their wigs draped over their shoulders. "Dimples," the Lord Mayor of London, was the first to take his chair. A judge in name only, he sat in the center. On his right was Lord Justice Reginald Arlington, the presiding judge, and on the other side sat Sir Percival Jersey, QC.

After a nod from Justice Arlington, the usher filled the arena once more with the sound of his voice. 'All persons who have anything further to do before Her Majesty the Queen's Justices of Oyer and Terminer and general gaol delivery for the jurisdiction of the Central Criminal Court, draw near and give your attendance. God save the Queen!'

There followed the business of swearing in the jurors,

one by one, all of whom gave their solemn oath that they would a true verdict give, according to the evidence.

'The accused will stand,' Justice Arlington said.

The Widow stood up.

'Mrs Beryl Baskerville,' Justice Arlington said, a stern frown on his face, 'you are charged that on the 28th day of September, in the City of London, you murdered Rodger Baskerville. How say you, Beryl Baskerville? Are you guilty, or not guilty?'

'I murdered no one,' she said. 'Not guilty.'

'You are further charged that, while married to Rodger Baskerville, with knowledge of your deceit, you were married to Peter, Lord Russell, the Baron of Somerset. How say you to the charge of bigamy, Beryl Baskerville? Are you guilty or not guilty?'

'Not guilty.'

'You may state the case for the Crown, Sir Guthrie,' Justice Arlington said, nodding at the robed and wigged figure before him.

'My Lords,' the Attorney-General said, standing to address the judges and the jury. A large man with a commanding presence, his voice penetrated even the cracks in the walls of Sessions House. 'Worthy counsel for the defence,' he said, acknowledging Jeremy who appeared to be doodling on the pad before him. 'Gentlemen of the jury.' The jurors attended to the words of the Attorney-General with great care, as though they were medical students, listening to a surgeon explain how he would perform surgery on the prisoner in the dock. 'Mrs Baskerville,' he said, speaking her name with solemn but awful tenderness. No longer a surgeon, he spoke her name as though she were lashed to the stake and stood on a pile of faggots, awaiting his command to light the torch.

All eyes fastened on her trembling magnificence.

The Attorney-General broke the spell by facing the jurors, commanding their attention. In a voice lined with velvet, he continued his address. 'A short two months ago, at approximately two o'clock in the morning of twenty-nine September, the woman who stands in the dock was seen by Constable Firstson of the Metropolitan Police, dragging what appeared to be a log--rather curiously wrapped in a blanket-- from the back door of her dress-making establishment into the alleyway behind. Some of you perhaps, and all of your wives most certainly, know of the business: *Fashions Sabor Brazilenos*, on Marylebone Lane.

'Constable Firstson had seen a dim light glowing from within, during the course of his patrol. After trying the main door and finding it locked, he suspected mischief. He secreted himself in the shadows, in the alleyway behind, and watched the back door.' Sir Guthrie's expression took on a secretive aspect.

'But rather than burglars with their arms filled with purloined goods, the person who softly moved through that doorway was known to him. Known not only to him, but to all England.' He held out his hand to the accused in the dock, as though he were the Master of Ceremonies, presenting the primary attraction. 'She was known to all of us--affectionately, I might add--as The Widow of Dartmoor.

'For she had found a hallowed place in our hearts, where she had nestled for more than a year. Nestled comfortably and, I might add, profitably.'

He invited all to look at her again.

'She had arrived in London in January of 1890, a woman of great enterprise, with money enough to start a dress-making shop. The name she chose to use as proprietress was Beryl Garcia. It was her maiden name. And so Marylebone Lane acquired *Fashions Sabor Brazilenos*, Beryl Garcia, proprietress.' He adopted the manner of the barker at a carnival. 'Artistic millineri, perfectly fitted gowns, dressmaking by native fitters, a touch of the exotic, a hint of the Caribbean, the flavor of Brazil.'

With a shrug of his shoulders, he dropped his pose. 'But in spite of her efforts, her business struggled . . . until a journalist for the *Times* revealed her past.

'All of us knew the dark happenings, chronicled by Dr John Watson in *The Hound of the Baskervilles*. That remarkable adventure began with the mysterious death of Sir Charles Baskerville. Sir Charles had been the baronet of Baskerville Hall, in far-away Devonshire. But until the article in the *Times*, few had realized that Beryl Garcia, dress-maker, was the widow of the villain who had murdered him.' He peered at her over his nose. 'Thereafter, she was known--not only as a woman of enterprise--but as a woman of intrigue. The Widow of Dartmoor.'

He smiled at the accused with seeming approval. 'The journalist reminded us of those dark events in Dartmoor in 1889. At their start, she was believed to be *Miss* Beryl Stapleton, the sister of Jack Stapleton. He in turn was thought to be only another of the rather eccentric characters who lived in that remote region. But as the mystery unfolded, Sherlock Holmes revealed her to be the *wife* of Jack Stapleton, not his sister. Her husband was shown to have murdered Sir Charles, and of attempting to murder Sir Henry Baskerville as well. Sir Henry was the lawful heir of Sir Charles and the new baronet of Baskerville Hall.

'The public knew, of course, that the murderer had not escaped. Dr Watson, in his factual account of the crime, told us he had not. It was believed that rather poetically, Stapleton had been sucked into the Grimpen Mire, leaving only a tell-tale boot floating on its surface to mark his passage.'

Sir Guthrie paused a moment, as though to collect his thoughts. 'Bravely, it seemed, the woman whom you see in the dock before you had endured the fury of her husband on that fateful night. Before unleashing the huge hound, its mouth washed with phosphorous to glow in the dark, Stapleton had silenced his wife by wrapping her up like a mummy and lashing her to a post. Had he not done so, she would most certainly have raised an alarm to save the life of Sir Henry.

'And just as bravely, after those events were concluded, she came to London quite alone, to open the doors of her fashionable *boutique*. And when this enterprising woman's tragic past was revealed, rather than being subjected to ridicule and scorn, she became the darling of London. The Widow of Dartmoor was more than a woman of enterprise. As well, she was a dramatic character immortalized in the pages of a book. And her fame and good fortune did not end there.' He smiled at the prisoner in the dock.

'In July of this year, Peter, Lord Russell, favoured her with a title. Lord Russell was known already to the public, and admired. Handsome, wealthy, a dashing sportsman and member of the House of Lords, he was renowned for his brave service to the Queen in India. He was renowned as well as a polo player without equal. Our Widow of Dartmoor captured his heart, and he made her his wife. When they were joined in marriage, an adoring public was delighted. Her tragic past had been replaced with a story-book ending.'

A pause. 'But alas. The story of her life took a rather sordid turn. They were married on a beautiful Sunday in early July of this year. As though to deflect the attention of the public, their wedding ceremony--a Saturday--was wedged between the arrival of the Emperor and Empress of Germany, the day before, and a royal wedding on the day after. Even so, all England applauded their marriage. Indeed, they appeared to have been made for one another.'

He raised a cautionary hand. 'But wait. Not even a month had passed, when Lady Russell,' and with a theatrical gesture, the Attorney-General drew attention to the accused, 'was seen at lunch, engaged in earnest conversation with another man. Quite trim in appearance, he was known to the scientific community of London as Professor Christian Vandeleur. A visiting lecturer from South Africa, he had secured a position at Queenland College for Women, in Essex. The meeting between Lady Russell and the professor was brought to the attention of Lord Russell, who thought it unseemly, perhaps, but innocent. Yet it bore a closer look.'

The accused bent her head, as though in shame. 'A closer look,' Sir Guthrie repeated, inviting the jurors to consider her distress. 'And so without the knowledge of either of them, a private detective agency was employed to follow them. One man discretely kept Lady Russell in view, and the other, Professor Vandeleur.'

Sir Guthrie was not in a hurry. He wanted everyone to witness the discomfort of the accused. 'The detectives, in the course of their employment, soon bumped into one another. You may have suspected that they would. One week later, Lady Russell and the charming professor were seen by the detectives at a fashionable restaurant. This time his hand came to rest on hers. And precisely one week after that--now it is the twelfth day of August--the two detectives saw them at lunch again.'

A disappointed sadness clouded the aspect of the

Attorney-General. 'Their next meeting was not at lunch,' he said. 'It was in the evening, one day more than a week from the time before. The *boutique* had closed for business, and all the customers and employees were gone. But Lady Russell had remained. When a well-dressed, obviously quite fit fellow came strolling down Marylebone Lane.' The shoulders of Sir Guthrie swung in rhythm as he acted the part. 'It was Professor Vandeleur! He reached the front door of the *boutique*, and-- rather than knock on the door to gain entrance--he pulled a key from his pocket! He opened it up, and let himself in.'

The Widow pulled the shawl more tightly around her shoulders, as if to hug herself. Sir Guthrie appeared for the moment to be reluctant to continue, as though he took no pleasure in salacious gossip, especially in the presence of the subject.

But he recovered. 'There is a flat above the *boutique*, quite nicely furnished with closets, a sink and bath, and a bed. The detectives were not in a position to see what transpired there, but they *were* in a position to see Professor Vandeleur leave the premises, an hour later. He appeared--how shall I put this. Pleased with himself?' There were smothered sounds of mirth. 'Quite satisfied?'

The comment drew laughter, allowed a moment until Justice Arlington motioned with his hands for silence. Sir Guthrie smiled at Jeremy, who did not acknowledge the levity. 'My learned friend is not amused,' Sir Guthrie said.

'Hardly,' was the reply. 'Saddened, perhaps.'

The jurors watched the interplay, of course. Sitting as I was beside them, I could not see the expressions of many, nor could I "read" those I saw. 'Not quite a week later,' the Attorney-General continued, 'the detectives happened upon one another again. Once more, those whom they followed shared a private lunch. Later that day, the good Professor boarded a ship for South Africa. He gave a series of lectures there, and did not return until late September.'

The Attorney-General paused, as though he must force himself to continue. 'And that brings us to their final encounter.

'On twenty-eight September, in the evening--again, after all the employees were gone--Professor Vandeleur let himself in the front door of *Fashions Sabor Brazilenos*. With a key. Lady Russell, we believe, waited for him. In any event, she alone remained.'

The Widow sat motionless, as though made of stone.

'The sleuths did not see Professor Vandeleur emerge from The Widow's place of business, as before, wearing a smile. At two in the morning, while one stayed at the front door, the other followed the constable, who had gone to watch the rear door. Without the constable's knowledge, I hasten to add.

'And so now we are back to the beginning of this tale. For *that* was the woman Constable Firstson saw, at two o'clock in the morning of twenty-nine September. Not miscreants sneaking out the back way, their arms filled with loot. Rather, it was Lady Russell, the proprietress of the establishment, dragging behind her a curious object.'

The jurors were most attentive to his words, as was I. 'When Constable Firstson slipped out of the shadows, wishing only to assist, it alarmed her, and she begged him to leave. The constable realized rather quickly that she dragged the body of a man, rolled in a blanket. In despair, Lady Russell gave up the name of the fellow. It was Professor Christian Vandeleur, she said.'

As though bemused, Sir Guthrie shook his head. 'The constable summoned the assistance of Scotland Yard, and the accused was taken to its headquarters by Inspector Lestrade. Later that morning, she provided him with a rather curious explanation of the matter. She told him that Professor Vandeleur had broken into the store the evening before, and put his hands on her. But in the course of his unwelcome advances, there was a knock on the door. It was the familiar rap-rap-rap of her husband.

'She answered the door. Did she tell her husband of her unwelcome visitor? She did not. They talked, he embraced her, and departed. She went back inside--to find Professor Vandeleur, on the floor of the cutting room, gushing blood from a wound to his throat. She tried to save him! This man who minutes before had forced himself upon her, died with his head on her lap. But while working to stem the flow of blood, what should happen but a pair of cutting shears suddenly landed on the floor before her!'

He allowed himself a smile, and a shrug. 'There is more to her statement, of which Inspector Lestrade will acquaint you. Let us turn to the cutting room, where this dreadful business occurred.'

Sir Guthrie gestured toward the table for exhibits, and the cutting shears. 'The evidence will show you that the shears bore no trace of the gore one might expect to have been on them, when they were taken that morning by the inspectors,' Sir Guthrie said. 'Rather, they were clean enough to have been used at supper. And the polished hardwood floor in the room where the victim expired was scrubbed and polished, a suitable platter to have carved your mutton on.

'And the man whom this woman of intrigue had said was Professor Christian Vandeleur? Later that day, he was positively identified by the headmistress of Queenland College as, indeed, Professor Vandeleur, a celebrated member of their faculty, lecturing on the natural sciences.

'Yet we know he was not the good Professor at all. That was kept secret.' He motioned toward the dock, where The Widow sat with her eyes cast down. 'By the accused.

'Before her secret came out, let us consider the evidence assembled to that point by Scotland Yard. Indeed, the case seemed clear enough. This most enterprising and beautiful woman, whom all London knew and loved as The Widow of Dartmoor, had risen above the tragedy in her life and been joined in marriage to the dashing Peter, Lord Russell. But she could not control her heart. After her marriage, she had taken a lover, and--as so frequently it will--the matter ended badly. She had murdered him. That, stripped to the bare essentials, appeared to be the crime the Crown would be called upon to prosecute.

'But the narrative took an unexpected twist. Wilkie Collins, that celebrated writer of mystery, could not have improved on the facts. For Professor Christian Vandeleur, the charming young naturalist, was not her lover. He was her husband.'

Sir Guthrie regarded the accused without pity. As though to avoid his inspection, she closed her eyes. 'The man whom we accuse this enterprising woman of murdering was not Professor Christian Vandeleur, as we had first believed. Nor was he Jack Stapleton, that eccentric young man who, with his sister, lived in the Dartmoor wilderness, where he chased butterflies. Vandeleur and Stapleton were identities assumed by Rodger Baskerville. And she had married Rodger Baskerville on the other side of the ocean, and followed him to England.'

He paused, and searched the eyes of the jurors.

'Ask yourselves, gentlemen of the jury. Did Mrs

Baskerville know who he was, when she told Constable Firstson his name was Christian Vandeleur?' His tone challenged them to say anything other than the obvious. 'How could she not know?' he asked. 'She had lived with the man ten years, sharing the same bedroom.'

Totally devoid of sympathy, the Attorney-General inspected her again. 'You might ask yourselves why she said nothing of this to Constable Firstson, or to Scotland Yard. Why did she choose to say nothing? What prompted her to keep the matter secret? Is not her reason obvious to you?' He showed them the palms of his hands. 'Consider the consequences of the truth. If the true identity of the victim were known, she would no longer be Lady Russell, the wife of Lord Russell. Her life would be stripped from her, and she would be revealed to all as a bigamist. The story-book quality of her new-found life of luxury, rubbing elbows with the titled and wealthy, would collapse.' With a gesture of his hand, he invited the jurors to look at The Widow again.

'If ever there was a motive for murder, this woman possessed one. And so it became the business of this enterprising woman to ensure that her secret should remain hers alone. That his true identity would never be known.'

The jurors inspected her too, as was their duty as subjects of the Queen. 'Perhaps it matters little, My Lords, and gentlemen of the jury. To the charge of murder, the Crown has added another: bigamy. As triers of the facts, you will determine the truth or falsity of that charge, as well.

'Is Mrs Beryl Baskerville guilty of bigamy, as well as murder?'

Chapter 10

The proceeding resumed at two o'clock, and Constable Firstson took the oath as the first witness for the Crown. He sat at attention in the witness box, a perfect brick of a man. The very uniform he wore radiated honesty, courage, and service to the Queen. 'You were on foot patrol on the night in question, in the early morning hours?' Sir Guthrie asked him.

'I was.'

'At two o'clock in the morning, were you in the vicinity of *Fashions Sabor Brazilenos*?'

'I was standin' right before her.'

'Will you tell us what you saw?'

The good man told of seeing the glow of a gas lamp from within, and noticing movement. His suspicions aroused, he tried the door and found it locked. He removed himself to the alleyway behind and positioned himself in the shadows, with a view of the back exit. Believing that a burglary was in progress, he readied himself for a confrontation with the miscreant.

The door opened 'quiet-like, you might say, a bit of a secret.' A head appeared, wearing a bonnet, and he recognized Lady Russell. Stifling an urge to ask if she required assistance, he watched her drag what appeared to be a heavy log, rather curiously wrapped in a blanket, onto the bricks.

Leaving the door ajar, she disappeared inside and the light was extinguished. She re-appeared, closed the door, and locked it. Then gripping a strap of some kind at one end of the object, she began to tug and pull her burden toward Marylebone Lane. Firstson stepped away from the shadow and offered to help.

Startled, she begged him to leave. But the blanket was

stained with blood, and a boot appeared at the end. It was clear to Constable Firstson that a body was wrapped inside. He opened the blanket enough to expose two booted feet, and Lady Russell sagged against the wall and sat down. '"Tis Christian Vandeleur," she told me,' Constable Firstson said.

The prisoner in the dock held one hand over her eyes, as though to shield herself from an awful vision. Few in the hall wore faces of sympathy. Most were formed into stern frowns.

As Firstson summoned assistance, he told the jurors that Lady Russell buried her face in her hands, and sobbed. Firstson took off his overcoat and wrapped it over her shoulders, for which she seemed grateful.

'Did anything further pass between you?'

'She had a wish to confess about her, Sir Guthrie. I seen that look before. Quick as a wink, I put me hand up and told her I would hear no more from her. Said I, Lady Russell, you need a lawyer. She asked for a name, and I said to her I said, if it were me I said, I'd want The Bastard.'

There was some tittering. 'Perhaps this is the proper place for me to end my examination,' Sir Guthrie said. He sat down.

Justice Arlington peered over the bench. 'Mr Holmes,' he said, with a perfectly straight face. 'May I suggest that you've been introduced to the witness?'

'Thank you, My Lord. So it would seem,' Jeremy said, standing easily, his robe hanging from his broad shoulders. He turned toward the constable. 'Constable Firstson, very kind of you indeed to think of me. I take it that you believed you were giving Lady Russell good advice?'

'That I was, sir.'

'And when you put your overcoat over her shoulders,

81

did you think she might take a chill?'

'I did,' Constable Firstson said.

'You were concerned for her welfare then?'

'I was that, sir. I wanted to help her. She had always showed me a kindness.'

'Yet later that evening, you placed her under arrest?'

'That I did, though I had no wish to do so.'

'My good man,' Justice Arlington said. 'Just answer the question. It is not at all necessary to adorn your answer with your attitude.'

'May I suggest, My Lord,' Jeremy said, 'that the attitude of the witness is for the jury to consider?'

'You may make the suggestion, Mr Holmes,' Sir Percival said sharply, from his chair on the left side of the bench. 'My Lord Arlington has directed the witness to confine his answers to his observations.'

Jeremy nodded, as though in approval. But as he ventured forward with his first examination in the cause, it became clear to all the barristers and solicitors in attendance that Justice Arlington and Sir Percival, working together, would have Jeremy seem awkward and inept. He was met with frequent interruptions and suggestions from them. "Dimples," the Lord Mayor, remained with his index finger along the side of his nose, looking judicious. As though stepping on stones to cross a swamp, Jeremy worked his way over and around the barriers that the judges put in his way.

After a struggle, Jeremy succeeded in drawing the testimony from the witness that he wanted. Firstson disclosed that he had seen Lord Russell, earlier that evening, at shortly after seven o'clock. The constable had watched Lord Russell, in his chauffeur-driven carriage, park in front of the shop. Wearing a cape, Lord Russell had disembarked from within, jumped lightly out, and knocked on the door. His wife had greeted him, and let him inside.

Justice Arlington chose that moment to explain to Jeremy that he should not allow the witness to mislead the jury, in that there was a question as to whether or not the accused had ever been the wife of Lord Russell.

Jeremy preceded his next question with a lengthy preamble. 'The woman who stands before you in the dock, whom you have identified as the woman you witnessed dragging a body into the alley behind an establishment known as *Fashions Sabor Brazilenos*, and who at that time was known to the general public as The Widow of Dartmoor, previously married to a man also known to the general public as a murderer who called himself Jack Stapleton, being as well the woman who had recently participated in a marriage ceremony with Peter, Lord Russell, and whom you believed to be his wife, Lady Beryl Russell. Will that satisfy you, My Lord?'

'Proceed, Mr Holmes,' Justice Arlington said, rather thinly.

Firstson, sitting at attention as though he was a soldier on parade, continued. After Lord Russell said good-night to Lady Russell, by which he meant the woman whom Constable Firstson believed to be Lord Russell's wife, she closed the door to her establishment. Lord Russell then climbed into his carriage and a woman rose up from her seat to greet him. 'Most anxious she was, I should say, sir.'

'"Anxious"?' Jeremy inquired. 'May I ask you to tell us precisely what it is that you mean, by "anxious"?'

'She had an eagerness about her, Mr Holmes,' the constable said. 'Not like a lady, I should say. She couldn't wait for him to begin the business she was about.'

Many of those in the courtroom were amused, but not

The Widow, who appeared not even to breathe. 'Can you describe her?' Jeremy asked.

'A woman of fashion, I would say, judging by her dress,' the constable said. 'She wore a necklace that sparkled it did, and her hair was done up in a rack studded with jewels.'

'How were you able to see her?' Jeremy asked.

'She opened the door to him,' he replied.

'What happened then?'

'As the chauffeur drove down the street, they was all wrapped up with each other, huggin' and kissin'.'

The Attorney-General majestically rose to his feet, as though troubled over something. 'May I suggest, My Lords, that we avoid the cumbersome methods adopted by my learned friend, when we refer to Mrs Baskerville?' he inquired. 'She is known to the public at large, and I'm sure to the gentlemen of the jury, as the widow of Dartmoor. Perhaps in this proceeding, she may be referred to as "The Widow."'

'An excellent suggestion,' Justice Arlington said. 'Do you agree, Mr Holmes?'

Jeremy recognized the "suggestion" of the Attorney-General for what it was: an effort to move away from the unseemly conduct of Lord Russell. 'If it please you, My Lord, I quite agree that we should clarify the name by which we refer to the accused, and most especially should we do so at this time.' He bowed his head with appreciation toward Sir Guthrie. 'For it would appear that when Lord Russell, thought to be the husband of The Widow, knocked on the door of The Widow's *boutique*, he was entangled in his own affair of the heart. It has also been suggested by my learned friend, in his statement of the case, that two detectives had seen the victim let himself in that same door, at very near the same time.'

Sir Guthrie tried to interrupt, but Jeremy raised his

hand at him and would not allow it.

'In view of the possibility of a connection between the presence of Lord Russell, and the detectives, all of whom were also at the scene when someone thrust cutting shears into the throat of the victim--at least to those who have difficulty in trusting coincidence--I agree fully that there be clear distinctions drawn, as to who is who.'

Sir Guthrie gazed at his "learned friend" with a flash of malevolence, then smiled and sat down.

'Mr Holmes,' Justice Arlington said, 'we can get along quite well without your commentary. You may proceed.'

'Of course, My Lord,' Jeremy said. 'May I assume as well that we may get along without further commentary from the Court, and the Crown?'

A stillness followed. 'You may assume, Mr Holmes,' Justice Arlington said, 'that the Queen's law shall be strictly, and fairly, applied in this courtroom. Proceed.'

'Thank you. And be assured that I shall refer to the accused as The Widow during the course of the trial, trusting the jurors to understand the relationship between her and Lord Russell.'

He turned toward the witness. 'Constable Firstson, after observing Lord Russell in his carriage, all wrapped up I believe you stated and hugging and kissing this woman as he drove away from the establishment of The Widow, did you see Lord Russell, or his paramour if I may so characterize his companion, again that night?'

'I did not, sir.'

'It has been suggested by my learned colleague, Sir Guthrie, that two detectives were also at *Fashions Sabor Brazilenos*, on Marylebone Lane. This would have been in the early evening, when you were there as well. Were you aware of them?'

'I was not, Mr Holmes. That comes to me as a great surprise.'

'Later, in the early morning, hours when you were with The Widow in the alleyway behind *Fashions Sabor Brazilenos*, did you have any knowledge of two detectives then?'

'I did not.'

Thus began our defensive maneuver. It lacked the subtlety that one might have expected from The Bastard, but clashes at the Old Bailey were not noted for their subtleties. There was not the least doubt that Sir Guthrie would use every opportunity thenceforward to defeat our strategy, just as Jeremy would seize on every opportunity to connect Lord Russell to the murder.

Along with the barristers and the solicitors, and other *aficionados* of the courts, I found the game a fascinating one. The majesty of the Queen's law, which had remained cloaked in the robes and wigs and elegance and courtesies of centuries ago, was perhaps the grandest game of all.

Chapter 11

The Crown called as its next witness Dr Allen Sutherland, a physician renowned for his testimony of a year ago. In that case, three persons who were accused of murder by poisoning were cleared of the charge. The eminent doctor had shown to the satisfaction of the jury that the agent causing the death of the victim was a food, not a poison.

Sir Guthrie began by leading the portly figure-- perpetually engaged in smoothing the whiskers on his face-- through his examination of the body of the man identified to him as Christian Vandeleur. The doctor described him as a slightly-built man in his mid-thirties, remarkably fit. He had been stabbed in the neck with a sharp object, severing his right common carotid artery. When the usher presented him with the cutting shears from the table, he agreed they could indeed have inflicted the wound. From its angle and position in the neck and throat, he thought it likely that the weapon had been held by the right hand, inflicting the trauma when the victim's head was turned, as if looking over his shoulder.

'The victim's neck was not sliced,' stated the doctor. 'The wound was a puncture. It penetrated the artery with sufficient force to sever it.' He went on to inform the jurors that once the artery was severed, the man could not possibly have survived. 'Where could one have applied a tourniquet?' he asked rhetorically, then held his throat with his hand, to illustrate the uselessness of the procedure. 'And with blood pumping out, how could one have done a surgical suture?' With an expressive lift of his shoulders, he expressed the utter hopelessness of such an operation. 'As a consequence, the man quite simply bled to death.' And yes, the thrust could have been delivered by a woman of sufficient strength.

When asked if The Widow appeared to him to be a woman of sufficient strength, he answered, 'Yes.'

Jeremy asked the doctor if he was acquainted with Peter, Lord Russell. 'I am not,' said the doctor, 'but I have seen him at a polo match. Remarkable.'

'Then you would agree that he too had the strength to inflict this injury?' Jeremy inquired.

'Mr Holmes,' Justice Arlington said, firmly. 'I find your question to be most extraordinary.'

'Would you have me re-phrase it, My Lord?'

'I would prefer that you withdraw it altogether.'

'Thank you but no. I should like it answered.'

'Allow me to remind you,' Justice Arlington said, 'that this matter is being reported and that your conduct is subject to review. I shall also interpose here my opinion of the question to the jurors.' He peered down upon them. 'Gentlemen, I find the question of Mr Holmes to be impertinent and insulting. It impugns the honour and integrity of a man who is not on trial here. You are not to be influenced in any way by the question, or by the answer.'

That said, he glared at Jeremy. 'You may proceed.'

Dangerous words indeed, I thought, as no doubt did others in the hall. Lord Russell was known throughout Britain as a duellist of the old school. It was as though Lord Arlington would compel Jeremy to either withdraw the question, or deliberately provoke a duel.

'Thank you, My Lord,' Jeremy said, quite satisfied by the manner in which the question had been challenged. It would magnify its importance, and lend to our strategy an added impetus. 'Doctor, is it your opinion then that Lord Russell is a man of sufficient strength to have inflicted the wound, suffered by the victim, with the cutting shears you have seen?' Jeremy asked.

'I should say so. Yes.'

The Crown's next witness, Dr James Mortimer of Devonshire, wore clothes more suited to the out-of-doors than to a courtroom. He brought with him the fresh air of the country, rather than the perfumes with which Londoners layered over the stenches that flourished in our great city. Dr Mortimer was from a small hamlet in Devonshire near Baskerville Hall, and was indeed the "Dr Mortimer" who had brought the strange case known as *The Hound of the Baskervilles* to Dr Watson and Sherlock Holmes.

Asked if he was acquainted with The Widow, he acknowledged that he was. But he had not known her as Mrs Rodger Baskerville. Rather, it was as Beryl Stapleton, the sister of Jack.

'Tell us, Dr Mortimer, of Jack Stapleton.'

A tall man with a nose like the beak of an eagle, the good doctor allowed that he had known Jack Stapleton quite well. Both men had an interest--more, a fascination--in an aspect of the natural sciences. 'Mr Stapleton was an entomologist, who had a most remarkable curiosity in moths and butterflies,' the witness said. 'Mine is the anatomy of the human skull.' His inquisitive eyes searched the visible portions of the Attorney-General's head with eagerness.

Dr Mortimer then told of being requested by Scotland Yard to view the body of a man exhumed from the grave. There had been some decomposition to the remains, but his facial features were easily recognizable. It was indeed the man known to him as Jack Stapleton.

The good doctor ventured to say that he was quite astonished, because of his certainty that the villain had perished in the Grimpen Mire. Yet he recalled, when first reading the news of the murder with which The Widow was charged, that he had recognized the name of the victim: Professor Christian Vandeleur. Earlier in the year, he had read an article in *New Review* authored by Vandeleur, on the evolution of an South African moth.

Thus, Mortimer knew Vandeleur to have been an entomologist, known to many at the British Museum. Mr Stapleton was also an entomologist, known to many at the British Museum. The good doctor had thought it curious that Lady Russell--rather, The Widow--who was remembered with fondness by all who had known her in Dartmoor, should have been charged with the murder of one with the same interests as her deceased husband.

Although Dr Mortimer had been cautious when questioned by Sir Guthrie, he brightened noticeably, on cross-examination, when Jeremy addressed him. Such was the change in his aspect that Justice Arlington remarked on it. 'Have you talked this matter out with Mr Holmes?' he asked.

'No, My Lord,' Dr Mortimer said. 'I have not met Mr Holmes, nor seen him for that matter, until this moment.'

'Have not met him! You act as though you know him quite well indeed.'

'I know *of* him, My Lord, as the barrister defending The Widow. And I have talked with Mr Greech, his solicitor.'

Justice Arlington continued to peer over the bench, as though he could not surrender his suspicion. His manner was not lost on the jurors. 'Please bear in mind, Dr Mortimer, that you are under an oath to tell the truth,' he said. 'And may I suggest that you make every attempt to be strictly objective.'

The witness was not chastised by the display of righteousness from the bench. Rather, he appeared to be offended.

'Dr Mortimer, it is quite true, is it not, that you and I did not meet until the moment you were called into the witness box?' Jeremy asked.

'That is true, Mr Holmes,' Mortimer said. 'We had not.'

'But you knew that I am the barrister for The Widow, and that Mr Edward Greech is her solicitor?'

'Yes,' he said.

'Have you talked with Mr Greech about this cause?'

'I have, Mr Holmes.'

'Will you be so kind as to inform His Lordship of everything, to the very best of your recollection, that was said?'

All those squeezed into Sessions House listened as Dr Mortimer, without interruption, recounted our brief conversations. The first occasion was a month ago, following his identification of the body. The second was on the following day, before his return to Devonshire. The third and last time had been the day before today. On all those occasions, he had been with Sir Henry Baskerville.

They had sought me out at the Bastriche Club, to ask me how they might assist in the defence of a woman for whom both men had a high regard. I had advised them to put their faith in British law, which was designed to protect the rights of persons accused of crime. I had also advised them to disclose everything they knew to Scotland Yard. When doing so, I had emphasized that they should guard against any temptation to do other than tell the absolute truth.

On the second occasion, also at the Bastriche Club, Dr Mortimer and Sir Henry had asked of me how the killing of an obvious monster could be regarded as a crime? To which I had replied that under the Queen's law, it was the taking of the life of one of her subjects that mattered, not the character of the deceased.

I had forgotten how noble were the sentiments I had expressed. But both Jeremy and I knew that some of those chosen by the Crown to prosecute a cause will probe a suspected impropriety between barrister and witness. Jeremy knew that I always took the precautions I had taken with Dr Mortimer and Sir Henry. He was not disappointed by the answer.

Sir Henry had offered to pay the expenses in the cause, Dr Mortimer said, to which I had replied it would be quite inappropriate because of the likelihood that, were he summoned to testify, bias in favour of The Widow would be suggested. Sir Henry had also asked if they might visit The Widow at Newgate, and I told them they could. I informed them that The Widow seemed comfortable enough in her quarters there, for which she must pay a considerable sum, but no amount of money could shield anyone in the prison from the powerful odors held captive inside its walls. Dr Mortimer was thorough enough to report that I advised them of the method I used to protect myself from the onslaught of those knee-buckling "perfumes." I prescribed for them liberal dosages of Irish whiskey. I had also asked them to convey any messages from her to me, and to assure her that her case was not as hopeless as it might seem.

I had further requested that they advise me of their future plans, and to wire me when they returned to London.

The third occasion had been the preceding day, in the rooms engaged by Sir Henry at the Manchester Hotel. Both men had told me that they had been summoned by the Crown to testify, and asked me for advice. I had taken them to Sessions House, showed them the witness box where they would sit, and the dock, and the bench. I advised them to listen closely to the questions, and to respond to them as fully and fairly as they could.

'Quite enough, Mr Holmes,' Justice Arlington said. 'Shall we move on?'

'If it please you, My Lord. Has the witness put to rest any questions you may have over the integrity of his testimony?'

'We will leave that to the judgment of the jury,' was the gruff reply of the chief justice.

The witness and the barrister then engaged in what might have been a friendly conversation, where one is curious about events in the life of the other. When asked to describe the Grimpen Mire, the doctor thought it a dreadful bog of swamp and reeds, concealing areas of unforgiving quicksand into which wild horses were pulled to their deaths. He expressed his amazement that Mr Stapleton could negotiate such a treacherous place in the fog. When asked whether the events in Dr Watson's chronicle accurately depicted the location, the characters, and the crime, Dr Mortimer replied that they had, including the brilliance of Sherlock Holmes in unravelling the mystery, as well as the shocking terror experienced by all at the sight of the hound. 'When it attacked Sir Henry, its ravenous mouth was aflame with phosphorous. A terrifying sight.'

Dr Mortimer then brought the narrative into the present. He had accompanied Sir Henry on a voyage round the world, taken to repair the psychic damage done to the latter by his encounter with the hound.

'There was also the matter of his broken heart, was there not?' Jeremy asked.

'Yes. Yes. That as well,' Dr Mortimer said, smiling at The Widow.

Upon their return, they were welcomed by Mr and Mrs

John Barrymore, faithful servants of Baskerville Hall. Mr James Frankland, the apoplectic retired lawyer who loved to sue his neighbors, was there as well. But in the spring of this year, Mr Frankland was taken unexpectedly from this life. 'He did not die of apoplexy,' Dr Mortimer recounted, a twinkle in his eyes. 'He fell from the roof of his home, with his telescope in his hand. He had initiated a suit at law against himself, for vexatious litigation. The coroner concluded that while engaged in spying on his own activities from the roof, he had twisted himself about in some fashion or other in an effort to watch himself through the glass. He lost his balance and fell off.'

'His telescope,' Jeremy said. 'Was that the instrument he had used to locate the escaped convict from Princeton, according to Dr Watson's account?'

'It was indeed, Mr Holmes. Perhaps he was fortunate not to have fallen then.'

The telescope was bequeathed to Mr Barrymore, Dr Mortimer said. The remainder of his estate had gone to his daughter, Mrs Laura Lyons.

'And what of Mrs Lyons?' Jeremy asked.

'She is now in London,' the doctor said. 'Sir Henry and I had dinner with her yesterday.' Mrs Lyons had given up her secretarial service in Coombe Tracey, Dr Mortimer added, to work for The Widow. 'Mrs Lyons also had psychic damage to overcome. That scoundrel Stapleton had used her badly. Quite despicably.'

'How so?' Jeremy inquired.

'It was through her that Sir Charles was unwittingly lured onto the moor, and to his death. Those scars remain with her still.'

The Widow, seated in the dock, sagged with weariness. Caroline, her concerned warder, held her by the shoulders as though to keep her from falling out of her chair. 'My Lords,' Jeremy asked, 'may I request a recess?'

'Are you quite finished with this witness?' Justice Arlington asked.

'I am not,' Jeremy said. 'But my client is near exhaustion.'

'I join in the request,' Sir Guthrie said, not to be outdone. 'My learned friend is quite right. She can hardly sit.'

Justice Arlington huddled a moment with his fellow judges, after which the three of them stood up. 'Gentlemen of the jury,' Justice Arlington said, 'you will attend at ten in the morning.'

As they filed toward their exit, the usher jumped to his feet. 'Upstand!' he proclaimed, loud enough to shatter stone. 'Upstand all!' He waited until the judges had disappeared from view. 'The Central Criminal Court is in recess. All persons who have anything further to do before Her Majesty the Queen's justices of Oyer and Terminer and general gaol delivery for the jurisdition of the Central Criminal Court may depart hence and give your attendance here again tomorrow morning at ten o'clock. God save the Queen!'

Chapter 12

The Widow and her warder were dropped into the dungeon below. I uncapped my flask and allowed the sweet fire of Irish whiskey to bring my throat to life. I watched Jeremy and Sir Guthrie exchange pleasantries as the gallery emptied. When the barristers were done congratulating one another on their splendid performances, Sir Guthrie left him, and Jeremy came over to me.

'I thought it went well enough,' Jeremy said, which was for the consumption of those who remained. 'Your business will go quickly, will it not?'

'I shall be brief,' I said.

He nodded. 'When you are done, let us meet at the club.'

I made my way to the witness room, a rather spacious chamber behind the Sessions House. Dr Mortimer and Sir Henry Baskerville were at a table. As witnesses for the Crown, they were not allowed to watch the trial. 'How do, gentlemen,' I said, and greetings were exchanged.

Sir Henry expressed the desire to see The Widow, and I told him that by all means, he should visit her. There was no need to be in the company of Dr Mortimer. He had seen Caroline, her massive gaoler, who regarded the prisoner as her mistress. Caroline was a most adequate guardian, a lioness protecting her young. Not even a duke of the realm would be allowed to force unwanted attention upon The Widow.

For Dr Mortimer, I had a special request. I asked him to examine the curtains in the room where the stabbing had taken place.

'What am I looking for?' he asked.

'Blood stains,' I told him.

'Would not Scotland Yard have searched the room and found anything of the sort?'

'The flooring in the room was most thoroughly inspected,' I said, 'and traces of blood were found. But their reports make no mention of the curtains. A rather fastidious customer, dressing while inside one of the curtained closets, noticed a discoloration to the fabric and brought it to the attention of Mrs Lyons. Perhaps it was stained with blood.'

A short time later, I mounted the steps at the Bastriche Club and found Jeremy in his corner, drawing furiously. The muscles of his jaws rippled, as though chewing raw meat. 'I must congratulate you,' I said. 'The seeds regarding Lord Russell have been planted, and thoroughly watered. But my dear fellow, are you sure it is wise to pursue him so openly?'

Jeremy paid no attention to my question. 'Sir Henry is not a cartoon,' he said, angry at himself. He ripped the sheet off the pad and let it flutter to the floor. 'His simplicity lends itself to caricature,' he said, starting anew, 'but he is more than just another pleasant fellow. Or is that all?'

'You have not answered my question,' I said. 'Is the life of The Widow worth your own?'

'You make too much of it,' Jeremy said. He worked with savage intensity on the sheet in front of him, but was clearly not satisfied.

'I hardly think so,' I said. 'It is as though Justice Arlington would challenge Lord Russell to call you out.'

'I am a bastard,' Jeremy said, paying little attention to me. 'Lord Russell would never stoop so low as to stain his hands with the blood of a bastard.'

'William the Conqueror was a bastard,' I said. 'You are hardly a commoner, Jeremy. You are a barrister, and your mother was of the house of Wendleton.'

'Then I shall remind him that dueling has been outlawed in England, and I have no intention of breaking the law.' He ripped that sheet off his pad and let it flutter to the floor, immediately starting on another.

'That will not matter in the least to Lord Russell,' I said. 'He will invite you to travel to the Continent, and will follow you like a bloodhound, and will humiliate you, until you give him the satisfaction his honour demands.'

Jeremy smiled. His eyes gleamed with a devilish playfulness, as though at a game of cat and mouse. 'Let us hope, when he finds me, that members of the jury are there,' he said, drawing more slowly, and with care. 'I should like to reveal his murderous tendencies to them. Those characteristics of his are cloaked, of course, in his code of honour. But perhaps I could take away the cloak. Will Dr Mortimer examine the curtains?'

'He will,' I told him, 'although I fail to see how it will help.'

'Suggest to him that perhaps the stains were made by someone wiping gore from the blades of cutting shears.' He drew with a renewed purpose.

It was then that I realized what the exercise might show. 'Especially if the stains are on the inside of the curtain, as though done by someone behind them?'

'I should like to suggest that someone was hidden behind them, Edward. Someone who watched The Widow go to the aid of the dying man.' He smiled at his work. 'The inferences one might draw from that fact, if we are fortunate enough to show it, point at an assassin, I should think. Not at The Widow.'

Jeremy's eyes were not those of his uncle. Though they frequently burned with anger--as, at some aspect of the law--

they were generally lighted with an odd, but intense, wonder.

And the rays from his eyes did not penetrate, as did those of Sherlock Holmes. Rather, they surrounded the object of their focus with something akin to an embrace. His gaze found me. 'We walk a narrow rail, in a storm, my friend,' he said. 'We must step carefully, or lose our footing. What I would do is present the jurors with a portrait of Lord Russell, but it must be most carefully drawn. It cannot show the shears in his hand, with him driving them into the throat of Baskerville. None of the jurors would accept such a picture.'

'What is it you would show them, then?'

'I would have them see Lord Russell as the mind behind the murder. But not the murder of Rodger Baskerville, of whom Lord Russell knew nothing. I would have them see Lord Russell as the mind behind the murder of Christian Vandeleur.' He returned to his work. 'The picture we draw together, that the jurors will draw with me, will be a devastating one, I hope,' he said. 'I would have them see Lord Russell as one who knew, when he stopped at the *boutique*, that both The Widow and Vandeleur were there. Lord Russell also knew that the sleuths whom he had hired, were at hand. Let the jurors see Lord Russell as one who parked in front of the store as a ruse, designed to separate his wife from Vandeleur, long enough for one of them to slip into the back of the store, and do his work.'

'Your artistry, no doubt, will fascinate them,' I said.

'Let us hope so. It will allow me to argue to the jurors that the vengeance of Lord Russell to the woman whom he believed was his wife knew no bounds, once he believed she had taken a lover. He would do more than simply punish her, by having her lover murdered. He would have her hang for his murder.'

A devastating picture indeed. How would Peter, Lord

Russell, respond to a poster of himself, displayed before all the world, as such a man? He would not suffer it. Jeremy would die. 'Allow me a toast to your funeral then,' I said, raising my flask to him.

Jeremy paid no heed to my words. With his eyes on his work and his mind on his thoughts, he continued to develop his tactic. 'I will show them a scene of The Widow, opening her front door to Lord Russell. But one of his sleuths will have been portrayed as an assassin, and he will slip in the back, and do the chap. And if Dr Mortimer finds blood on the inside of the curtain, the jurors will watch the fellow hide behind it, wipe off the blade while The Widow tries to save the life of Professor Vandeleur, then slip out of the room, showing nothing but his cape. You must watch the scenes I draw when I offer them in court, Edward. You must tell me if a draw what I intend.'

'What you propose is madness,' I said. 'Do you know who Lord Russell is?'

'Of course,' Jeremy said. 'You found him for me. He is a most appealing alternative suspect.'

'Lord Russell was a professional soldier, and is now a member of the House of Lords. His honour means more to him than his life. He is skilled in the use of pistols, has faced the bravest of men in duels, and has killed them.'

'You could not have done better for The Widow than to have found such a man.'

'If you pursue your course, you will die.'

He shrugged. 'Perhaps.' He continued to draw.

'Your funeral will be well-attended, of course. *Listen* to me!'

'How can I not?' he asked. 'Your voice is loud enough to be heard in Bristol.'

'All the lovely scoundrels and rogues of London will be

there,' I said, lowering the volume of my remarks. 'I would hope to be one of those invited to speak, and would tell of your courage and dedication to justice for the oppressed.'

'Ah! What a pity that I am dead. How I should love to attend.' He stepped back from his work. 'I think I have him.'

'Sir Henry?' I asked, standing to look.

'Sir Guthrie will call him tomorrow,' he said. 'Do I know him? Is this the man you see?'

Sir Henry's crooked smile greeted me from under the brim of a cowboy hat. 'A solitary-looking chap,' I suggested. 'He belongs on a horse.'

'I quite agree,' Jeremy said. 'The isolation of those raised in wide open spaces becomes a part of them. I know it well.'

'You do?'

'Yes,' he said. 'My mother . . .' I waited for him to continue, but he stopped. With a nod of his head, he turned my attention back to the portrait of Sir Henry. 'The British may speak the same language as the Canadians,' he said, 'but their hearts are not the same.'

'An odd thing to say. What do you mean?'

'The Canadians do not depend on others. Those wide open spaces create in them a spirit of independence, quite unlike the British sense of family.' He looked at Sir Henry. 'It is no wonder they chafe to be free of British rule. Like the Americans, they can be *citizens*, perhaps, of a country. But never *subjects*, who owe their allegiance to the Queen.'

I nodded at the sketch. 'Yes. You have caught that quality in him,' I said. 'What else do you see?'

He frowned. 'One who had always believed that he had the courage to face the most extreme danger. But the terror he experienced recently--no doubt when the hound was at his

101

throat--humbled him.'

I frowned at the work. The soul of Sir Henry was exposed. I had seen it without knowing what I saw. 'That too,' I said, humbled also by a dawning awareness of mine. Jeremy was not mad. It was I, who was obtuse. 'Is there more?'

'He has doubts now,' Jeremy said. 'Is his manhood a mask? He does not know.'

Chapter 13

It was Friday, the second day of trial. I worked my way through the crowd in front of the Old Bailey and into the Sessions House. The jurors were in their places and The Widow--more simply dressed than the day before, but with the same woolen shawl draped over her shoulders--had been raised from the depths below and sat in the dock. Caroline, her warder, sat behind her. The Widow seemed at peace with herself, as if prepared to meet her Maker.

Jeremy, more fit in appearance than others dressed in robes and powdered wigs, chatted amicably with Sir Guthrie and his colleague, Mr Roberts. When the judges in their silken scarlet robes filed solemnly into the courtroom, the barristers moved to their places. 'Up stand! Upstand all!' boomed the usher, his voice the crash of a cannon. 'All persons who have anything further to do before Her Majesty the Queen's Justices of Oyer and Terminer and general gaol delivery for the jurisdiction of the Central Criminal Court draw near and give your attendance. God Save the Queen!'

At Jeremy's request, Dr Mortimer did not resume his place in the witness box. Jeremy would call him later, as a witness for the defence. The Crown called Sir Henry Baskerville as its next witness.

'I swear by almighty God that the evidence that I shall give shall be the truth, the whole truth, and nothing but the truth,' he said, then handed the Bible to the usher. When he took his chair, his dark eyes seemed to caress The Widow.

Sir Henry identified himself as the baronet of Baskerville Hall. The estate had devolved to him on the death of his uncle, Sir Charles Baskerville. He confirmed the accuracy of *The Hound of the Baskervilles*, and--as had Dr Mortimer--

expressed his total astonishment at viewing the body of the man known to him as Jack Stapleton. Along with everyone who had been involved in those dark events, he had believed the fellow had perished in the Grimpen Mire. 'At that time then, you knew the accused?'

'I did. And I do still, Sir Guthrie.'

'Yes, of course. After meeting her in Dartmoor, you proposed marriage to her, did you not?'

'I did, sir.'

'When you offered her your hand in marriage, you believed her to be the sister of Jack Stapleton?'

'Yes.'

'May I assume that you were in love with her, when you proposed to her?' Sir Guthrie asked, rather unexpectedly.

Sir Henry blushed slightly. 'I was indeed.'

'Forgive me for asking you the obvious, but while on your voyage with Dr Mortimer, did you believe The Widow to be free of her marriage bonds?'

'I did.'

'Did you renew your marriage proposal then?'

'I did not.'

'During your voyage, and after your return to Dartmoor, did you have any contact with The Widow?'

He shook his head. 'No.'

'When did you return to England, Sir Henry, if I may ask?'

'In February of this year.'

'And are you healed, from the psychic damage done you by that fearful apparition?'

'I am, sir. I feel very fit and healthy.'

But he was not healed. Jeremy's sketch had deepened my insight into the man. I could see terror, buried in his heart.

'Thank you Sir Henry,' the prosecutor said, and sat down.

Jeremy rose slowly, as does one who is at a bit of a loss. 'Sir Henry, we have not met, have we?'

'We have not, Mr Holmes.'

'But you have had conversations with my instructing solicitor, Mr Edward Greech?'

'I have.' Sir Henry found me in the gallery next to the jurors, and nodded.

'It is my pleasure to meet you, Sir Henry, and kind of Sir Guthrie to call you as a witness. There is not the slightest doubt in your mind that the corpse you viewed recently, at the request of Scotland Yard, was that of the man known to you as Jack Stapleton?'

'Absolutely none.'

'Thank you, Sir Henry.'

The witness stood down.

Why had Sir Henry been called, I wondered? He added nothing to the case for the Crown. Would Sir Guthrie use his love for The Widow in his summation? Would he give to her the powers of a witch?

Inspector Lestrade, of Scotland Yard, was next brought to the witness box by the usher, and sworn in as a witness for the Crown. A small, wiry man endowed with the jaw of a bulldog, he sat attentively, very alert to his surroundings, his hands resting on his knees. He responded to the questions of Sir Guthrie in the clear, terse dialect of a professional solver of crime. 'On the night of twenty-eight September and morning of twenty-nine,' he boldly informed the jurors, 'I had the duty, and was at rest on my cot at Scotland Yard, Whitehall, when I was called to action. The body of a man rolled into a blanket was in the alleyway behind a dress-making shop at Marylebone Lane.'

When he arrived, he found that the constable at the location had detained a woman. 'It was the accused, and I recognized her. I had come to know her in Dartmoor, as Mrs Jack Stapleton, in the company of Sherlock Holmes. And I was aware of the fact that she had come to London afterwards, and was married to the Baron of Somerset. It was in all the papers.' The Attorney-General interrupted, and asked him to refer to the accused as The Widow. 'Right, Sir Guthrie,' Lestade said. 'It was The Widow who had been detained by the constable in the alleyway behind Marylebone Lane. I had the confidence that she would remember me well, because in Dartmoor, I had saved her life.'

Lestrade assigned to himself the delicate role of interrogating The Widow. Inspector Brogarth of the Yard would conduct the investigation at *Fashions Sabor Brazilenos*. Lestrade and The Widow took a carriage to Scotland Yard.

'She remembered me, as I had thought she would,' Lestrade said. 'One does not forget the man who saved one's life.' When asked by Sir Guthrie if her statement was given of her own free will, he said it was. A secretary transcribed her words, which were typed up and read over by her. 'She was invited to make corrections, and did so, to which she affixed her initials.'

The questioning of her, and the proper recording of her statement, took up much of the early morning hours, Lestrade said. But at seven o'clock the morning of 29 September, he escorted The Widow to the Police Court at Greater Marleborough Street. The magistrate considered her statement, as well as other evidence assembled by the Yard. He then charged her with the murder of Professor Christian Vandeleur.

'The jury will have her signed account of the matter to

consider,' Sir Guthrie said, 'but will you be so kind as to tell us what was in her statement?'

He would indeed. 'She identified herself as the wife of Peter, Lord Russell, and as the owner of *Fashions Sabor Brazilenos*. By her husband's grace, she was permitted to operate her business after their marriage. It was dear to her, she said, and told me of her closeness to those in her employ. Spanish ladies they was for the most part, without means. She had developed a fondness for them and had no wish to abandon them.'

On the evening of the day before, she had remained in her office after all her employees had gone. 'A fashion show of some importance would begin in Paris that week, which she must attend. It was her intention to stay that night in her rooms above her business. But while in her office, immersed in work, this fellow made his appearance. It was most unexpected, and she had not invited him to do so in the least.'

Lestrade pursed his lips. 'She knew the man. His name was Christian Vandeleur, and she had met him through her husband. He frightened her, she said, but it was his uncalled-for presumption that bothered her the most. It angered her.'

Lestrade asked her how Vandeleur had come inside without her knowledge, but she could not explain how he had done so. 'She thought perhaps he had entered earlier in the day, then hidden in some corner until the others had gone.'

'She said nothing of a key to the front door then?' Sir Guthrie asked.

'She did not.' Later, when The Widow told the man to leave, 'Mr Vandeleur would not budge. Rather, he attempted to take her into his arms.'

Had she cried out then, Sir Guthrie asked? 'She did not,' was the reply. 'No one was there to hear, she maintained, though she agreed that perhaps her voice might have carried as far as the streets.'

'And then?'

'There was a knock on the door. She recognized the rap by the sound of it, and knew it was her husband,' Lestrade said. 'For which she expressed great relief. She wasted no time in disengaging herself from the fellow's amourous advances, and made for the front door.'

'He let her go?'

'So she said, Sir Guthrie. She firmly believed Vandeleur would seize the opportunity to make his escape out the back. So she opened the front door and invited her husband inside.' The bemused expression of Lestrade was not lost on the jurors. 'They spoke of her trip, after which he had embraced her, and departed.'

'Did she alert Lord Russell of the unwelcome presence of Professor Vandeleur?'

'No sir. The men were acquainted with one another, she said, and her husband was a man of passionate temper.' He wiped at his nose. 'She had no wish to create a scene, or to cause trouble, so she let it pass.'

At first, it appeared to The Widow that Vandeleur had gone, Lestrade continued. 'But noises from the fitting room gave her alarm.' He described the room as a large space, given over to sewing machines and tables on which implements used by the dress-makers rested, such as cutting shears. 'The room is in the back of the establishment, and it was with great trepidation that she went in.'

She was greeted with an awful scene. 'Noises as from a drowning man greeted her she said, and on the floor was Professor Vandeleur, twisting this way and that way, hands at his neck. Blood in large quantities pushed out of his neck as from a hole in a dyke.' She rushed to his aid. She took strips of cloth from a table nearby, and wrapped them round his neck-- when a pair of cutting shears landed on the floor, quite near her.

'She told you that?' Sir Guthrie asked, as though incredulous.

'And more, sir. At that very moment the door at the back of the room slammed shut. But she thought she caught a glimpse of a figure wearing a cape.' The witness displayed a mischievous smile. 'She assumed it was a man, but not to swear to. Professor Vandeleur, of course, was quite done.'

She then acknowledged to Lestrade that she had made a dreadful mistake. The barest of smiles continued to tug at his mouth as he testified. She spoke of her concern over the appearance of the situation, considering the prominence of her husband, and his family.

'And so she chose to cover the matter over,' Lestrade said, a twinkle in his eye. 'She would clean up the cutting room as only a woman can, and herself as well. Then she would wait until the early morning hours, to avoid being seen at her business, and at the right time she would transport the body of Christian Vandeleur to Regent's Park in her carriage. It was not a great distance from her business on Marylebone Lane, and she knew it well. Her husband was a member of the Toxopholite Society and she had seen him in some competitions there.'

'What is the Toxopholite Society?' the Attorney-General asked.

'They are sportsmen, who engage in archery. They have a green at Regents Park.' He pursed his lips to keep from smiling. 'When the body was found on the grounds, with a wound in the throat, she thought perhaps it would appear that

Professor Vandeleur had been pierced with an arrow, as from a stray shot.' He frowned, perhaps to avoid a smile. 'She would then go to Paris, as though nothing had happened.'

Lestrade commented that throughout the interview, The Widow was in control of her emotions. Although one might expect her to be in a fragile state of mind, 'there were not the signs of weakness or agitation as one might expect from a member of her sex, after mopping up blood and scrubbing a floor of its fearful stain. Her companion as she worked through the night was the man who had bled to death in her arms, spread out on the floor. As she told me of it, Sir Guthrie, she did not so much as shed a tear.'

Sir Guthrie took his chair.

'Inspector, I know *of* you, as do all in London who can read the papers, but we have not met,' Jeremy said. 'It is my pleasure.'

'The pleasure is mine, Mr Holmes,' Inspector Lestrade said. 'Your uncle speaks highly of your abilities in the courtroom.'

'Do you refer to Sherlock Holmes, the consulting detective?'

'I do,' Lestrade said. 'We would have asked him to view the body of Rodger Baskerville, but he is on serious business now, on the continent.'

'Mr Holmes. Inspector Lestrade,' Justice Arlington said sharply. 'You are not to engage in gratuitous pleasantries here.'

'Thank you My Lord,' Jeremy said. To Lestrade, 'Should you see Mr Sherlock Holmes, tell him I am indeed complimented.'

'Mr Holmes!' Justice Arlington said. 'We have business here. Be so kind as to have your conversation with the witness another time.'

'Of course, My Lord.'

Jeremy asked Lestrade if the part he had played in Dartmoor, two years before, was as Dr Watson had described it in his account. Lestrade hesitated a moment before he replied. 'I must say that I had some reservations,' he said. When asked to elaborate on his comment, Lestrade replied that when the hound first appeared on the heels of Sir Henry, with fire dripping from its jaws, 'I did indeed stumble and fall to the ground, as Dr Watson wrote of it. But it was not out of fright, Mr Holmes, not at all. I had slipped in my eagerness to confront the beast.'

When he bounced to his feet, Lestrade continued, he had his pistol out and was shooting at the fearful apparition. 'Though furthest away, it was my unerring aim that wounded the hound, Mr Holmes. I hit it as it leaped on Sir Henry.' He nodded his head as though to emphasize the point. 'Had the animal not been grievously wounded by my bullet, it would have torn away the throat of Sir Henry.'

Unlike others who had testified, the inspector was of the opinion that the chronicles of Dr Watson did not always describe an adventure with accuracy. 'His reverence for Mr Holmes resulted in some unfortunate distortions of the facts ... . If one was to rely on the pen of Dr Watson, one would never know that Sherlock Holmes had a bastard for a nephew, or that one of his brothers had a bastard for a son.'

In Dr Watson's account of the Baskerville case, 'my work was buried out of view,' Lestrade said. 'Yet it was I who found Mrs Stapleton, all wrapped in blankets and bound tight in the mouth, quite near to suffocation, she was. Had I not found her in time, she would have died.' Again, the rocking of his head emphasized his words. 'The woman bore many signs

111

of mistreatment, not merely a weal on her cheek from a lash, and bruises on her arms. Dr Watson did not fully describe the terrible extent of her abuse, as will come when a person is all but torn limb from limb. It was indeed fortunate that a man of my experience was there to direct the early stages of her recovery.'

Immediately after the witness stood down, Justice Arlington called for a short recess. I scurried in great haste for the privy.

Chapter 14

Inspector Brogarth was in the witness box when I returned to my place. A large man with a florid face, he quite filled up the box, yet in spite of his size, he spoke with a high-pitched timidity.

The premises known as *Fashions Sabor Brazilenos* was thoroughly searched, he told the jurors, and a search warrant obtained for the rooms above. A bloodied dress, known to have been worn by The Widow that day, was found inside a laundry bag that had been stuffed in a large drawer in the bedroom closet.

Two large trunks were in the bedroom, placed along the wall nearest the stairway. The trunks had been carefully and neatly packed with fine clothing, toiletries, and other objects. There were framed photographs of Lord Russell, with inscriptions on them from him, one of which showed him engaged in a polo match, and another standing beside a target with three arrows in the center. There were letters written in Spanish, signed by "Mama". A bracelet of polished rubies was there, and other jewelry that appeared to have been crafted in India. There was a butter-fly net, a painting of a manor house in the English country-side, and three notebooks of dress patterns. Also quite carefully packaged, there were wedding photographs of The Widow and Lord Russell. 'Lady Russell was to travel to Paris for a fashion show,' Brogarth said, 'but one hardly needs two trunks for such a trip.'

'Would one take letters from one's mother if one expected to return in a week?' Sir Guthrie queried. 'And why would one take wedding pictures on a short business trip?'

Jeremy smiled at the Attorney-General, but gave no indication of an objection. 'If I may say so sir,' Inspector

Brogarth said, 'it was as though she wasn't coming back.'

Later when Sir Guthrie requested the witness to refer to the accused as The Widow, in that her marriage to Lord Russell was null and void, Justice Arlington suffered a change of attitude. 'You may address the accused as Lady Russell, or as Beryl Stapleton, when required to do so by the context,' he said. 'I am quite sure the jurors are not confused. Please proceed.'

The mistaken identification of the victim did not embarrass him, Brogarth said. During the early stages of the investigation, it was clear that the deceased was Professor Christian Vandeleur. Lady Russell had volunteered his name to Constable Firstson, and she referred to him by that name when interviewed by Inspector Lestrade. A search of his body substantiated her identification.

In the man's pockets were found two letters, both addressed to Professor Christian Vandeleur. The British Museum had granted him an unlimited use of its facilities, and the headmistress at Queenland College for Women written to Professor Vandeleur in the other, telling him how thrilled she was that he had agreed to present a series of lectures on the moths of South Africa at her "humble school for girls."

'In his front pocket, we found a ring of keys,' Brogarth said. 'One of the keys opened the main door of *Fashions Sabor Brazilenos.* Another, a flat in Essex, let to Professor Christian Vandeleur, and the last was to his office at Queenland College. When his body was positively identified by the headmistress at Queenland College as that of Professor Vandeleur, we had no cause to question his identification.'

The inspector then summarized the balance of the evidence presented to the magistrate at the Marlborough Street Police Court. The abstracts of the notes of two detectives, employed by the Fleet Street Investigative Agency, disclosed that from early August until the murder, Professor Vandeleur and Lady Russell were seen together on many occasions. Later in August, they had been alone, for more than an hour, at *Fashions Sabor Brazilenos*. On the evening of 28 September, they were also alone for what may have been many hours. 'The matter had the look of a lover's quarrel,' Inspector Brogarth said, to which Jeremy did not protest. 'With a disastrous consequence.'

Four pairs of cutting shears, located on the sewing tables in the cutting room, were examined under microscopes at the Scotland Yard laboratory. One had minute flakes of human blood in the steel springs that operated its hinges. 'Lady Russell volunteered to the magistrate that they were quite like the shears dropped on the cutting room floor, by an unknown person,' Brogarth said. 'She also told the magistrate that the bloody clothing in the laundry bag found in her rooms above, did indeed belong to her.' Though the cutting room floor had been thoroughly scrubbed, blood stains were still discernible, and traces of blood were found in the thin fissures between the boards.

The magistrate found the evidence quite enough to charge Lady Russell with the murder of Professor Christian Vandeleur. The Attorney-General took his chair.

'Scotland Yard, then, was not the least bit embarrassed by its mistaken identification of the victim?' Jeremy asked.

'Perhaps a bit, Mr Holmes,' Brogarth responded.

Jeremy reminded Brogarth that he had said, '"the matter had the look of a lover's quarrel, with a disastrous consequence."' There followed questions from Jeremy suggesting that perhaps another "disastrous consequence" had occurred, because of the mistaken identification of the victim. 'The murder would not have had the look of a lover's quarrel,

115

with a disastrous consequence, had the Yard known that the victim was Rodger Baskerville, would it?' Inspector Brogarth was asked.

'Perhaps it would not have had the same aspect,' Brogarth replied.

'The Yard--and certainly Inspector Lestrade--knew that Rodger Baskerville had murdered Sir Charles Baskerville?'

'I am quite sure all of those at the Yard knew as much.'

'Then will you agree with me that had you known the victim was Rodger Baskerville, the investigation would have started down an entirely different path?'

'Mr Holmes, that is precisely the path we followed, when we discovered our mistake,' Brogarth said.

'Then you will agree with me that the Yard did not start down the right path until three weeks after the murder?' Jeremy asked.

'The facts are the facts, Mr Holmes,' Brogarth said.

'They are indeed,' Jeremy said. 'Would you be so good as to describe the corners of the cutting room?'

'Each had been converted into a small closet,' Brogarth said, 'with drapes as doorways. Shelves were hung on the walls, as were hooks to hold clothing. Two of the closets had large mirrors affixed to the walls. The ladies could change clothes in the closets quite comfortably,' the inspector squeaked in his high voice.

'Were these corner closets searched?'

'They were,' was the reply. 'Nothing was found in any of them of consequence to our investigation.'

'Did you know, when you conducted your search of the closets, that Lady Russell had told of a person dropping cutting shears on the floor, and leaving the room?'

'I did.'

'Had it occurred to you that such a person might have been hiding in one of the closets, when Lady Russell came into the room?'

'It most certainly occurred to me, Mr Holmes. I found nothing in any of the closets that would suggest the presence of such a person.'

'Then you examined the drapes?'

'I gave them a visual inspection,' Brogarth said.

'Did you take them into your hands, and pull apart the pleats, and go over them inch by inch?'

'I did not, Mr Holmes.'

'You looked at them then,' Jeremy said. 'What did you see?'

'I saw nothing to remark on.'

'Were they taken down, to be examined at the laboratories at the Yard, for that which your visual inspection might not have seen?'

'They were not.'

He was asked to stand down.

The next witness called by the Crown, dressed in the suit of a gentleman, wore as well the wariness of a burglar at work. A former bobby in Bristol, my inquiries had shown that Mr Edward Longstreet was hardly a paragon of virtue. He had beaten a dog to death with his nightstick, and had given up his badge to avoid charges. In London, he obtained employment as a detective for Fleet Street Investigations.

When Sir Guthrie introduced him to the jurors, he dwelled on his background as a bobby, without mentioning the unpleasantness. Mr Longstreet was asked if he could identify the accused, and he said he could. 'Have you met her?'

'No, sir, but I knows her well enough.'

'Does she know you?'

'Doubts it, sir. She never laid her eyes on me.'

'Explain yourself, please. May I suggest that you tell us who your client was, the purpose of your hire, and then in a chronological fashion, detail your contacts and your observations of the accused?'

His client was a solicitor whose chamber was at Staple Inn, Holborn. Longstreet was instructed to follow Lady Russell, wherever she might go. 'Not into places of privacy, Sir Guthrie. The game was to show that she met up with a bloke name of Professor Christian Vandeleur. If they bumped up to one another, our job was to see and report the whole of it.'

'You did not work alone then?'

'The way of it sir, I tagged Lady Russell, me pal Madan Asan of the Orient tagged Professor Vandeleur.'

'May I ask if there was a reason that you were assigned to Lady Russell, and Madan Asan was assigned to Professor Vandeleur?'

'Madan Asan had a considerable edge on me in the game,' Longstreet said, 'so he took the sex that has the greater awareness of his surroundings, I the female gender. If I may say so,' he added, 'I ha'nt never seen the likes of Madan Asan. Times he would disappear before your very eyes.'

The agency prepared them well, Longstreet said. The targets became family members, as easy to spot as a brother or sister. He then listed the time and place of the meetings of Vandeleur and Lady Russell. On Wednesday, 5 August, they met for lunch at the Bridgewater House near Green Park. The following Wednesday, 12 August, they lunched in the intimacy of a booth at Crosby Hall. On Thursday evening, 20 August, they were alone with one another for an hour, at *Fashions Sabor Brazilenos*. On Wednesday, 26 August, they had lunch again at Crosby Hall, and they were together for their final time on Tuesday, 28 September, in the evening.

'Will you describe their manner toward one another on these occasions?' Sir Guthrie asked.

'At Bridgewater House, I observed a bit of hesitation by Lady Russell at the start of it. But she had no objection when he held her hand. At Crosby Hall, they bent toward one another and held hands, as does couples who have romance in their minds.'

The two occasions when they met at Lady Russell's place of business? Sir Guthrie asked. 'I could not see them. They was inside and not visible through the window. But perhaps I seen enough. The first time, after Professor Vandeleur let himself in the door, he departed after an hour with a pleased look about him.' Mr Longstreet rubbed a hand under his chin, and the smile on his face was quite suggestive. 'The last time, the lamp in the room above the business, which we knew to be the bedroom, was lit up for a minute or two, and then it went out.'

'There was a month between their last two meetings,' Sir Guthrie said. 'They met for lunch on August 26, and then were together again on September 28. Can you account for such an extended separation?'

'Professor Vandeleur had gone to South Africa, Sir Guthrie. He was gone away from England from twenty-six August until twenty-five   September, when he was back.'

Jeremy chose not to question Longstreet over the circumstances surrounding his discharge, for which the detective appeared grateful, having expected the worst. Jeremy asked if Lady Russell had given any indication that she was aware of him, such as an evasive manoeuver or a backwards glance. 'None of it, Mr Holmes,' the witness said. 'Not a hint.'

'Take us through your activities in connection with this matter on twenty-eight September, if you will, Mr Longstreet,' Jeremy said.

The detective had picked up Lady Russell at her home in Kensington at 9:30 A.M. She was driven to her *boutique* by her chauffeur, arriving at 10:25 A.M., entering through the main door, as was her habit. Once inside, the detective waited for her to show herself. He positioned himself at the north end of Marylebone Lane, in such a way that he could see the main door of the *boutique* clearly, as well as the entrance to the alleyway behind. There was construction in the alleyway, obstructing the passage of anyone who might wish to go out the south end. Though Longstreet could not see the back exit of the store, anyone leaving the alleyway must come out the north end, thus he was in a position to see them.

He did not see Lady Russell again until a richly-appointed carriage pulled up in front, out of which jumped a fine-looking gentleman. The man had not waited for the chauffeur to open the carriage door. 'The toff tapped with his knuckles on the door of the business and Lady Russell opened it up, she did, and let him inside.'

'And you saw her then?' Jeremy asked.

'I did.'

'At what time did that occur?'

''Twas ten minutes after seven P.M.,' the witness said.

'Then earlier that evening, you had watched Professor Vandeleur let himself in?' Jeremy asked.

'Correct, Mr Holmes.'

'What time did Professor Vandeleur go inside?'

'Quite close in time it was. Perhaps ten minutes before the coach stopped there.'

'Then at least three people were inside the *boutique*

120

while the carriage stood in front of it?' Jeremy asked.

'They was indeed, Mr Holmes. There was three inside.'

'The gentleman was not inside for long, was he?'

'No,' was the reply. 'A minute or two.'

'Then he drove away?' Jeremy asked.

'He did, sir.'

'Was he alone in the carriage when he drove away?' Jeremy asked.

'No sir,' Longstreet said. 'A woman was there. She climbed on top of him, one might say, when he was in. Most anxious she was to embrace him.'

'Most anxious, was she?' Jeremy asked.

'Indeed she was, sir.'

'You told Sir Guthrie that you had seen a light go on in the bedroom above the *boutique*,' Jeremy said, 'and that it was on a minute or two. When was that?' Jeremy asked.

'I made no note of the time, but it was later in the evening,' the detective said. 'The lamps on Marylebone Lane had been lit by then, and it was dark outside.'

'Then it was perhaps half an hour after the gentleman in the carriage, under a woman who had climbed on top of him, had gone?'

'I should say it was at least that.'

When asked if Peter, Lord Russell, had engaged the solicitor who hired Fleet Street Investigations, the detective said he had no knowledge of that. He gave his reports to the solicitor who had instructed him, and had no interest in who had engaged the solicitor.

Was his partner Madan Asan stationed in front of the business, when the carriage pulled up? Jeremy inquired of the witness. Mr Longstreet did not know. Yet he remembered quite clearly that when Professor Vandeleur had let himself in

121

the door, 'Madan Asan gave me a sign. Then he vanished.'

'He vanished,' Jeremy said. 'Then he may have gone round to the back of the building?' Jeremy asked.

The detective nodded his head. 'He might well have done so.'

'May I ask you as to the manner of Madan Asan's dress at that time?'

'He was not someone you would notice,' Longstreet said. 'The clothes he wore was dark.'

'He was difficult to see when inside a shadow then?' Jeremy suggested.

'More than difficult, Mr Holmes. Careful as you might look for him, he was hard to spot.'

'Did he cover his shoulders?' Jeremy asked, knowing the answer, which I had provided him.

'He did, Mr Holmes. They was covered over with a black cape.'

'You are quite certain that he wore a black cape?' Jeremy asked.

'Quite certain, sir.'

'Mr Longstreet, to your knowledge, has Madan Asan ever hired out as an assassin?'

Sir Guthrie rose to his feet, as though to register an objection, but said nothing.

'Mr Longstreet, should I repeat the question?' Jeremy asked.

The witness looked toward Sir Guthrie.

'You do not need the permission of the Attorney-General to answer the question,' Jeremy said. 'Do you know whether or not Mr Madan Asan has ever been an assassin for hire?'

'I knows nothin' of that sort about 'im, Mr Holmes.'

'Would it surprise you?'

'My Lords,' Sir Guthrie said, his hand raised as though to shield the jurors from further testimony, 'surely my learned friend knows better than to ask Mr Longstreet to speculate on such a matter.'

'I quite agree,' Justice Arlington said. 'Have you anything further of this witness, Mr Holmes?'

'No, My Lord.'

'The witness may stand down,' Justice Arlington said, who then nodded at the usher. 'We shall adjourn, for lunch.'

Chapter 15

I lunched alone, at the King's Tavern, on a steaming platter of Welsh rarebit. For drink, I enjoyed a mug of Bass Pale Ale. The day was overcast when I returned to the Sessions House, and the overhead lamps had been turned up. The light from them radiated down on the chamber as Madan Asan was brought into the witness box.

Perhaps because of the expectations created by Detective Longstreet, one could readily believe that the slightly-built Oriental could blend himself into his surroundings, and render himself invisible. Sir Guthrie approached him with his customary good cheer and aplomb, but it was apparent to me that he hoped to quickly have done with the rather sinister detective. The small man could not more perfectly have worn the face of an inscrutable member of the yellow race. It was a blank slate.

In simplified English, he said he was from India, and had been employed by the Fleet Street Investigative Agency for three years. When questioned about the meetings between Vandeleur and Lady Russell, he verified the testimony of Longstreet. When asked to tell what he had seen on the evening of 28 September, his contributions differed only slightly from those of Longstreet. 'I follow Professor Vandeleur. He approach *Fashions Sabor Brazilenos*. He hold key in hand. He unlock front door. He open door. He go inside.'

'And then?' asked Sir Guthrie.

'I wait.'

The witness told the jurors that he had remained on Marylebone Lane, in the shadows across the street from *Fashions Sabor Brazilenos*, until the early morning hours of 29

September. 'Did you go round to the back at any time?' he was asked.

'Yes,' was the reply. When the constable went round the back into the alleyway behind, he had followed him. But he had not done so until then.

Madan Asan had also seen Lady Russell come out the back door, dragging a body wrapped in a blanket into the alleyway. He remained out of sight until after the lady had gone off in a carriage with an inspector from Scotland Yard. A wagon was brought for the corpse, and as it was lifted in, the inspector in charge had opened the blanket. Madan Asan saw the face of Vandeleur.

'My business done,' he said, quite without a change of expression. He returned to the Fleet Street Investigative Agency and wrote his final report. Later that morning he delivered his report to the solicitor.

With an approving nod at the witness, the Attorney-General sat down.

Jeremy thoughtfully considered his sketch of the small man, then turned it over. 'You are a man of many languages, are you not?' he asked.

'Yes.'

Thus began a most remarkable examination. Though Jeremy knew nothing of the small Oriental, he drew from him a history that fit our strategy as closely as do the gloves on one's hands. In his youth, Madan Asan had lived a simple life in India. But the small village that had been his home was ravaged by bandits, and his family murdered. He escaped by hiding from them. After, he made his way to the Kingdom of Nepal where he trained in a society of monks. He became proficient in the martial arts, the use of silent and deadly weaponry, and matters of stealth. He readily agreed with

125

Jeremy that he was quite skilled in the use of daggers, and dress that allowed of concealment.

'The bandits who murdered your family. What of them?' Jeremy asked.

'No more,' Madan Asan replied, impassively. 'Gone.'

'They are gone,' Jeremy said. 'Do you mean, they no longer are alive?'

'Yes.'

Jeremy waited a moment, as though watching for a change of expression on the face of the witness. There was none. 'Were they dispatched by your hand?' he asked.

'I not answer.'

Jeremy nodded. 'Were they turned over to your police and executed?'

'No.'

'Yet, they are gone?'

'Yes.'

The jurors nearest me appeared to be captivated by the little yellow man, as were the judges. Their expressions showed fascination, with a dash of distaste.

'On twenty-eight September, as you followed the man known to you as Christian Vandeleur, were you dressed in a manner that would allow you to conceal yourself, if the occasion demanded it?'

He was so dressed, with a black cape over his shoulders to allow him to blend into shadows. He further testified that he could easily have entered *Fashions Sabor Brazilenos* through either the front door, or the back. But he had not done so. Oddly, he denied any awareness of the occupants of the carriage that had parked in front of the *boutique*. In accordance with his training, his concentration was only on the man he followed.

'You have followed many people then, other than Professor Vandeleur?' Jeremy asked.

'Yes.'

'Have you ever lost a person whom you followed?'

'Not understand.'

'At any time, has someone you followed become aware of your presence, and given you the slip?'

'No.'

'Have any such persons tried to give you the slip?'

'Yes.'

'May I assume then, that you are able to determine whether or not the person whom you follow is aware of being followed?'

'Yes.'

When asked to describe the tell-tale signs, the witness said that their manner of walking would change, as did their facial expressions. The body had a language of its own, which Madan Asan said he had learned to read. What of Professor Vandeleur, Jeremy asked? Did he know he was being followed?

'Yes.'

'Did he try to give you the slip?'

'No.'

How very odd, I thought, as Jeremy took his chair. The expressions of many of those in the hall were also unsettled.

Lord Arlington addressed Sir Guthrie, as the Attorney-General got to his feet. 'The day grows dark,' he said. 'Can you give us a weather forecast, so to speak? Would now be a good time to adjourn for the week-end?'

'If that is your wish, My Lord,' Sir Guthrie said. 'The evidence thus far has been in proof of the charge of murder, lodged against the accused. But if it please you, let me suggest that the balance of the day should be quite sufficient to address the charge of bigamy.'

Lord Arlington nodded at him. 'Please proceed then,' he said.

Sir Guthrie began by producing a document in the Spanish language, which--when translated into proper English--was a Certificate of Marriage. Issued by a court of record from Costa Rica, the English translation was read to the jurors by Mr Roberts. It proclaimed that on 19 February, 1882, John Rodger Baskerville and Beryl Garcia had been joined together in marriage as man and wife.

Mrs Laura Lyons was next led in by the usher, and took her chair in the witness box. When I saw her pretty face, I realized that I had formed an attachment to the woman. It rather surprised me. As the instructing solicitor for the defence, I should never have socialized with a witness. Although I might possibly be able to justify our dinners as necessary to prepare for trial, in truth, my pleasure in her company had swept away my judgment. Her taste in whiskey may have gone beyond the lovely bite of my fine Irish blends, but I saw that as only a minor blemish in her character. She would take my arm when we walked, and when we dined, would smile at me across the table, and laugh at my feeble jokes. I was taken with her.

She smiled at me from the witness box, and it quite warmed me. Dressed stylishly in clothes that would have served her well at the opera, her responses to the questions of the Attorney-General were delivered in the soft, well-modulated voice of an educated woman.

Sir Guthrie introduced her as the personal secretary and principal assistant of The Widow. But two years before, the witness told the jurors that she had known both the victim, and the accused. That was in Dartmoor, Mrs Lyons said, where the victim and the accused were known as Jack and Beryl Stapleton, brother and sister. Shortly before the so-called hound of the Baskervilles was killed, Mrs Lyons had learned they were not brother and sister. She had been informed by Mr Sherlock Holmes that they were married.

Mrs Lyons had frequent conversations with Lady Russell in the latter part of 1889, after the death of Jack Stapleton. The two women had grown close to one another. 'Beryl told me of her marriage to Rodger Baskerville in Costa Rica,' Mrs Lyons said, 'and even admitted to a brief period of happiness with him. But that light was soon put out. Underneath his charm, and even his brilliant mind, she found an incomprehensible layer of greed, and cruelty.'

'Was more said to you on the subject?' Sir Guthrie asked.

'She wanted to rid herself of the name of Baskerville,' the witness said. 'She wanted never to use it again. When she came to London in January, she took her maiden name. That of Beryl Garcia.'

'What of her subsequent' . . . and the Attorney-General put quotation marks around the next word with his fingers . . . '"marriage" to Lord Russell? Did she speak to you of it?'

'Oh yes,' my dear Laura said. 'She glowed with love, if I may say so, as only a woman can. She spoke to me of her great happiness, when first she married Lord Russell in July.'

'Did she ever acknowledge to you, before twenty-eight September, that she knew she was . . . "married" . . . to both men?'

With reluctance, Mrs Lyons nodded her head in the affirmative. 'Her new-found happiness with her husband was shattered, after less than two weeks,' she said. 'Lord Russell took her to the British Museum to a lecture of great interest, and introduced her to the speaker. The speaker was Professor Christian Vandeleur, from South Africa. To her horror, she found that the man was her first husband, Rodger Baskerville.'

'Is that what she told you?' the Attorney-General asked.

'It is, Sir Guthrie.' Mrs Lyons had not believed her, and had questioned her closely about this unthinkable development. 'I told her it was not possible,' the witness said. 'Her first husband had drowned in the Grimpen Mire. I suggested to her that perhaps he had a brother, with identical features.'

Sir Guthrie nodded at my dear Laura. 'My Lords,' he said, 'there is no purpose to be served in further testimony of the witness.' He began to take his chair.

'You are done with me?' Mrs Lyons asked.

'I am,' the Attorney-General replied.

'Sir Guthrie, what you do here is dreadful. My lady is innocent. You must believe her. You must!'

The Attorney-General smiled with great cordiality at the witness. 'Of course you believe as you do,' he said. 'You love her dearly, do you not?' He took his chair.

Jeremy had been sketching the witness, as was his habit, to ready himself for his examination. He glanced at his sketch and stood up. 'You are quite certain that The Widow has been falsely accused of this crime then?' he asked.

'I am indeed,' she said, with a fervor I had not known her to possess.

Jeremy had no other questions of her, and she was asked to stand down.

Peter, Lord Russell was called as the next and final witness for the Crown. The moment had come that Jeremy had been waiting for.

Chapter 16

As I have said before, Jeremy had a unique method to prepare for trial. Rather than write out lists of questions and rehearse his arguments before a mirror, he drew pictures. He knew the crime scene as well as anyone at Scotland Yard, because he had drawn it from various angles, even though he had seen it but once. In the same way, he had come to know Lord Russell.

'What do you see, Edward?' he had asked me the night before, when showing me his drawing of the man.

A handsome fellow, dashing, a long thin scar on his left cheek. From a duel, perhaps? His eyes blazed with arrogance and danger. 'Not someone I would trifle with,' I said. 'If he wanted the sidewalk, I would give it to him. And you?'

'He is not afraid to die. But as a lad, he was ruled by the terrors of his imagination. Through the power of his will, he has rooted them out.'

'How could he do such a thing?' I asked.

'His picture does not reveal to me his method. Perhaps he chained himself to a tree in a thunderstorm, daring the lightning to strike him. I only see that he has done so.' He nodded at the sketch, as though to confirm what he saw there. 'I also see a man who is absolutely loyal to his Queen, but not particularly burdened with concern for her subjects.'

'Not a Socialist then?' I asked, and he had laughed.

But no one laughed now, as Lord Russell took the stand. The oldest son of the Baron of Somerset, he told the jurors he had soldiered in India out of a need for adventure. Upon the death of his father, he had retired from the Army to take his father's place as a member of the House of Lords. Never had he been quick to take offence, he volunteered, but he would die before allowing a stain on his honour.

Such was his reputation that the jurors knew to what he alluded. It was to the duels in which he was known to have engaged. As he spoke, with a light but dangerous smile, he regarded Jeremy.

Jeremy seemed quite unaware of the attention Lord Russell paid him. With his head down, he appeared to be taking notes, and listening to every word.

In response to the questions of the Attorney-General, Lord Russell said that in the course of his service to the Queen, he had formed a passion he hoped to pursue with his last breath. The passion was for the sport of polo. He had played it on the fields in India, and brought it to England. It was at a match near a family estate in Oxfordshire that he met Beryl Garcia. 'Quite by accident, I'm sure,' Sir Guthrie said.

'Not in the least,' Lord Russell replied, his eyes resting on the accused. 'I saw her with a group of ladies and was quite taken by her beauty. I wanted to meet her.'

'Did she make it easy for you? Or difficult?' Sir Guthrie asked.

'Most difficult,' Lord Russell said. 'Do not think for a moment that she put herself in my path. She wanted nothing to do with me.'

But he pursued her with success. They were married on Sunday, 5 July of this the year of 1891, at the estate of his uncle in Oxfordshire. It had been a rather small gathering of perhaps a hundred, and the date had been selected to make it so. The Emperor and Empress of Germany had arrived in London the day before, and a royal wedding had been held on Monday.

'I could not have been more proud of my lovely bride,' he said. 'She was the most beautiful woman I had ever seen.' A gentle blush caressed the cheeks of the accused, who listened with her eyes averted. 'I knew myself to be the envy of every man in Briton. In the whole of the Empire.'

Of course, he was familiar with her background. From Costa Rica and Brazil in the Americas, her maiden name--and her business name, before their marriage--had been Beryl Garcia.

After a moment with his colleague, who appeared to have reservations, Sir Guthrie again turned to Lord Russell. 'Lord Russell, were you acquainted with Rodger Baskerville, the victim in this case?'

The question surprised me. I had thought Sir Guthrie would make it difficult for Jeremy to inquire into the relations between the two men. It was as though he would invite Jeremy to pursue his strategy.

'I was, Sir Guthrie. But I knew him as Professor Christian Vandeleur, not as my wife's--rather, Beryl's--husband.'

When asked how they met, he replied, 'It was at cards. My uncle, Sir Alfred Russell, introduced me to him.' Sir Alfred had endowed a chair at Oxford College, Lord Russell added, and was known there. 'He had met a visiting professor from South Africa, and found him a most engaging fellow.'

Then at a lecture at the British Museum, Lord Russell had introduced Professor Vandeleur to Beryl. 'It was shortly after our marriage,' Lord Russell said. 'The fellow had lived in Brazil, and I thought Beryl should like to meet him.' Your impression of the man? 'A bold fellow, I thought. In my presence, he asked Beryl out to lunch.' He smiled at that. 'I thought it a splendid idea.'

'To your knowledge, did the matter stop there?'

Lord Russell shrugged, his gaze on Jeremy. 'Sir Alfred

informed me that my wife and the professor were seen at lunch on a second occasion, but I found that amusing. Nothing more.' The Attorney-General took his chair.

Jeremy consulted his drawing of Lord Russell a moment longer than was usual, then rose to conduct his examination. A charge of electricity filled the chamber. Foremost in my mind was the admonishment of Lord Arlington to the jurors, regarding a question Jeremy had posed to the coroner: ". . . it impugns the honour and integrity of a man not on trial here."

When Jeremy nodded at Lord Russell, the gesture was met with a cool smile. It was as though their swords had crossed. Jeremy took a moment to remind the jurors of the testimony of Constable Firstson and Detective Longstreet, both of whom had watched a richly-appointed carriage stop at the door of *Fashions Sabor Brazileos* in the evening of 28 September. When the man got back in the coach, ' . . . the constable saw a woman rise up to greet him. The Fleet Street detective saw a woman climb on top of him, and embrace him most anxiously.' He addressed the witness. 'Were you that man, Lord Russell?'

He was. Lord Russell readily admitted that when he stopped by 'her little dress shop,' he was with a woman. He did not know her name because they had not been properly introduced. Clearly it was a matter, in Lord Russell's mind, of no consequence.

But The Widow was saddened by his words. With a glance in her direction, Jeremy brought her distress to the jurors--after which he thrust questions at Lord Russell as would a fencer, on the attack. His questions were tipped with innuendo and suggestion, alarming the jurors and offending the judges, who waited for a sign from the Attorney-General. Sir Guthrie, however, appeared to be enjoying the performance.

Jeremy dared to remind Lord Russell that as a man of honour, he was bound to tell the truth. 'Do you question my honour, sir?' Lord Russell demanded.

'Allow me to remind you that it is my place to ask the questions, Lord Russell,' Jeremy said, 'and yours to answer them truthfully. Is it not true, sir, that you believed your wife was having an affair with Professor Vandeleur?'

'I did not believe that of her.'

'Yet you were informed, by your uncle, that they continued to lunch together?' Jeremy asked.

'Yes.'

'And you thought nothing of it?' Lord Russell shrugged. 'You knew that detectives followed the woman whom you believed was your wife, did you not? And Professor Vandeleur?'

'I knew nothing of the sort.'

'Allow me to remind you, Lord Russell, that you are under an oath to tell the truth.'

'Do not insult me, Mr Holmes.'

Jeremy turned his back on the witness, expressing his disbelief. Then he engaged with him again. 'You are of noble birth, are you not?' he asked.

'I am.'

'There is a tenet in the law, known rather loosely as the doctrine of the nobility of blood. Do you know it?'

'I have heard of it.'

'Those of noble blood put commoners beneath them, do they not?'

Lord Russell supposed that was so, in some instances.

'You would never challenge a commoner to a duel, would you, Lord Russell?'

'What is it that you suggest?'

'You have engaged in duels with deadly weapons in the past, have you not?'

'Admitted most readily, my good man.'

'Have you ever duelled a commoner, meaning a man not of the nobility?'

Lord Russell, quite at his ease, smiled at Jeremy. 'Pardon my question, Mr Holmes,' he said 'but it is true, is it not, that your mother was of the house of Wendleton?'

The Attorney-General stood up, but Jeremy raised a hand to him. He smiled at Lord Russell in perfect imitation of Lord Russell's expression. 'Is that a warning, Lord Russell?' Jeremy asked. 'Do you suggest that I am not a commoner, and am therefore one with whom you would duel?'

'I make no such suggestion, Mr Holmes.'

'What is it then that you suggest by your reference to my heritage?' Jeremy asked.

'Allow me to withdraw the question then,' Lord Russell said.

Jeremy smiled at the man. 'Permission granted, sir,' he said. 'You believed Professor Vandeleur to be a commoner, did you not?'

Lord Russell shrugged. 'I had no beliefs whatever about his lineage. It meant nothing to me.'

'As a commoner, you would not have challenged Professor Vandeleur to a duel?'

'An absurd question.'

'Your answer, Lord Russell, to my absurd question?' There was no response. 'I will consider your silence to be a "yes."'

Lord Russell crossed his arms and stared at Jeremy with a terrible resolve. As he did so, a light smile lifted the corners of his mouth. 'It is true, is it not,' Jeremy said, 'that you formed a passionate hatred of the man whom you thought was Christian Vandeleur?'

'That is not true,' he said. 'I rather liked the fellow.'

'Even after you were told of his affair with your wife?'

'A damnable lie, sir.'

'Is it not true that on twenty-eight September, when you drove your carriage in front of the door of her little dress shop, that you did so for a reason?'

'Yes. To bid her adieu, for she would leave the next morning for Paris.'

'Your purpose was more than that, was it not?' Jeremy asked. 'Your purpose was to send a signal to Madan Asan, an assassin, letting him know your wife was engaged at the front door, so that he could enter the back door while she was distracted and apart from him, and dispatch Professor Vandeleur. Is that not true?'

Lord Russell laughed. 'You are blessed with an extraordinary imagination, Mr Holmes.'

'Your laughter is not from your belly, Lord Russell,' Jeremy said. 'Have I provoked you, sir?'

'You have.'

'Did you laugh with an equal amount of mirth when you drove away from your wife's "little store," in the arms of a woman whose name you do not know?'

Lord Russell did not respond. After waiting a moment, Jeremy nodded at him and sat down.

The chamber was still. 'Are you quite done?' Lord Arlington asked.

'I am,' Jeremy replied.

Lord Arlington frowned at Jeremy. 'I shall refrain at this time from comment,' he said. 'You may stand down, Lord Russell.'

The long, lean figure stopped for a moment by Jeremy's chair, touched his forehead in a mocking salute, and moved on.

The day had become evening. Neither the daylight nor the lamps overhead were enough to illuminate the reflector panels aimed, at The Widow. Her expressions were not discernible. 'Sir Guthrie?' Lord Arlington asked. 'Have you anything more?'

'I have nothing further at this time,' was the reply.

'Does the Crown rest its case then?'

'It does not, My Lord,' Sir Guthrie said. 'It is possible we shall have another witness.'

Lord Arlington frowned at him, then looked toward the usher. 'You may inform the jurors that we shall meet on Monday morning at ten.' He stood up, along with Dimples, and Sir Percival.

'Upstand!' proclaimed the usher, as all those in the Sessions House rose to their feet. After the robed judges had disappeared, the usher launched into his recital, ending with a booming, 'God save the Queen!'

The chamber erupted into excitement, as though a beehive had been swatted with a stick. Everyone expressed their wonder, or their horror, at the exchange between Jeremy and Lord Russell. I waited for a sign from Jeremy, when he was quite unceremoniously approached by a loathsome, repulsive old hag. How had the creature managed to gain an entrance, not only into Sessions House, but through the bar? Sir Guthrie and Mr Roberts closed up their brief cases and hurried off, leaving Jeremy to deal with her.

Jeremy motioned for me to join him, as the chamber quickly emptied. I made my way to the floor, prepared to restrain the agitated woman who showed signs of madness. 'Greech, would you be so kind as to give my lady a drink from your flask?' Jeremy asked.

'Of course,' I said. Obviously Jeremy was humouring the wretched woman. 'To your health,' I said to her, after opening my flask and drinking enough to see me through the next hour. I handed it to her, knowing I should have to boil the container before drinking from it, after it had touched her filthy lips.

'Thank-ee thank-ee thank-ee,' she said, gripping it eagerly with both hands. She smelled of the foulest of the London alleyways.

'This is Lady Somerset, Edward. She has information for us, but there is a price. I must draw her likeness.'

'Yes, yes, yes,' she said, her thin twig-like fingers combing her grotesque hair, with flask in hand. 'I am of the same house as Peter, Lord Russell,' she said, then sucked whiskey into her mouth. 'Lord Russell has much to hide!' She cackled, then struck a pose.

'My flask, Lady Somerset?' I asked. 'A portrait of you with a flask in your hand would not become you.'

'You are right, my good man,' she said, jerking toward me, but when she went to hand me the flask, it dropped from her trembling hands. 'Pick it up, my good man,' she said.

'What does Lord Russell have to hide?' I asked of her, as I picked up the offending flask. Jeremy sketched rapidly, hardly looking at his pad, but watching her with care. It was as though his hand was guided by unseen spirits.

'Not another word, not another word, no, no, no. Not another word on that subject,' she said. 'First you must pay the price.'

I was baffled by her manner. She alternated between madness and lucidity. I was annoyed as well by Jeremy, who had permitted this old human wreck to interrupt our work.

'My friend,' I said to him, 'have we nothing better to do?'

'There is nobility here,' Jeremy said. 'It runs deeper than her blood. Her royal presence glows from within, Greech.'

'Of course it does,' the creature said. Lifting her skirt, she curtsied toward him.

'I only hope I can capture a glimpse of that royal grace, my lady,' Jeremy said. With a flourish, he raised his hand, then bowed to her. 'I am done.'

'So soon?' she asked. 'Hardly time enough to do a caricature.' But when Jeremy pulled his work off his pad, she snatched it from his hand.

Her eyes opened wide. Then she emitted a sound most difficult to describe. It was a joyous cackle, what one might have heard from the goose when she laid the golden egg. 'Ah, my dear nephew,' she said, her voice still the tremulous quiver of an old woman. 'Greech, you must see this!'

The face Jeremy had drawn was that of Sherlock Holmes! On his head, he wore a crown!

'You will know me then, when next you see me,' the disreputable old creature said, scuttling away.

And then she was someone else. A tired, over-worked cleaning woman, wearing bonnet and apron, found a bucket with a mop against the wall, and trudged out of sight. 'Was that Sherlock Holmes?' I asked.

'That was an unlovely old woman,' Jeremy said. 'Sherlock Holmes is on the continent.'

'He does not want it known that he is in England then?' I asked. 'Does he come to help us?'

Jeremy shrugged. 'One should not jump to conclusions,' he said. 'Shall I see you later at the club?'

'If you wish it,' I said. 'Will you be there soon?'

'You will have time enough to thoroughly clean your

flask,' he said, 'and to re-fill it.' He walked away.

Chapter 17

Lord Russell stood in the center of the great hall at the Old Bailey, his posture that of a hunter, waiting for prey. Most of those who had attended the day's proceedings had gone, but several men remained. Although no one stood next to Lord Russell, many of us managed to mill about near him.

All ears it seemed were pointed at him, though no one looked his way. A tall man, elegantly attired, he held thin leather gloves in one hand, with which he swatted the other. 'Ah,' he said, as Jeremy hurriedly walked for the main door. 'The Bastard.' He stood in his way. 'You have kept me waiting, sir.'

Jeremy was not as tall as Lord Russell. He carried a briefcase full of sketches with his left hand, and wore a coat made of buffalo hide over his suit. 'Forgive me, my lord. Had I known...'

With a sudden move, Lord Russell lashed the gloves at Jeremy's face. In the same instant, Jeremy's right arm blocked the gesture. Russell's other hand flicked upward, knocking the cap off Jeremy's head.

'Rather tiresome of you, my lord,' Jeremy said, having dropped his briefcase. With his hands hanging loosely at his side, he faced his antagonist. 'Will you allow me to pick up my hat? I should not like it stepped on.'

'I find your insolence and your innuendo to be intolerable, sir. I demand an apology.'

No one ventured close to Jeremy's cap. 'May we discuss this after the trial?' Jeremy asked, mildly. 'Perhaps then...'

'We may not,' Russell said. 'I will have your apology now.'

Jeremy's eyes blazed suddenly with that reckless joy I

had seen in them before, when first we met. Then he had fought rowdy boys in an alley, but the man he faced now was hardly that. 'And if I refuse, then you would have us duel with swords, or pistols?'

'I would. On a field of honour,' Lord Russell said.

'Rather, a field of assassination,' Jeremy said. 'You are trained in the use of swords and pistols. What you would have us engage in would not be a duel. It would be murder.'

'So. The lawyer in you has come out,' Lord Russell said. 'You would reason with me and erect a barricade of argument, to hide behind. Are you a coward, sir?'

Jeremy was quite still. 'As you say, sir, I am a lawyer. I am more than willing to negotiate with you. Allow me to propose an alternative to swords and pistols.'

Lord Russell smiled at him with irony. 'Do so then.'

'You are a member of the Toxopholite Society, are you not?' Jeremy asked.

Lord Russell's face relaxed slightly into something like amusement. 'Are you mad? Bows and arrows? Surely you know of my skills as an archer.'

'They are legendary,' Jeremy said. 'As are your skills at polo. Would you be adverse to a real test of your most sacred honour? A duel like no other, but one to remember.'

'I am intrigued.'

'Let it be mounted then,' Jeremy said. 'As archers.'

Lord Russell smiled with delight. 'Splendid!' he said. 'You do not disappoint, sir.'

In perfect imitation of Lord Russell, Jeremy saw fit to smile with delight. 'Splendid!' he said. 'You do not disappoint, sir.'

'Do you mock me?'

'My lord, I am engaged in a trial,' Jeremy said. 'It

commands virtually all of my attention, and it would be most inconvenient for me to die before it is over. However, if you should kill me, then perhaps I will have made my point.'

Lord Russell laughed heartily. 'You are a rare one. I would have you know, my laughter at your remark was from my belly.'

'You compliment me then,' Jeremy said. 'How nice of you.'

'There is a field of honour at Calais, large enough to accommodate your choice of weaponry,' Lord Russell said. 'I shall be most happy to meet you there on Sunday, at day-break.' The eagerness in his manner accented his words. 'Will you be so good as to have your attendant--that fellow Greech, I assume--call on my uncle?'

I had not thought he knew who I was. But his cold, insolent eyes found me in the knot of silent men who listened. They froze my face.

'I have no intention of involving my good friend in this business,' Jeremy said. 'I would suggest that your uncle, Sir Alfred, call on Richard, Lord Wendleton.'

Lord Russell looked sharply at Jeremy, followed by a sardonic salute. 'I shall instruct him to do so.' He stepped to Jeremy's side, bent down, and picked up his cap. 'Fox?' he asked, handing it to Jeremy.

'No,' Jeremy said. 'I have more regard for fox than to make hats of them. It is made from squirrel hides.'

Russell roared again, with laughter. Slapping his gloves into his bare hand, he strode off.

As did Jeremy, after a nod at me. I made no effort to catch up to him. What madness, I thought, pulling the stopper from my flask. What absolute madness.

#

A short while later, after Jeremy had stopped at his Inn, we met at the Bastriche Club. He had set up his easel and was at work on a sketch. 'Do you think of the trial at a time like this?' I asked.

'Tell me, old sot. Where do we stand?'

'You have been in far worse difficulty, and prevailed. The seeds you wished to plant in the minds of the jurors are there. They can readily visualize that small Indian fellow in his black cape responding to the signal of Lord Russell. All that is needed is the manure you are so capable of spreading, for them to take root.' I had a nip from my flask. 'But I question whether you will ever work the stuff into the soil. Rather, your blood will have enriched the soil at Calais.'

'Why has Sir Guthrie made it easy for me?' he asked. 'I am not confident.'

'I do not agree. Until today, you have been forced to tack into a hurricane to set the stage.'

'But today, he invited my attack on Lord Russell.'

'Knowing you would provoke a duel?' I asked. 'Secure in the knowledge that you will die?'

His head leaned to one side. 'That's odd.'

'What?' I glanced at his work. My lady-friend smiled at me. 'You have made Mrs Lyons into a most alluring woman,' I said. 'Will you bequeath it to me?'

He laughed with good nature. 'Your concern is touching, but do not fear for my safety,' he said. 'Lord Russell is in more danger than am I. I should be ashamed, perhaps, at the manner in which I have tricked him, but I am a bastard and quite without shame.'

'You delude yourself,' I told him. 'Lord Russell could not be happier. Those I have talked to cannot comprehend your rashness. He has never lost a contest for marksmanship at the Toxopholite Society, and is heads and shoulders over anyone in England at polo.'

'Has he hunted on horseback with bows and arrows?'

'I don't expect it of you, Jeremy, but you are not making sense to me. What do you mean?'

'As a child, I lived on the back of a horse. I have hunted buffalo, and counted coup.'

'You have said nothing of this to me before,' I said. 'What on earth are you talking about?'

But his attention was on his work. 'You've formed an attachment to Mrs Lyons,' he said. 'Was that wise?'

'You know of it, then.'

'Of course,' Jeremy said. 'So do Sir Guthrie and Mr Roberts.' He looked at me. 'Do you know her well?'

'Not as well as you, I am sure. I am not able to draw.'

'That is unfortunate,' Jeremy said. 'I should exercise care, if I were you.'

'Do you warn me?' I asked. 'What harm could she possibly do to me?'

'She is a witness, Edward. I should not like to have you called to the stand to explain your association with her. I should not like to have her testimony compromised, or you defrocked.'

'You are the last person to warn me of impropriety,' I said.

His gentle eyes regarded me with a quiet understanding, then returned to his work. 'She toys with you, Edward.'

'Of course. I am used to being toyed with, by the fairer sex. Why do you draw her?'

'I will call her on Monday as a witness.'

'If you are among the living,' I said. 'Surely a duel

against one who has led a light brigade in battle is a more deadly business than hunting the wild buffalo.'

'They are very alike, old sot.'

'"Old sot"!' I demanded. Suddenly, an anger within me that I was not even aware of, flared up. 'Do you get some kind of malicious pleasure out of calling me "old sot"?'

He looked at me with surprise. 'I apologize to you, Edward. I meant no offense. I have great affection for you.'

'Yet you choose to exclude me from going with you to Calais.'

He gave me his full attention. 'I do not exclude you at all,' he said. 'I should be pleased to have you there, if you wish to go. But I would spare you the aggravation of involvement in the matter.'

'You would have Lord Wendleton as your second, before me,' I said. 'I am offended. I thought . . .' I stopped, unable to say more.

'He is my grandfather,' Jeremy said.

'But he refuses to acknowledge you.'

'He cannot,' Jeremy said. 'His wife--my grandmother-- does not know I exist. He also stables my horses, and has the resources that are needed for me to engage in this adventure.'

'You would have your own horse at Calais?' I asked, thinking of the cost.

'Yes,' Jeremy said. 'As will Lord Russell. Will you come, Edward?' he asked. 'I should like to have you in my corner.'

'I will indeed,' I said, lifting my flask. 'To your success there.'

'Allow me to join you?' he asked.

'My word.' I gave it to him, and he took a most healthy pull.   I was quite touched by his gesture, but said nothing of it, of course.

But I saw his work. As always, I was amazed at its clarity. There was a quality in Laura that I could not define, and that he had captured. 'Tell me, Jeremy. What do you see?'

'Torment.'

Chapter 18

'May I join you?'

'Sir?' The voice I heard sounded oddly like that of Jeremy, but the man who addressed me was not him. 'Have we met?'

'We have not, Mr Greech, but I know you.' An older man, dressed for warmth rather than fashion, leaned against the rail of the passenger deck near me with familiarity. We were on the deck of a steamer that carried passengers from Dover to Calais. 'I have seen you in court.'

'Indeed. Then you must know that I carry the brief for The Bastard, and that I drink.'

'The Bastard is my grandson,' he said. 'I am Lord Wendleton.'

I lifted my flask. 'To your health, my lord.'

He smiled. 'Quite nice of you. Isn't it glorious?'

'What is, my lord?' I asked, uncertainly.

'The sky. The sea.' There were tears in his eyes. 'The abundance of life. See how the dolphin play.' Were tears of emotion welling up in him? 'Old age may be the curse of life,' he said, a moment later, 'but there are comforts, one of which is invisibility. No longer am I seen in the courtyards of London. I have disappeared.'

'I hardly think so, my lord.'

'Time also acquires a remarkable elasticity. It can drag endlessly, or rush past one in a blur. I am caught in its pocket at this moment, as are you, I suspect. Quite filled with the ambivalence of anticipation and dread.'

My words would not have comforted him, for I feared the worst. I held my peace.

'May I talk to you in confidence, Mr Greech?'

'Of course.'

'To be shared with no one. Not even Jeremy.'

'My lord, I cannot promise that.'

He smiled. There was a holiness about his smile. It was a comfort to me: a blessing. 'You are a good man, Mr Greech,' he said. 'I shall trust in your love of him then, knowing it will guide your discretion.'

My love of him? Surely he did not think . . . And yet, I *did* love him. How could that be?

More tears had gathered in Lord Wendleton's eyes. 'I will confess to you what I have to no other man,' he said. 'I have many regrets.'

Thus it was that in the passage between Dover and Calais, I came to a deeper understanding of Jeremy Holmes. What I had believed the source of his courtroom brilliance, was not madness at all. It was genius, nourished by tragedy.

#

Lord Wendleton had raged, when learning that Cecilia, his fifteen-year-old daughter, was pregnant. An only child, he and Lady Wendleton had expected of her a virginal perfection. But in June of 1862, they learned of her condition from her very own lips. She had been bedded by Sherrinford Holmes.

They vowed to keep her disgrace from the world. Not even their trusted servants would know. But Lord Wendleton alone would make the decisions. His wife wanted only the assurance that no one would know. The course of action he chose to take, in retrospect, was extreme; but at the time, it seemed the perfect solution.

Two years before, with some good fellows, he had gone on safari to the Dakota Territory in America. He would take Cecilia to that remote country, and she would have her baby there. He would then surrender the child to wild Indians, and bring his daughter back to the English countryside, and the life that was hers.

They boarded a steamship in Bristol and in a fortnight, they were in New York. America was embroiled in a war of secession then, but he had been assured the conflict would not spread into the vastness of the northern and western territories. By the time they reached their destination, his daughter was quite obviously with child.

His anger toward the fifteen-year-old girl had abated, perhaps because of her frequent tears. She loved the feeling of life within her, and knew she carried a handsome boy. How could she give him away? she would ask him. Why could not she remain in America with her son?

He humoured her, but was firm in his resolve to take her back to England after her child was born. She would marry well, he would see to that. She would reclaim the life her foolishness might otherwise have destroyed.

They disembarked from a paddle-wheel steamboat onto the dock at Yankton, a small village on the Missouri River, named for an Indian tribe that had befriended the white man. When there before, he had stayed with his companions in a thinly-disguised bordello. It was the home of Rose Thorn, an Indian woman of surprising accomplishment and grace, and was staffed with maidens of exotic complexions. Rose was beyond the reach of the gentlemen with rooms there, but he had bedded her. When their hunt for the wild buffaloe was over and they returned to England, he had maintained a discrete correspondence with the woman. There was a post office in Yankton, and letters were routed through his business agent in New York City.

It was to her that he turned, for assistance.

A Cheyenne Indian woman, Rose had been sold by her

father for whiskey, to a white trapper who brought her to Yankton, then abandoned her. Endowed with beauty, intelligence, resolve, and a facility for language, she had succeeded in making her own way. Lord Wendleton thought she would make the perfect companion for Cecilia, and so she was. The Indian woman's heart reached out to the girl and folded her in comfort.

By the standards of the Dakota Territory, Rose's home was palatial. On a bluff that looked over the Missouri River, its windows reflected the sun. A wide verandah surrounded the log building, and the rooms inside were equipped with lamps, fireplaces, and books.

Lord Wendleton returned to England, letting it out that his daughter was enrolled in a school for young women at Troy, in the state of New York. When the child was born in January of 1863, Cecilia was 16. He returned to Yankton in April of that year, intending to leave the infant with Rose, and bring his daughter home.

But when he saw the boy with his mother, he wavered in his desire to take her away. She had named the infant "Jeremy," after a playful uncle who had lost his life at sea, in whom she saw a likeness. Lord Wendleton was persuaded that he saw it too. The infant struck him as playful and bright, yet in need of his mother. Cecilia promised that she could give him up easily, when the boy was weaned. Rose Thorn sided with his daughter, of course.

Rose too had changed. She fancied herself a lady, not a whore. With the money he had sent to her, her house had been transformed into a garden of her creation, in a primitive desert. There was a piano, a violin, and a library of books, as well as guests of her choosing. Of many colors and talents, they were alive with an eagerness to explore emerging ideas. He enjoyed himself there, with his mistress, and abandoned himself to the vibrancy of her home.

Three Indian girls suckled babes, as did Cecilia. Caught in the congeniality of the place, he remained for several months, participating in hunts with trusted savages, whom he had befriended.

In England that fall, he contrived a story that no one questioned. Cecilia had been hospitalized with a rare disease, and could not travel. He would return in the spring of 1864-- which he did, only to be confounded with an intolerable development. His seventeen-year-old daughter, wonderfully vivacious and devoted to her son, was in love with an Ogallala Sioux Indian.

He absolutely forbade any exchange between her and the young brave. Although his grandson was indeed the "handsome boy" Cecilia had known he would be, and even though he was not yet fully weaned, Lord Wendleton ordered Cecilia to abandon the child at once. She would return with him to England.

She refused. Rose Thorn would not intervene, telling him that the decision was not his to make. It belonged to his daughter.

Lord Wendleton could not tolerate such nonsense. He hired two large Indian women, who literally tore the suckling babe from Cecilia's breast. They dragged her on board the steamboat to St. Joseph, and the howling infant was given to Rose Thorne. At times the guards were forced to bind and gag his daughter to secure her compliance, and they stayed with her until she was on board a Bristol-bound steamer. At that point, after her promise to behave, he released her.

In the middle of the Atlantic Ocean, his beautiful, head-strong daughter who had incorporated into her nature some characteristics of the wild Indian, was seized with the despair of the young. On a star-filled night, she dropped into the cold Atlantic water, putting an end to her despair.

As Lord Wendleton spoke of it, I feared he might follow her into the sea. The manner of his daughter's death had not been disclosed to anyone, he said, not even to Jeremy. Lord Wendleton returned to his estates, alone. His wife, an increasingly fragile woman with age, had surrendered her mind to religion. He told her only that her daughter had died unexpectedly on the voyage back to England. The lingering effects of the disease with which she'd been afflicted had taken her from them, he had said, and she was buried at sea. A ceremony was held for Cecilia at their manor.

There was Indian trouble in the Dakota Territory, which Lord Wendleton followed in the papers. Over the years, he wrote to Rose Thorn, but there were no replies. The wars with the Indians continued after the rebellion had ended, and he read of them with grave concern. In 1876, Indians of the Sioux and Cheyenne nations had massacred an army of soldiers at a hunting ground called The Little Bighorn.

Within months of that disaster, he received a letter from Rose Thorn. She thanked him for his letters to her and told him why she had not answered them. Her home in Yankton had been burned and destroyed soon after he and Cecilia were gone. The Indians responsible were led by the young Sioux warrior Cecilia had loved. Rose and Jeremy were taken to the other side of the Holy Mountains (called "Black Hills" by the Whites) and sold to a band of Cheyenne Indians.

Lord Wendleton became animated when he told me of what Rose had written, as though he had been there too. She was never their slave, he said. An old one recognized her, and knew her story. Rose and Jeremy lived with the grandmothers, and her place in the tribe became that of a wise one. She knew the tongue of the white man, and the so-called Cheyenne "dog soldiers" would bring her newspapers to read, taken during raids on the foolish whites. She read the stories about the fights out loud for all to hear, as the young warriors strutted and preened.

Jeremy became a favorite of the tribe. They called him "White Horse," a name he earned before he could walk, when he crawled through a herd of horses who seemed to know him. At three, he could ride. He shot a duck out of the sky with an arrow at six, killed a buffalo at eleven, and counted coup on a surprised Crow warrior at twelve.

But many regarded him with suspicion. He had too many tongues, they said. He spoke Sioux as easily as he did Cheyenne, and could talk the language of the whites. When the dog soldiers gave Rose newspapers to read, soon he could read them too. And when a warrior brought her coloured pencils and a large tablet of paper, on which there were drawings of faces and flowers and distant mountains, White Horse watched her make crude drawings on the pages.

She let him try, and there was magic in his fingers. He lost himself in his drawings, doing likenesses of many of those in the village--and was overwhelmed, and humbled, by what he saw. What happens when an image passes through me? he asked his Indian mother. She did not know. But some of the Indians claimed that after he had drawn them, they were not the same. It was as though he had pulled out their essence.

The Cheyenne people were camped on the banks of the Little Bighorn, when they were attacked by Custer, the yellow-haired general. Crazy Horse, a Sioux warrior known for his daring, led the Sioux and Cheyenne braves into the fight. White Horse, whose voice had just begun to change, was not allowed

155

to ride with them. But when a small war party rode out to join Crazy Horse, he mounted his pony and followed them.

He came upon a wounded young bluecoat, whom he readied himself to kill, when the bluecoat spoke to him in English. The young soldier was not much older than White Horse. He did not beg for his life, but he did not want to die. White Horse wanted to know him, to draw his picture. He put the bluecoat on his horse and was leading him back to Rose . . . when three mounted Sioux warriors surrounded them. They pulled the bluecoat off the horse and made him stand. When White Horse tried to stop them, they knocked him down.

With gestures, the warriors let the bluecoat know he must run. The Sioux shot arrows at his feet, to make him run faster. But they tired of their game when the boy stumbled and fell--and the Sioux were filled with a terrible lust. They charged him, attacking with lance and hatchet, and stabbed him and hacked at him and covered themselves with his blood. They scalped him, then took his boots, his belt and dagger, and the brass buttons off his bloody coat. One of them put on the blue cap, and they rode away.

White horse ran over to the boy, who still breathed, but not for long. With blood oozing from his mouth and flies swarming over his hairless, gleaming skull, his eyes lost their focus, and he died.

Rose saw White Horse later that day, leading his horse slowly toward the Sioux camp. She ran out to him. A roughly-built travois dragged along behind his horse, on which lay the body of the bluecoat. He would take it to the Sioux camp, he told her, and dump it there. Then he would challenge them all to fight, knowing they would kill him too. He wanted to die.

Rose told him he must kill her first. White Horse charged at her, knocking her down. But when he tried to lift her up, he began to cry. She held him, and he let her comfort him.

But soon he broke away and ran off into the prairie. She dropped the travois and its burden, mounted his horse, and caught up to him. He surprised her then, by telling her he hoped she would stay with him. In awe, she watched the boy open his mind and his heart to the wonder and the pain of existence. He chose to confront his anguish, rather than shield himself from it in a protective dream. But he could not go back to their camp until he knew the Cheyenne people from the outside, he said, and asked her to help him understand.

Who were his people? he asked her. Was he Jeremy, of a nation he knew little about, or White Horse, a Cheyenne Indian? Why did the white people want the land when it belonged to no one? Why would they put the Cheyenne nation behind fences? How could the Cheyenne, and the Sioux, peel the hides off their enemies, and watch them die?

She rode back to the Cheyenne camp on the edge of the river, gathered some provisions, and bought a horse from an old one whose picture White Horse had drawn. They knew of the bluecoat, having been shown his scalp by the Sioux warriors. She told them White Horse could not come back to the tribe until his heart was right.

She rode back to White Horse, who had buried the bluecoat in a small ravine. They rode toward the Holy Mountains, camping on the bank of a stream. She told him what she thought was true. The Cheyenne and Sioux nations would be over-run by the whites, and it would be better for him to ride away forever.

Her words silenced him. Finally he spoke to her, saying only that he would seek a vision, or die. He asked her not to follow, and told her he would find her later, if only in a dream.

That night, he rode away.

He did not eat or drink for four days until, in the Holy Mountains, he had a vision. It was of him, White Horse, standing before three tribal elders, dressed as a warrior but with a book in his hand. A bluecoat was tied to a pole, who White Horse knew was his brother. He begged for the life of the young soldier, but the elders refused his plea. White Horse rode away from his past, hearing the screams of his brother as he was put to death.

He found his Indian mother and together, they rode to Yankton, living off the land. There were wagon trains of whites, on the east side of the Holy Mountains, which they did not approach. She told him all she knew of him. In Yankton, many of the letters from Lord Wendleton were at the post office, and she replied to him. As a squaw who could speak and write in English, she took a job with a lawyer. The man would have apprenticed Jeremy to learn the law, but in November, she received a letter from Lord Wendleton. With funds enclosed, he asked them both to come to England.

'My Indian mistress chose to stay with the lawyer,' Lord Wendleton said, 'where she remains to this day. I secured lodging in London for Jeremy, and provided him with a tutor. He had a most remarkable eagerness to learn of his English heritage and to satisfy his curiosities about . . . I know not what. But he embraced me as his grandfather.'

At last, he smiled. 'He comes to Wendleton Manor, whenever it suits him. But when there, he lives in the forest, or in the stable with his horses. His grandmother is rather fond of the young visitor from America, who will sit with her, and listen to her, and draw pictures for her of those places of which she speaks. Perhaps, in her heart, she knows who he is.'

'And you made a barrister of him?'

'I encouraged him to embrace his vision.'

Chapter 19

At Calais, there were designated fields of honour, available for a price. Arrangements were made for the largest one, the size of a polo field, but not level. Its undulating terrain was pock-marked with rock and a scattering of low bushes that could sustain themselves with little soil. The field sloped downward, from the south to the north, and was enclosed in a low wall of stone. A light snow lay upon the grassed surfaces and when the thin fog lifted, the sun shone over the horizon at a low angle.

I did not think it a day for a duel. It was far too beautiful for that. There were flocks of birds in the pure blue air, and the day breathed of life. It was made for a wedding.

'Gentlemen, is there movement toward a settlement?' the arbitour asked. A tall, well-dressed man in a top hat, he spoke to those of us assembled near the two figures who stood by their horses. Spectators had gathered along the stone walls.

Lord Russell scoffed at the suggestion. 'My opponent may be of noble birth, but he is not a gentleman. He is a bastard.'

'If I may say so, sir, this perhaps is not the time for such observation,' the arbitour said.

'Peter,' Sir Alfred Russell added, standing near his nephew. 'Your anger will not work to your advantage.'

'Look at him,' Lord Russell said, his voice a sneer. 'He mocks us all. Is this to be a duel, or an act from that recent entertainment inflicted on our queen by that American buffoon, Buffalo Bill?'

Jeremy indeed was a spectacle. His clothes, made of buckskin, were a loose shirt that covered his elbows, trousers that reached just below his knees, and leather sandals. His muscled body was quite exposed to the cold. A beaded belt held his hair in place, and on his cheeks were lines of red and blue. He wore paint! A quiver holding three arrows was over his shoulder, and--with a rather ordinary-looking bow in one hand--he stood casually beside his horse.

The animal pushed at Jeremy with his nose. Brown and black splashes covered the horse as though they were large blots, on a white canvas. The horse wore no saddle, nor was there a bridle and bit in his mouth. A short rope hung from his neck, with which Jeremy led him.

I did not wonder at Lord Russell's protestations. 'Am I to fight a savage?' he asked.

'The rules were agreed to,' Lord Wendleton said. 'You were present when they were drawn. I ask you sir, was the manner of dress a subject of discussion? Rather, it was specifically excluded at the request of your uncle.'

'My lord, were it not for your age, I should challenge you next,' Lord Russell said.

'And my insult?' Lord Wendleton replied. 'To your intelligence perhaps?'

'Bah!'

Lord Russell stood beside a magnificent white stallion, over which lay the light saddle used in polo. He wore woolen trousers and a thick woolen blouse, heavy enough to absorb an arrow that did not squarely hit its mark. A fur cap was pulled down over his ears. He held a well-crafted recurve bow in his hand, and his quiver hung from his saddle.

At the Toxopholite Society, Lord Russell would hit the center of his target at fifty yards, nine times out of ten. He was insulted beyond endurance by Jeremy, and wanted the duel to end in Jeremy's death. I feared greatly for the life of my friend.

'The rules, sir?' Lord Wendleton asked of the arbitour.

161

'My lords, is there no rapprochement?'

'I can assure you,' Lord Wendleton said, 'that Mr Holmes is open to an honourable settlement.'

'Lord Russell?' the arbitour asked.

He stared at Jeremy. 'I would not accept an apology for his many insults,' he said, 'if he were to offer them to me, on his knees.'

Jeremy smiled, and remained silent.

'Very well,' the arbitour said. 'The rules are these. The combatants will take their positions, Mr Holmes at the north wall, Lord Russell at the south. Each will have three arrows. Upon my signal, they may be discharged at will. It is forbidden to pierce an animal with an arrow. Should that occur, the opponent will have an unobstructed shot at the violator from ten yards.' He took a deep breath. 'The duel is to the death, or serious injury, to be declared by the representatives.'

'If the arrows are mutually exhausted, without injury or death?' Sir Alfred asked.

'The combatants are entitled to three more, under the same terms. Combat to continue thus until death or serious injury, or the representatives agree to an end.' He closed his tablet. 'To your horses, gentlemen. May God be with you.'

We followed him to a small opening in the wall as the duellists mounted their horses and took their positions at opposite ends of the field. Though it was the luck of the draw, Lord Russell--at the high side, with the sun to his back--had all the advantage.

'Begin!' the arbitour called out, his right hand slashing the air.

Lord Russell began a cautious approach, urging his horse forward, touching its flank with a limb of his bow, as with a crop. Crouched on a saddle, he guided him lightly with the reins, keeping the high ground.

Without a saddle, Jeremy sat easily on his steed, allowing his horse to pick its own path. He had removed the rope with which he led the animal when on foot, and his legs hung comfortably down its flanks. His right hand rested in the wealth of long hair along the neck of the horse, and his left hand carried his bow. How would he guide the animal, I wondered? But when Jeremy shifted his weight and leaned to his left, his horse seemed to know what was wanted.

As they approached one another, Lord Russell maintained his position on higher ground, intent on keeping his advantage. Though Jeremy also moved forward, both he and his horse appeared to concentrate on the ground, as though to understand it. Suddenly at fifty yards, Jeremy sat upright and with his right hand, was having difficulty pulling an arrow from the quiver on his back--when there was a snap from the bow of Lord Russell! Jeremy fell!

Or so it appeared. He had rolled to his steed's flank and the arrow passed over his knee! Then as though he would join a friend, Jeremy's horse picked its way toward the white steed of Lord Russell, along a rib of rocks, avoiding the pockets of snow. Drawing closer to Lord Russell, who had notched another arrow in his bow and drawn the string, Jeremy's horse whinnied, as though to say 'Ha-lo!'

In some fashion, from thirty yards away and from under the long neck of his animal, Jeremy shot an arrow at Lord Russell. It carried off his hat!

In great surprise, Lord Russell jerked his bow and reached upward, releasing the arrow and sending it into the sky. 'My compliments, noble savage,' he said. With a light smile on his face, his last arrow was notched into his bow.

With no urging from Jeremy--indeed, the animal was in

charge--they closed the gap! Was Jeremy mad? Lord Russell prodded his horse onto a hollowed level of grass covered with snow, maneuvering to get a shot, when of a sudden, Jeremy's horse stood on its back legs and kicked its front hooves at the white steed! Jeremy stayed on the back of his animal as though glued to him, but the great white animal of Lord Russell reared up in terror. The last arrow of Lord Russell was discharged into the ground, as he clung to the back of his horse--when we heard a loud snap.

The animal cried out. A back leg had been thrust into a hole under the snow, and it was broken. The animal crashed down.

Lord Russell tried to clear himself from the beast, but his foot was caught in a stirrup. He landed with a thud, on his back.

In an instant, Jeremy was off his horse, and was there.

Our small party was quite close, and we ran toward them. Lord Russell could not move. His great white horse began to scream, its left hind leg at a grotesque angle, with bone from his broken leg poking through the skin.

A second later, an arrow from Jeremy's bow entered the animal's eye. It penetrated several inches into his head, and the screams were echoes that yielded to silence.

With an expression of dismissive insolence, Lord Russell smiled at Jeremy. 'You have an arrow left,' he said. 'End this adventure.' He sat up slowly and opened his clothing, presenting his chest.

'No, my lord,' Jeremy said. He handed his bow and the remaining arrow to Lord Russell. 'I have broken the rules.' My friend was crying! 'My arrow pierced your horse. It is your place to end it.'

'Do you weep sir? Over a horse?'

'I do.'

Lord Russell, seated in the snow, drew back the string of the bow at less than ten yards. He let the arrow fly. It creased Jeremy's left shoulder, drawing a line of blood.

With a salute, Lord Russell nodded at Jeremy. 'I am satisfied.'

Chapter 20

On Monday morning, I met early with Jeremy at the Bastriche Club, before he went to his chamber at Lincoln's Inn. There was much to go over, but little time. The Crown had not rested, yet all the witnesses whom Sir Guthrie had listed on the indictment had testified. 'Will he call a mystery witness, one that was not listed?' Jeremy asked.

'Even Lord Arlington would not allow that,' I said. 'Perhaps Sir Guthrie hoped to find something for Lord Russell to testify about, to put him in a better light. But Lord Russell was carried off the field at Calais and I cannot imagine that he will attend today. I for one will not miss him. Will you?'

Jeremy touched his arm where the arrow had creased his arm. 'He could have killed me. We do him an injustice.'

'Do you pity him?' I asked. 'Bah! His absence will strengthen our position that he orchestrated the murder.'

Jeremy nodded his agreement, and stood up, prepared to leave. 'Is all in readiness then?' he asked.

'Our witnesses are few,' I said. 'Dr Mortimer, Sir Henry if you choose to call him, and Mrs Lyons.' I smiled as I thought of her.

'Tell me, old fellow. What is between you and Mrs Lyons?'

'I find her an attractive woman.'

'You continue to see her then?'

I smiled. 'I am very discrete about it, Jeremy. You will understand, I hope. You too have stepped on the rules.'

He examined me carefully. 'Do you love her?' he asked.

'It is hardly important,' I said, then shrugged. 'I am not overly familiar with the emotion. But it is possible, I suppose.'

'Greech, I do not like it,' Jeremy said. 'Rest assured that

Mr Roberts and Sir Guthrie are aware of your impropriety.'

'I hardly think that you are in a position to lecture me about my conduct,' I said.

'Perhaps not,' he said. He opened the door, and left.

When I arrived at the Old Bailey, the sky above London had cleared and the ground sparkled with snow. There were gaps in the crowd that had gathered in front. A knot of ruffians sang a bawdy lyric, borrowing a tune from *Trial By Jury*. Its dreadful rhymes told of viewing the hanging of The Widow, while looking up her skirts.

Inside, in the Sessions House, there was a delay. The jurors were in their places at ten, but neither the judges nor the barristers were there. Yet The Widow had been lifted from the gloomy depths below, into the dock. Her hair lay in coils on her head, exposing her delicate neck. Carolyn of the big bosoms sat behind her.

The barristers in their powdered wigs and flowing gowns filed in from the robing room. There had been a conference, and it was done. When Jeremy looked at me, he shrugged his shoulders. The message he sent was clear enough. The business in the conference room had not gone well.

That message was accented by the triumphant buoyancy in the stride of the Attorney-General. At their places, Sir Guthrie offered Jeremy a triumphant smile.

There was a knock on the door on the judge's platform. 'Upstand!' boomed the usher, as the judges filed into the chamber. 'Upstand all!' He waited until the robed-in-scarlet figures in their long white wigs were seated, then launched into his ancient ritual, ending with a resounding 'God save the Queen!'

When all in the chamber were seated, Lord Arlington

leaned forward and addressed the jurors. 'Gentlemen,' he said, 'this cause has steered into a heavy sea. So that you may follow the course we take, I shall offer the following by way of explanation.'

The jurors listened with great attention.

'The Attorney-General has requested permission to call a witness who was not listed on the indictment. Normally the Crown cannot call such a witness, but where the trial court is confronted with special circumstances, exceptions are allowed.'

Lord Arlington looked toward Jeremy. 'On Friday, counsel for the accused greatly enlarged the scope of the examination of Lord Russell. In that examination, Mr Holmes virtually requested you, the jurors, to entertain an explanation of the count of murder that suggested that Lord Russell had orchestrated the crime.'

Lord Arlington returned his attention back to the jurors. 'It is the considered judgment of all'--and he extended his arms to include Sir Percival, and Dimples--'that this is a special circumstance. Sir Guthrie will therefore be allowed to call a witness not shown on the indictment, but for one purpose only.'

He consulted a note on his tablet. 'The evidence showed that the victim and the accused were followed by detectives, up to the time of the crime,' he said. 'Did Lord Russell know of it? He testified he did not, but his veracity was severely challenged. Sir Guthrie will offer a witness to address one question only. Did Lord Russell know that the victim and the accused were followed by detectives? Both the Crown and the defence shall limit their examinations to that issue alone.'

Sir Alfred Russell, an older and softer version of Peter, Lord Russell, climbed into the witness box. He did not look any the worse for wear, after the weekend in Calais. His testimony was delivered with devastating clarity. After identifying himself as the uncle of Peter, Lord Russell, he quite destroyed our efforts to suggest that his nephew was responsible for the crime.

There was not the slightest possibility that Lord Russell could have known that either The Widow, or Professor Christian Vandeleur, were being followed, Sir Alfred explained. It was he who had hired the Fleet Street agency, and he had gone to great lengths to keep the information from his nephew.

The meticulous man produced a notebook, which he identified as a calendar he maintained for his own use. On 22 July, he had attended a gathering at the British Museum with his nephew and his nephew's newly-wed wife. Professor Vandeleur, an entomologist of note, was there. The fellow had travelled extensively in Brazil, and Lord Russell thought his wife should like to meet him. Thus, Beryl and Christian Vandeleur were introduced to one another.

Sir Alfred had witnessed their introduction, and was struck by what he saw. Lady Beryl appeared to recognize the man, although she pretended otherwise. And though Vandeleur expressed himself in the words of one meeting another for the first time, it was clear to Sir Alfred that Vandeleur knew her.

'My nephew, Lord Russell, has not the social instincts, perhaps, to be aware of such subtleties,' Sir Alfred continued. 'He sees only the surface.' When Professor Vandeleur suggested to The Widow that they should have lunch together, 'Lord Russell thought it a capital idea. He encouraged his wife to do so.'

Thus The Widow agreed to meet Vandeleur for lunch a week later, Sir Alfred told the jurors. 'I thought perhaps I should also be there,' he said. 'For if a scandal involving the house of Russell was in the making, I should like to be in a position to prevent it.' And so he lunched there too, but secreted himself from their sight.

His suspicions were confirmed. 'There was an intensity to their discussion that could not have occurred had they not known one another.' Furthermore, 'the hand of Professor Vandeleur hand rested on that of Lady Russell. And she permitted the familiarity.'

Sir Alfred told his nephew that an acquaintance had seen his wife and Professor Vandeleur at lunch together, and thought they showed an unbecoming closeness. 'Quite characteristically, my nephew shrugged it off. My wife most certainly should be allowed to have friendships among members of the opposite sex, he said. He saw no harm.'

At that point, Sir Alfred determined to have them followed. 'I quite frankly suspected the worst. I thought Lady Russell and the professor had at some point in their lives been lovers. Would their earlier passions for one another again assert themselves?'

The matter was not arranged by him personally, of course. 'My solicitor made the contact with a Fleet Street detective agency, and my solicitor alone received the reports from the detectives.' Sir Alfred thus learned of their meetings. He kept the business totally beyond the awareness of his nephew, because he knew him to be a man of temper who acted on impulse. 'It would not do to excite an action on his part that all might come to regret.'

Sir Alfred further told the jurors that he never told his nephew what he himself suspected, which was that Lady Russell and Vandeleur were lovers. He did not do so because he knew of his nephew's nature, and wanted to avoid any scandal that might arise. It had been his purpose to gather unmistakable proof of the affair, then confront Lady Russell with it, in the hope that she could be induced to leave at once, and allow a divorce.

I could listen to no more. My attention was on the jurors. Some wore expressions of a dashed hope, others were more judgmental. But all appeared to agree that The Widow had committed a murder, then sought to blame the deed on an innocent man.

They would have her hang.

Chapter 21

From the reign of William the Conqueror, our law has vacillated on the question of whether the accused may testify in his own defence. In the regnal year 35 Victoria, which was also the calendar year 1891, we were in a swale between waves. It was the Queen's law that the accused may make a statement immediately after the Crown had rested. However, the statement was not evidence, and could not be subjected to the rigor of cross-examination.

Nor were the witnesses for the accused permitted to hear it. If an accused wished to speak in his defence, all the witnesses for the accused were to be excluded.

That time, for The Widow, was now. Our witnesses were in the witness room, and I told them they must remain there until they were called. 'It does not go well for Beryl, does it?' Laura said.

My heart went out to her. I had not known, until meeting her, that I had a heart. 'We must not give up hope,' I said. But in my association with Jeremy, I had never seen him in so deep a hole.

I returned to my chair in Sessions House, and sat in the expectant stillness. The Widow stood bravely in the dock, illuminated by the light from the reflector panels, and--so it seemed, even to my jaded old soul--from within.

'Mrs Baskerville,' Lord Arlington said, 'you may begin, if it is your desire.'

'It is, sir. But am I not to take an oath to tell the truth?'

'That is not our practice.'

'But My Lord, I wish the jurors to know that I tell the truth.'

'Proceed, my good woman.'

172

The Widow faced the jurors, and spoke with touching earnestness. 'Dear gentlemen, I swear to you, before God, that I speak the truth. I will not lie to you and if the judges will permit it, I will answer any questions that you have of me. They will be addressed as fully and as truthfully as I am able. I am also anxious to be questioned--to be examined--by Sir Guthrie.'

Sir Percival rose from his chair. 'Mr Holmes, the suggestions of your client are most unusual,' he said. 'Have you prepared her to speak thus? And are we now to be subjected to the carefully-rehearsed performance of an actress, under your direction?'

The observation by Sir Percival was most inappropriate, and Lord Arlington should never have allowed it. He was obviously disturbed by the behavior of his colleague. But Jeremy had risen to his feet, and Lord Arlington chose not to intervene. 'I have talked with my client at some length, Sir Percival,' Jeremy said, slow enough to cleanse the anger that I, for one, watched ripple through his frame. 'The practice is customary in the defence of one charged with murder. I will confess to you that I have also drawn her portrait. That is a device of mine, and I have persuaded myself that it enables me better to know a person. I have asked her many questions, to clarify her account of things in my mind. And she has asked questions of me, to which I have responded. Nothing more.'

Sir Percival sat down, wearing a frown. When Jeremy took his chair, he carefully avoided looking at The Widow, out of concern that--after the observation of Sir Percival--it might be construed by the jurors as a signal.

The Widow watched him sit down, then looked at the jurors. 'My dear gentlemen, I do not know what Sir Percival would have you believe. But at no time did Mr Holmes suggest to me that I engage in theatre. He greatly encouraged me to make a statement to you, but neither did he dictate its terms, nor rehearse me in any way. Though he knows much of what I will say, I have not told him everything. And as God is my witness, you shall hear the whole of it.'

Some of the jurors watched her with care, but others could no longer look at her. She seemed to sense their disquiet. 'Mr Holmes told me that my only hope lies in the truth,' she continued, 'but he quite realistically advised me that it is but a hope. I am aware that my account may not be accepted by any of you. But the truth has a life of its own, he said to me. It can radiate out of one's heart. Perhaps some of you will listen with your hearts, as well as your ears. Perhaps some of you will know I speak truly.'

The poisonous remark of Sir Percival appeared to have registered with them, however. They settled in their chairs as though for entertainment, yet their attitudes were grim.

She began by 'acquainting them with a realization' which she had but lately come to, about herself. She was 'drawn to dangerous men.' That quite obviously had been the case with Rodger Baskerville, who when they were first married, she had loved with all her heart--in spite of her dawning awareness that his reckless and quite fearless adventures were often far more than mischievous. They were criminal.

It was equally so with Peter, Lord Russell, she said, allowing her gaze to rest on the man himself. I had not seen him come in, and was quite astonished to find him attending the trial. He had been carried off the field at Calais the day before, after having been thrown from a horse. Yet he sat with indolent grandeur in a section reserved for the privileged.

The jurors were afforded a side-show. The soft

feminine sorrow in the expression of The Widow was not met by Lord Russell with sympathy. It was stopped by a heavy wall of sardonic, masculine superiority.

The Widow looked down. In a soft voice that vibrated with intensity, she told us that when the two of them were married, she had never been so in love.

She had thrilled to his electrifying performances on the polo fields. When others suffered injury, Lord Russell was at his most magnificent. She had seen him risk his life to save a fellow sportsman from harm. His spontaneous reactions in the battlegrounds of thundering horses and swinging mallets were quite simply heroic. As though we were all her confidantes, she told of being irresistibly drawn to him, and yielding to him as his willing, and loving slave.

At that point, The Widow interrupted her narrative to state that she was certain, in her heart, that Lord Russell could never have acted in the manner suggested by Mr Holmes. She knew Lord Russell as a man of honour. Her sorrow-filled eyes found Jeremy then. 'Had I known his defence of me was built around that which I know to be impossible, I would not have allowed it.'

Yet, perhaps, it was because of her devotion to Lord Russell that she had lost her way. After the events in Dartmoor chronicled by Dr Watson, there had not been the slightest doubt in her mind that Rodger Baskerville, her husband, was dead. And though God send her to Hell, her reaction to his death was not for the loss of him to whom she had been bonded in holy matrimony. Her reaction to his death was joy, an exuberant joy. She relished--even celebrated--his death.

It was with joy that she left her friends in Dartmoor, and struck out for London. On becoming a part of the vibrance of this great city, she waited with great expectation for the dawn of each day. For she was free to do what she was made to do. Her mother had been a dress-maker in Brazil, and Beryl had always had an eye for fashion. She loved the business she created, and took personal interest in those whom she employed, knowing instinctively what each was best suited for. They loved her in return.

Her enthusiasm for life was boundless then. She knew her enterprise would succeed. Success was hastened by the article in *The Times*, for which she was most grateful, but it would have come without it. Then to meet--to be pursued--by the handsomest man in the realm: her joy and gratitude for life, and for God, was greater than anything she had known . . .

When two weeks after her marriage to Lord Russell, with a dreadful suddenness, the man who had been the scourge of her life stood before her! At an earlier time in her life, the man known to all in Dartmoor as Jack Stapleton, had been Professor Christian Vandeleur at a school in Yorkshire. Now Professor Vandeleur was introduced to her by the man to whom she given her soul, and her heart.

As I watched The Widow, I had no doubt of her sincerity. Yet I wondered if perhaps it was too much. Some of the jurors were transfixed, though others smiled only with the pleasure of a patron of the theatre who appreciates a good performance.

Lord Russell had thought it would please her to meet the fellow. He had told him that he was familiar with the vastness of Brazil, where he had searched for butterflies. She had roamed through those meadows too. But following the introduction, The Widow told the jurors that she knew not how she had lived through that day. Had it not been for the comforting arms of Laura Lyons, she would never have survived. Mrs Lyons had also known Vandeleur in Dartmoor, but not by that name. She had known him as Jack Stapleton. 'She refused to believe me,' The Widow said, 'and insisted I was mistaken.'

Before The Widow had lunch with Christian Vandeleur the next week, she had persuaded herself that he was an impostor. 'I had made myself believe that Rodger Baskerville, whom I had married in Costa Rica, had a brother or a cousin whom I had not known, with identical features. Perhaps the fellow would attempt some form of blackmail, in exchange for money. That was my fervent hope.'

But it was not so. 'You are mine,' Rodger Baskerville demanded of her, sitting across a table at lunch, her hand quite helpless in his grip. 'You belong to me.' Under the threat of immediate disclosure of her untenable situation to Lord Russell, she met with Baskerville regularly thereafter for lunch. She could not recall the dates of their meetings with accuracy, but had no quarrel with the testimony presented, as to times and locations. In a daze, she wandered through one day and into the next.

At the beginning of her dreadful ordeal, she at least had her dear friend Laura to confide in. But even that solace was taken away. At their first meeting, it was as though Rodger knew she had confided in someone. He ordered her to speak to no one of him and threatened her over the matter, reminding her that she knew him well, and knew his power. If she should dare to tell another living soul of their meeting together, he would know it. He would find those persons, and destroy them.

In their subsequent meetings, he frightened her more. 'There was a madness about him,' she said. Such madness was made distressingly apparent when he revealed his grandiose scheme to her.

After he was done at Queenland College, he would return to South Africa as Professor Vandeleur, where he had carved out a niche that admirably suited his talents. There was the prestige that came with his position on the faculty of a University, and the freedom to be a thief. It afforded him the delicious excitement on which he thrived, in purloining the keys to another man's treasure, then relieving him of it.

But when November came, he informed her, with his hand firmly gripping her own, she would join him there. They would remain in South Africa for two years, then return to Baskerville Hall as its baron, and lady. His cousin Sir Henry would have met with an accident by then, 'and the estate will be mine.'

Before, he had wanted only the money, but now he wanted more. He would be Sir Rodger Baskerville, the baronet of Baskerville Hall, and rub his presence in the faces of all those who had wanted to bring him down. He would invite Sherlock Holmes and Dr Watson to dine with him at Baskerville Hall. There was never enough evidence to charge him with the murder of Sir Charles, and there was not sufficient evidence to charge him with the attempted murder of Sir Henry, even now. The world's foremost detective would know he had met his match. Nothing would give him greater pleasure than to live with his lady at Baskerville Hall, a flagrant symbol to the failure of the genius of Sherlock Holmes.

She appealed to God for help, then came to a desperate decision. What could he do to her without exposing himself as the murderer of Sir Charles Baskerville? She determined not to go to their next scheduled lunch. Her best course of action quite simply was to cut him forever out of her life.

It was a course of action for which she paid dearly. The very next night, he gained entrance into the *boutique* without her consent. Then he forced himself upon her.

How could there be a question in anyone's mind, as The Widow struggled to tell of the incident, that as she spoke of it, she relived its horror? She told of her awful humiliation at being subjected to the hatred and rage of his person, and of his strength, and her inability to prevent him from ripping apart her legs and forcing himself inside her, bruising and tearing her womanly possession in his fury, then flooding her with his disgusting fluids. After he had done with her, he literally crowed in exultation. He believed, in his madness, that he had impregnated her, and that she would have his son. When he returned to Baskerville Hall as its Baron, he would bring with him not only his lady, but an heir.

Then he had slapped her, and ordered her to dry her tears, which were only those of a foolish woman. He had done no more than exercise his marital right. Never again will you disobey me, he told her then. To do so would risk more than her life. He knew what she held precious, and threatened to destroy all of it, and her as well. Before leaving that night, he ordered her to meet him the coming Wednesday, for lunch.

That he could break so easily into her store did not surprise her, for she knew of his skills. The evidence at the trial had shown that he had a key to her door, and she did not question it. For him to obtain one would not have been difficult. But, she assured the jurors, he did not get it from her.

She knew she must meet him the following week for lunch. His threats were not idle words. There was no one to whom she could appeal for help, and she knew not how to extricate herself from his insane desire. May God forgive her, she said, trembling in the dock. She considered suicide.

Peter, her dear husband, had to have sensed her distraction, though he said nothing. As an animal with a foot in the steel jaws of a trap, she knew she must do as Rodger had ordered, and so she met him for lunch. To him, she was once again his possession. And at that lunch, he gave flesh to his insane plan.

He would leave for South Africa on the 2d of September, to return in the middle of October when his business there was done: a series of lectures, concerning what some of the fools at the University considered his brilliant proofs of the theory of evolution of Charles Darwin. As Professor Vandeleur, he had documented the changes in a species of moth that allowed them to hide from, and survive, a predatory bird that was new to the location.

She told the jurors how, in spite of his malevolence, she marvelled at the workings of his mind. Moths fascinated him, and in his desire to know and understand them it was as though he could become one. Perhaps that was the source of his genius. Yet he regarded all those who stood in awe of his discoveries as fools. He used them with the same pleasure he gained from using her. For they led him to treasures of many kinds, and the dangerous excitement enjoyed by the professional thief.

As for her, she knew her life in England had come to an end. His absence would give her time, she told the jurors, to develop a strategy that would permit her to surrender all that was dear to her, and to escape from him. How desperately she wanted to be free!

An annual fashion show in Paris would begin on the last day of September. She made it seem, to all her employees and to her husband, that she would go. Her husband had given his consent with reluctance, and her staff made all the necessary arrangements.

Then she told Laura Lyons, for whom she had a special

affection, that soon Laura would inherit *Fashions Sabor Brazilenos*. But it must be their secret. For, so she explained, her life as Lady Russell had come to mean more to her than she ever imagined. Peter would meet her in Paris, and after the show, they would sail to the islands of Greece. Her solicitor would have prepared all the documents for the transfer, and her only condition was that those presently employed would share in its ownership.

Her husband, for so she continued to think of Lord Russell, knew nothing of her deceit, nor did Laura. For she had no intention of going to Paris, she told the hushed assemblage in Sessions House. She would pack her trunks with memories, and drive away from *Fashions Sabor Brazilenos* on the morning of 29 September, in her carriage.

The carriage was stabled at the Portland Hotel. Her chauffeur--also at the hotel--was to pick her up at seven that morning and take her to the ferry for the mainland. But the old soldier was quite loyal to her wishes, and she would give him five hundred pounds, then tell him she must have the carriage for herself. She was certain he could be persuaded to say nothing of the matter for a one-week period.

Then she would drive her carriage by herself, which she was quite capable of doing, to Dartmoor. There she would warn Sir Henry of his danger, in that his cousin Rodger still lived. She would advise him to contact the authorities at once, allowing them time to use their resources to locate the fraudulent Christian Vandeleur in South Africa, and arrest him for his crimes.

After, she would drive to Bristol, there to take a ship and sail to America. From Bristol, she would post a letter to her dear husband, another to her solicitor, and a third to her dear friend Laura. Her intention on the last night in her beloved *boutique* had been to compose them . . .

When Rodger stood in the doorway to her office. 'I am back early,' he said. 'Surely you have been anxiously waiting for me.'

Words passed between them, many of which The Widow could not recall. But Rodger insisted in his madness that his son, the heir to Baskerville Hall, was growing in her womb, and he wanted to feel him.

She could not stand his touch and looked frantically about her. He blocked the doorway. He saw her alarm and discomfiture, which--as always--gave him satisfaction. And then there was the rap on the front door, the familiar knock of her husband.

'Who is that?' he had asked.

'My husband,' she had replied.

'I am your husband,' he had said. 'Get rid of that impostor.'

She slid past Rodger to answer the door, telling him that he must leave. At once.

And she thought he had.

When she opened the door to Peter, her heart was breaking. She knew she would never see him again. And then she told the jurors that they had already heard the words that passed between them from Lord Russell, and that everything he had told them was true. He was a man of honour, without the capacity for deceit.

I glanced at Lord Russell, who sat in his chair, his head gently rocking and eyes half-closed. What were his thoughts? I wondered.

The Widow then spoke of the chaos in her heart as she closed the door to Lord Russell. And then she heard those awful sounds, from the cutting room, and went in. Blood gushed from Rodger's throat as he twisted on the floor. Seeing him thus, she did what any woman would have done. She tried to save him. It mattered not who he was, or what he had done to her in the past. Such thoughts are not in the mind of a woman at such a time. Her instincts, if you will, compelled her to do what she could . . .

But it was no use. As the jurors had been informed by the pathologist, the damage to his throat was beyond repair. All she managed to do was bloody her dress, as well as dress-making materials which she had used as rags.

Most of the jurors watched with fascination as they sat in judgment of her every expression. Some wore faces that reflected their suspicions. Others looked away.

She told of hardly being aware of the cutting shears as they rattled on the hardwood floor, so occupied was she with her hopeless task. And then of her fleeting glimpse of the cape as it disappeared from her view, followed by her awful realization that the man was dead.

Perhaps it is different for a woman than it is for a man, she said, still speaking--it seemed to me--with incomparable honesty, from her heart. Perhaps a woman feels more deeply than does a man. When a woman is witness to the loss of life, it does not matter to her that the man whose head is in her lap was evil. Moments before, blood had coursed through his veins, through his heart.

But those thoughts did not remain with her long. Others crowded them out. Peter knew this man as Christian Vandeleur, the brilliant entomologist from South Africa. Others at the British Museum knew him by that name too, for Rodger had used it before. For him to be found in *Fashions* was out of the question. Not only would it bring scandal and harm to her, so would it to the house of Russell. She could not allow that to happen . . .

When it came to her that she was free of him. Rodger Baskerville was dead! There could be no mistake. He was not presumed dead, as before. His body was there, on the floor. The man who had made her life a hell on Earth in Dartmoor, and who had then invaded the magical world she had found in London, transforming it from wonder into terror and despair-- that man was dead! Could she have her life back? For the man on the floor was not Rodger Baskerville to anyone but her! To everyone else, he was Christian Vandeleur!

The wonder of it gripped her, flooding her with hope. With Rodger truly gone, there was no need to warn Sir Henry. Nor was there a reason to call in the authorities. And the world need never know she had been a bigamist, however unwittingly.

Her sorrowful gaze found Lord Russell, who appeared to be lost in thought. She could remain Lady Beryl Russell, she told the jurors. She need not sail off to America with nothing but memories of what might have been. Rather, in the morning, she would go to Paris! Perhaps she could entice her husband to meet her there, then show her the isles of Greece. They would travel even to America. She thrilled at the possibilities that unfolded before her. Oh, what a wondrous sense of exhilaration she did feel.

But could she deceive the authorities? Was it possible for her to move the body of Christian Vandeleur to a location that would not throw suspicion on her?

She would enlist the assistance of her trusted chauffeur. It would be so simple, she persuaded herself. She would tell him that Christian Vandeleur had broken into her store and tried to rape her. She would tell him she had stabbed the man to stop the outrage. Then she would put the old soldier on his honour to tell no one, in that she had not the heart to let Lord Russell know of it. She could not endure a scandal, or risk a trial. He would swear to her never to disclose the events of her evening's work. And of course, she would pay him handsomely. If need be, she would continue to pay him the remainder of his life.

But what could they do with the body? As if in answer to her prayers, a plan occurred to her. The wound in his throat had come from an arrow! Did it not have that appearance? Take the body to Regent's Park, the grounds used by the archers! Place it there, and leave it for others to explain. She shudders now, she told the jurors, to admit to such common and low deceit.

And so she worked with vigor and purpose through the night, with something of the joy she had experienced in Dartmoor when she first believed him dead. She cleansed the room of any sign of disorder, cleaned and bathed herself, disposed of the bloodied clothing and rags--when she was beset with doubts. She must not be seen, and so she waited until well after midnight, then dragged the remains outside . . .

When her dream, as though a fragile boat, smashed into the rocky shore of reality. The jurors knew the sorry ending to her efforts. Inspector Lestrade spoke truly, regarding her statement to him. She knew not why she did not tell him that the murdered man was Rodger Baskerville. Perhaps because at that time, in her mind, he was not. And though she appeared to those with whom she talked to be in control of herself, in truth her emotions were in a dreadful state. But for long years with Rodger Baskerville, she had learned to wear a mask, to hide her true feelings from . . .

With an abrupt suddenness, The Widow sat down. Perhaps she saw the cynical smiles of some of the jurors. 'I am done,' she said. 'Before God, I have told you the truth.'

Lord Arlington's gavel came down on the table. 'There will be no questions of the accused,' he announced. 'We are adjourned until the hour of two o'clock.' Majestically, he and the other judges rose and filed toward their door.

Chapter 22

The dock disappeared into the depths below with the exhausted and trembling Widow of Dartmoor, and Caroline, her warder. I had expected Jeremy would lunch with me, following the dramatic statement of The Widow. He would want my opinion on whether the jurors had been swayed by her eloquence, and my assurance that our witnesses were ready to be called.

But it was not to be. With a welcoming gesture, Jeremy saluted Lord Russell, who stood in his place in the gallery. Lord Russell let it be known with a gesture of his own that Jeremy should wait a moment.

I was disgusted by the spectacle. One hears of the deep friendships that blossom into being after two men have duelled, but I would never have believed that Jeremy and Lord Russell would fall into one another's arms.

As the elegantly-attired man who a day ago had tried to kill him made his way to the table for the barristers, Jeremy walked over to me. 'Is all in readiness?' he asked.

'Of course.'

'You must excuse me then,' he said. 'I am lunching with Lord Russell.'

Thus I was dismissed. It angered me that he should treat me as his vassal. Was I being punished for my association with Laura? With my arms folded over my stomach, I watched them leave.

I had no desire to lunch at the King's Tavern, there to suffer the sarcasms of the barristers and solicitors who would crowd near me and talk of the splendid defence mounted by The Bastard, or to be forced to hear their witticisms, regarding the fate of The Widow. I walked to the Bastriche Club, to lunch there with fellow bastards. The fare was fish and chips that day, but the conversation was suitably inane.

At two o'clock, well-fortified with Irish whiskey, I was at my post when the jurors filed into their places. The Widow sat quietly in the dock, like a rose on a bush, awaiting the scissors. But there was a wariness about Jeremy when he acknowledged me. Perhaps I only imagined it. After receiving assurances from me that our witnesses were ready, he assumed the center of the stage.

'Upstand! Upstand all!' boomed the usher, and the final act to the tragedy began.

In accordance with the practice of that day in the Old Bailey, the defence did not open its cause with a statement of the case, as did the Crown. Without a preamble or any indication of its destination, the cause for the accused simply pushed away from the shore, and set sail. Jeremy called Dr John Mortimer, the first witness for the defence.

The good doctor was reminded by Lord Arlington that-- though his testimony had been interrupted--he was still under an oath to tell the truth. Jeremy asked him whether, after his testimony of Thursday, he had gone to *Fashions Sabor Brazilenos*, and if so, for what purpose?

'Your solicitor, Mr Greech, asked me to examine the curtains in one of the rooms for signs of blood.'

He was met there on Saturday, by Inspector Brogarth of Scotland Yard. That good man believed the exercise to be a futile one, but he had been requested by the Attorney-General to attend, and so he did. The men did indeed find what appeared to be a bloodstain on a curtain. With the permission of Mrs Lyons, Inspector Brogarth cut away a sufficient patch from the curtain for testing purposes, which he took to the laboratories at Scotland Yard. Dr Mortimer was allowed to tell the jurors the results of the tests. 'The stain of blood on the curtain was from a human being,' he said.

Mortimer was next asked to describe the appearance of the stain. Was it a large blot, as though spilled from a jar, or perhaps a spatter, with small drops, as from a spray?

Neither of those, said the doctor. 'It appeared that the curtain had been folded, or cupped if you will, over an object, then used as one might use a rag, to wipe it clean.'

'A knife-blade perhaps? Or a cutting shears?' Jeremy asked.

'Really,' Sir Guthrie said. 'My learned friend knows better.'

When Sir Guthrie addressed the witness, he was clearly bored. 'Could the tests determine when the stain was put on the curtain?' he asked. 'Or who put it there?'

'They could not,' Dr Mortimer said. After which, he was asked to stand down.

As Laura Lyons took her place in the witness box, Jeremy examined a sketch of her he had done, which he turned over and laid face down on the table. She smiled at both him and The Widow. And then, bless her soul, her radiant expression found me.

Lord Arlington reminded her that she was still under an oath to speak the truth. Jeremy, in his easy fashion, inquired more deeply into her background than had Sir Guthrie when she had testified for the Crown.

For much of her life, she had lived in Dartmoor with her father, a lawyer of a difficult turn of mind. He had not approved of her marriage to Mr Lyons, who was an artist. They were not married long, when Mr Lyons drifted away from their rooms in Coombe Tracey. Her father was quite without sympathy for her situation, and would not take her back in his house. 'Fortunately, I had acquired the skills of a secretary,' she said. 'When one needed a letter, I would type it up. But I hardly earned enough to live on, and leaned heavily on others for support.'

'Was one of those on whom you leaned the victim in this case?' Jeremy asked.

'It was,' she said. In a voice clouded with lingering bitterness, she told of the manner in which the man had used her, by inducing her to lure Sir Charles Baskerville out of the Manor at night, to her ever-lasting regret. The ruse he had used was a false promise of marriage.

She had not known Beryl until after the attempted murder of Sir Henry Baskerville. It was after that dreadful affair that Sherlock Holmes revealed Jack Stapleton to be Rodger Baskerville, the cousin of Sir Henry. 'Mr Holmes--indeed, everyone--thought Jack Stapleton had perished in Grimpen Mire, and no tears were shed over his demise,' Mrs Lyons told the jurors. A look of immense satisfaction covered her face. 'None.'

'How did you meet The Widow?' Jeremy asked.

'We met for tea,' Mrs Lyons said. 'We had each been wronged by Stapleton, whom I then, for the first time, knew to be Rodger Baskerville. Beryl and I reached out for one another, as women will do. We became quite close. When Beryl moved to London, we corresponded,' she continued, 'and when her business began to grow, she wanted a secretary and an assistant.' The women exchanged glances, recalling that happier time. 'But I was more than her secretary. I was her dear friend.'

Had she worked on the day The Widow and Lord Russell were married? 'I did not,' the witness replied. 'I had received an invitation to the wedding, and attended it. It was a most happy occasion.'

'Rodger Baskerville was a man of many places and identities,' Jeremy said. 'Born in the America's, his true name was Rodger Baskerville. When first in England, he was Master Vanderleur, a teacher of natural sciences at a school in Yorkshire. Then in Dartmoor, he took the name of Jack Stapleton. Most recently, in South Africa, he resumed the identity of Vanderleur. Did The Widow speak to you of Christian Vandeleur?'

There was one such conversation only, Mrs Lyons said. It occurred on 22 July, a Wednesday, and 'a date of which I am certain, in that I kept my lady's diary of appointments. . . She had gone to a lecture at the British Museum that day and it was in the afternoon, on her return to work, that we spoke of him.' Had she gone to the museum alone? 'No. She was with her husband and his uncle, Sir Alfred Russell.'

When she returned, 'she came at once into my office, shut the door, and burst into tears. While in my arms, she told me what I simply could not believe.'

Her husband had introduced her to Christian Vandeleur, '"a most engaging fellow," her husband had said.' But the man was Rodger! With characteristic effrontery, he had asked her to lunch in the presence of her husband and his uncle! '"Do go, my dear," Lord Russell had said to her. "It will be good for you to speak with one who knows your homeland." And so they arranged to meet the following Wednesday!

'My lady was frantic,' Mrs Lyons told the jurors. 'I suggested to her that the fellow was an impostor. Did Rodger Baskerville have a twin, or a brother who resembled him closely? She seized upon my thoughts. They were her most desperate hope.'

It was with fear and expectation, the following

Wednesday, that The Widow set off for lunch. Yet on her return that afternoon, 'though clearly in anguish, she said little. "I was mistaken," she said to me. "Let us speak no more about it." And she held her peace, from that moment until she was locked in gaol.'

Yet there were indications that they continued to meet. 'My lady was not the same.' And on Wednesdays, she often was gone from the store, with no explanation.

But in the early days of September, 'the sparkle came back to her eyes.' An annual fashion show in Paris seemed to account for it. The most stylish of winter apparel would be on display, and the show would be attended by the most discriminating buyers of ladies' clothing in Europe. 'The spark of life that none of us had seen for months, was back,' she told the jurors. With a flurry of activity, The Widow made plans to attend. 'I was closely involved in those arrangements,' the witness said. 'It was I who alerted the sponsors that Lady Beryl would attend, and I who located a comfortable suite for her in a nearby hotel.' She smiled at The Widow, who sat quietly in the dock. 'When very close to the day of her departure, she drew me aside. There was a sadness about her, but a joy as well. What she told me was to be our secret.'

'What did she tell you?' Jeremy asked.

'She would not return from Paris.' My frequent companion at dinner gazed with sorrowful eyes at the jurors. 'I was to have her store. Lord Russell was to meet her in Paris, and they would travel to the isles of Greece. She had engaged a solicitor, who would draw up the documents of transfer.'

'Did she give you his name?' Jeremy asked.

'No. She would send his name to me by post, after her departure.'

'And when was she to depart?'

'In the morning of twenty-nine September. She would spend the night in the rooms above *Fashions Sabor*, and leave the following day.'

'Were you to meet with her in the morning before her departure?'

'No, Mr Holmes. She was to leave at seven. I am there at eight, and open the doors at nine.'

'May I assume you were at work at your usual hour?'

'I ... Yes, of course.'

There was a minor disruption in the gallery. The tall figure of Lord Russell stood in the section for the privileged, intent on his own business, with no regard to the business at hand. He tapped his uncle, Sir Alfred, on the shoulder with his riding crop and motioned with his head. Sir Alfred registered alarm, but got up quickly and followed Lord Russell out of the gallery.

Lord Arlington had been hesitant to call for order, no doubt out of respect for their rank. Before he could act in the matter, they were gone.

'Where are your lodgings, Mrs Lyons, if I may be so bold?' Jeremy asked, his attention on the witness.

She gave him an address I knew quite well, though I had been there only as her escort of an evening. It was on Granville Place near Portman Square.

'Had you come from there to work, that morning of twenty-nine September?'

'Yes.'

'Were you there at eight?'

'Yes. Of course.'

Jeremy had more than one drawing of the witness. There were three that he consulted on the table in front of him. Why were there three? I wondered. I had only seen one.

'Your landlady is Mrs Thimble, if I am not mistaken,' he said, after a moment.

The question surprised me. How had Jeremy come to know her name? As a barrister, he would never have made the inquiry himself, and I had not given it to him.

'Yes,' the witness replied.

'Would it surprise you if I were to tell you that Mrs Thimble was quite worried for your welfare that morning, in that you did not go to work, and remained in your rooms until after the lunch hour?'

What was Jeremy suggesting with the question? How could he know that Mrs Thimble had worried over such a thing? He could not have made any inquiries of her. They would have been made by me, his instructing solicitor, and I had not questioned the woman.

'That is not true,' Mrs Lyons said. 'She is mistaken.'

My dear drinking companion, from her chair in the witness box, had the aspect of one who was not at all certain of what to expect. She was on her guard. I did not know what to expect either. I wanted to scream at Jeremy, to demand of him, what do you do?

'Then you were at work, at eight, on twenty-nine September?' Jeremy asked.

'Perhaps it was later,' Mrs Lyons answered. 'I do not recall.'

'But you did go to *Fashions Sabor Brazilenos* that morning before nine, to open the doors?'

'Yes,' she said, rather vaguely. 'I am sure of it.'

'Will you be so kind as to tell the jurors whether or not you had any difficulty getting into the store?'

Laura looked to me, in distress. But I was as dismayed by the questions as was she. 'What do you mean, Mr Holmes?'

194

'I mean that I find it odd,' Jeremy said. 'The inspectors from Scotland Yard were at *Fashions Sabor Brazilenos* at three o'clock that morning, and they remained there all that day. Their reports make no mention of your being there.' He glanced at his drawings, then to the witness. 'Are you quite certain you were there before nine, to open the doors?'

'Forgive my lapse of memory,' she said. 'That morning is one I have tried to forget. I recall now that when I arrived, the door was blocked by a constable. There were people milling about on the street in front and I had a most fearful presentiment that something was terribly wrong. I chose to leave immediately, to go back to my rooms.'

Her answer wrang hollow, even to me. I felt, rather than saw, the questioning expressions on the faces of the jurors.

'Did you not fear that your presentiment concerned your dear friend Beryl?'

'Mr Holmes,' she said, 'I must confess to you that I was not thinking clearly. I could not stay there.'

'Were there people milling about in the street?' Jeremy asked.

'Yes.'

'Did you hear what was said?'

'I did not, Mr Holmes. I left at once.'

'And you made no inquiries of anyone?' Jeremy asked.

'No. I was terribly distressed, and was possessed by a sense of dread.'

'Is it fair to say that you ran away?' Jeremy asked.

'It is indeed,' Mrs Lyons said. 'I literally ran from there.'

'As you had the evening before, from the rear exit?' Jeremy asked, using the same conversational tone.

'No!' my lady friend exclaimed. 'What do you suggest?'

'I suggest that you were not at *Fashions Sabor Brazilenos*, before nine, to open the doors on twenty-nine September,' Jeremy said. 'I suggest that you knew a murder had occurred there the evening before, and it did not occur to you to go to work. I suggest that a moment ago, when you said, "I literally ran from there," that you spoke the truth. But in your mind, you saw yourself running from the back door, as you had the evening before.'

'That is not true!' she exclaimed. 'None of it is true!'

Sir Guthrie rose to his feet. I wanted to rise to mine. 'Your Lordships,' Sir Guthrie said, 'I hesitate to interfere with the examination of my learned friend, but perhaps he should be reminded that the witness is his.'

'I quite agree with the observation of the Attorney-General,' Sir Percival said, standing and pre-empting Lord Arlington. 'The manner employed by learned counsel in the questioning of his own witness is hardly appropriate.'

Lord Arlington frowned, but not at Jeremy. Rather, he directed his disapproval at Sir Percival! Quite clearly, Lord Arlington was not pleased by the behavior of his learned colleague, though he chose not to say as much in words. He waited until Sir Percival was seated, then he smiled at Jeremy. 'Mr Holmes, do you care to respond?'

'With your leave, My Lord, I should like no more than to continue the examination in my own clumsy way.'

'Please proceed.'

In his most engaging manner, Jeremy asked the witness and the jurors to indulge him in a fantasy of his. It was his habit to draw a likeness of those who would be called to testify, in his own somewhat in-artful manner. By drawing their portrait, he believed he came to know them. 'I have drawn more than one of you, Mrs Lyons, and confess to having been struck by what I have seen in each of them. My Lord, may I show Mrs Lyons one of the drawings?' he asked Lord Arlington.

'A most unusual request, Mr Holmes,' Lord Arlington said. 'Sir Guthrie, have you any objection?'

'The fantasy of my learned friend is known to me,' the Attorney-General said. 'As long as the jurors know of it, as do I, as a fantasy, I have no objection.'

'Proceed then, Mr Holmes,' Lord Arlington said.

The picture he showed Laura was the one I had seen. It portrayed her as a lovely woman of deep intelligence. She looked at it closely, but said nothing.

'Is that your likeness, Mrs Lyons?' he asked.

'I am flattered by it, Mr Holmes,' she said. 'You make me a handsome woman. But I fail to see what is striking about it. What strikes you so?'

'Do I see torment in your expression?' Jeremy asked.

Mrs Lyons made no reply.

'Are you in torment, Mrs Lyons?' Jeremy asked.

'Of course,' she said. 'My dearest friend may go to the gallows. The prospect is more than I can bear.'

'Let me suggest that your torment runs even deeper than that. For you *know* her to be innocent. Yet you are prevented . . .'

'I *believe* her to be innocent,' Mrs Lyons said, correcting her examiner. 'With all my heart.'

'Do you bring nothing to your face other than your *belief* in her innocense?' Jeremy asked. With a gesture, he brought her expression to the attention of the jurors.

'That is all,' she replied. But did her eyes waiver as she spoke?

'Your habit last summer, in the evenings, was to wear a black cape, was it not?'

'What an odd question,' she said. 'I do not own a black cape."

'But you owned one last summer?'

'No,' she said. 'I did not.'

'Then your landlady is mistaken about that, also?'

'Yes,' Mrs Lyons said, firmly.

He nodded at Laura in apparent agreement. 'Mrs Lyons, I would ask you to take yourself back to that night in Dartmoor, when everyone supposed Jack Stapleton was drowned in Grimpen Mire. You knew otherwise, did you not?'

My lady-friend's face went white for a moment, then coloured with anger. 'I did not!' she replied. 'I knew nothing of the sort!'

'Did he not let himself into your lodgings at Coombe Tracey, and did you not give him safe haven, until he could make his escape?'

'Preposterous!' she said. 'You have no proof!' Then for a moment, she looked as though she would faint.

Jeremy regarded her with great concern. 'Are you well, Mrs Lyons?' he asked.

'I am not.' Her voice sounded as though it was coated with sand. 'I am not.'

'Perhaps water would help?' Jeremy asked, with a glance at the usher.

'It would not. I feel as though I might faint.'

'My Lords,' Jeremy said. 'May I suggest a short recess? Or perhaps, in view of the hour, that we adjourn for the night?'

Sir Guthrie quickly stood up. 'I quite agree with my learned friend,' he said. 'The witness obviously cannot continue, and the hour is late.'

The witness sagged in her chair. 'I beg of you, My Lord,' she managed to say.

Lord Arlington frowned at her, and then at Jeremy. 'Is it your wish to interrupt your examination at this point?' he asked.

'It is, My Lord. I am concerned over the welfare of the witness.'

'Very well,' Lord Arlington said. 'It is after four. We are in the middle of an examination, but we shall adjourn for the day.' The witness was greatly relieved. 'Mrs Lyons,' he said to her, 'you may stand down. Your testimony will resume tomorrow, at ten in the morning.' To the usher, he said, 'You may so advise all who may attend.' The judges began their solemn procession to their door.

'Upstand!' boomed the usher. 'Upstand all!'

I stood, as did everyone in the chamber. My dear lady-friend found me watching her. She wore an appealing, helpless expression. 'Wait for me,' I mouthed, motioning with my head, signing her to stay a moment in the Great Hall, outside the Sessions House. The usher performed his centuries-old littany, after which Sessions House began to empty.

Jeremy came over to me. Others listened, but I cared not a whit. 'Is this your new strategy?' I demanded of him. 'Having failed with Lord Russell, do you now use this good woman as an alternative suspect?'

'I must speak to you in private,' he said. 'Please, my friend. It is a matter of urgency.'

We met in the hallway. 'Go to her at once,' Jeremy said. 'Suggest to her that her best course is to leave England.'

'What! Why on earth should she do that?'

'Tomorrow, her landlady will testify,' Jeremy said. 'Mrs Thimble has in her possession, and can clearly identify, the cape that Mrs Lyons wore the evening of the murder. Mrs Thimble is also quite clear in her recollection of the morning of the next day. Mrs Lyons did not go to the store to open it, as she testified. Rather, she was in her rooms early the night before, and remained in them until noon.'

'How do you know what Mrs Thimble will testify to, Jeremy? Surely you did not make the inquiries. Who made them for you?'

'You did, Edward.'

'I did nothing of the kind!'

'We will also show that Rodger Baskerville stayed with her at her lodgings in Coombe Tracey, *after* he was presumed to have drowned in the Grimpen Mire. Additionally, we will show he stayed with her at her rooms in London.' I stared at him. 'Edward, you must do as I ask,' he said. 'Unless you would rather see her hang.'

My lady was in tears when I found her, huddled and alone on a bench in the ante-chamber in the Great Hall. 'My dear man,' she said. 'What does The Bastard do?'

I uncapped my flask and offered her refreshment, which she took most readily. 'He would use you, I fear,' I said.

She returned my flask, and I drank deeply. 'How would he use me?' she asked.

'Tomorrow, he intends to produce your black cape.'

'But I threw it away!' Then she glared at me, as though to challenge me to make something of her words.

I was made numb by them. There was no longer a doubt. My Laura had driven the cutting shears into the villain's throat. I drank deeper, but there was not drink enough in London to quench the despair that wanted me.

And then I cared not what she had done. To me, she was still my dear Laura and I would rather die than have her hang. 'He will also show that Rodger Baskerville has been to your lodgings at Portman Square.'

'How could he know?' Then there was realization in her expression. 'The detective. Jack was followed by a detective.'

I thanked the stars for the manner in which Irish whiskey could at least soften the harshness of reality. 'My dear Laura,' I said, handing her the flask, 'I knew nothing of what he would do. Had I known of it . . .' I could not finish my thought.

'What would you have done?' she asked.

What did it matter? 'The Bastard thought that perhaps I should suggest to you that your best course would be to leave me.'

'Leave you?' She tipped my flask, then stood up. Her tears were quite gone.

'Leave England,' I said, correcting myself.

'I shall miss you, dear man,' she said, returning the flask to me.

And then she vanished from my sight.

Chapter 23

When she had gone, I tried to stand up, but could not. What was wrong with me? Where did I hurt? I should have walked to the Bastriche Club, but had no desire to tell Jeremy of my conversation with Laura, or to see him.

'Greech, old fellow!' a barrister who had watched the spectacle in court said to me. He and another nob stood in front of me. 'Who will you and The Bastard throw it off on next?'

'Her chauffeur!' his companion said. 'The old soldier! Have you not seen it coming?'

'Join us, Greech!' the barrister said, loudly. 'We will raise our glasses to you and The Bastard. You have made a game of it!'

'I cannot,' I said, 'but kind of you to ask.' I reached for a mantle of propriety and respectability, and put it on. 'The Bastard and I have much to do.'

'Off with you then, my good man!' said one of them.

'Blacken Sir Guthrie's eye!' said the other, as they hurried away.

When I arrived at the club, Jeremy had an old photograph of Rodger Baskerville on the table before him, and a sketch-pad in his knee. Caricatures of faces: some hideous, some of great intelligence, others desolate and lonely: framed the border. Yet the features in each quite clearly were of the man in the photograph.

In the center of the pad emerged a portrait of the scoundrel himself. Somehow all the cartoons were drawn together. 'Remarkable,' I said. 'The drawing you have of my dear Laura. Is it also a composite?'

'Is she still your dear Laura?' Jeremy asked.

'You *are* a bastard,' I said. 'In the unlovely sense of the word.'

I had thought he would be insulted, but he was not. He put the sketches of Baskerville aside and found the portraits he had done of Laura. 'Will she be there tomorrow?' he asked.

'I would be surprised.'

He put one of the drawings on his easel. 'Do you love her still?'

'That does not concern you.'

'Edward, she has compromised you.' He looked at the drawing. 'I do not want her to hang, nor would I have you suffer for her. Let me show you who she is.'

I could do no more than to stare at him.

'In court, I spoke of her tormented heart,' he said, 'but there is more I could have said. My drawings of her quite clearly show that she was betrayed, and overwhelmed with rage. She is now free of the rage, but not the torment.'

When I looked at the pictures, I saw nothing of such things. I saw only her smile. 'Would you have me believe that you can you see her passions?'

'In a manner of speaking, yes. I would have you see them, too. I would have you do more than that. I would have you dare to feel them.'

'That is impossible.'

'I disagree. Her passions resonate in me when I draw her. I would have you see her, as I do.'

All at once, I wanted nothing more. 'Help me then,' I begged of him.

'Your dear Laura is indeed a woman of passion,' he said, 'but they are hidden from view. Yet they surge in her, and freeze her, and have twisted more than her soul. They have transformed her face into one that has become quite malleable.

It can promise every man she is with, what he wants most in a woman. Her passions as well have given her limbs the beauty of a statue of marble.'

'How can you know this of her?' I asked.

'How can I *not* know?' he replied. 'When I drew her, she flowed from the tips of my fingers, through my eyes and ears and heart, and on to the paper before me. It was more than a window into her soul that I drew, Edward. It was as though my hands felt the throbbing of her heart.' His expression asked me to understand his words, and perhaps I did. 'I experienced the hugeness of her rage. I felt her satisfaction when she was freed from it. It was not a great leap of the imagination to imagine what led to her rage, and what rid her of it.'

'Stabbing Rodger Baskerville with shears?'

'Yes. Yet there remains in her the torment of a conflict she cannot resolve.' Critically, he examined the drawing. 'It is rooted in love. Her face does not reveal *who* she loves, but one can surmise as much. The Widow.'

'The Widow!' I exclaimed. 'I had hoped...'

'No. You are a tool to her, Edward. An implement she uses to shape her unlovely world.' I shielded myself from his words. 'Perhaps she feels some affection for you,' he added.

'Does she love The Widow as she would a man?'

He shook his head. 'There is closeness, something akin to the tenderness of a mother for her child. But it is not sexual. It is rooted in caring for another, not desire.'

'Poppy-cock,' I said, suddenly. 'I refuse to believe you. It is not possible that such secrets are revealed to you in your art.'

'Yet you see the same thing.'

'I do not!' I said. 'Your visions are no more than the

intuitions of a woman, not the product of a logical mind. There is nothing rational about them. I do not believe you can know what you claim to know about Laura, by drawing her.'

He would not be provoked. 'Edward, there is no longer a doubt in my mind that Mrs Lyons committed what some might consider an act of mercy, though it was done in a rage. Is there any doubt in yours?'

'You must prove it!' I said. 'I will not believe that of her!'

'Will you help me?'

'Help you!' I said, angrily. 'You ask for my help? I should like to know, why? You do not need me, Jeremy. Your questioning of Laura was quite enough for even a dullard, such as me, to deduce that another does the work of your solicitor now. Go to him.'

'I cannot,' Jeremy said, looking about the room. There were others who could not keep from overhearing us. 'May we continue this conversation in the privacy of your sitting room?'

'If that is your wish.'

My sitting room was comfortable enough for me. There were papers strewn about on the carpeted floor, which awaited the attention of a servant. The cushioned chairs were made of leather, and were gathered around a solid table in the center, as though they were friends, playing cards. There was a fireplace on an inner wall, windows to let in the light, and lamps on the walls to use at night. My library of books was not remarkable. They were on shelves, on a wall. A small table under a window was filled with magazines. I turned up the lamps, sat down, and let Jeremy find his own chair.

My attitude was not that of an instructing solicitor, in conference with a barrister. The cause of The Widow was not foremost in my mind. "I shall miss you, dear man," my Laura had said, and her words had filled me with despair. Would I see her again? A wall had also grown between me and the man who sat across from me.

'After you have heard me, you may choose to disassociate yourself from me,' Jeremy said. 'If you do, I will not blame you, or love you the less. But I beg of you to hear me, and to help me. For I need your help.'

'I am listening,' I said.

'The old hag whose portrait I drew on Friday, at the close of proceedings for the day, was indeed Sherlock Holmes. He had been on the continent, engaged in a case of great importance. By chance, he saw an article in a paper about our trial. The facts were a great surprise to him, and he came to London at once. In his rather pawkish way, he let me know he was in attendance.'

'I thought as much,' I said. 'Yet you are only telling me now.'

'This morning, I saw him again in the gallery. He was there in the section reserved for the privileged as Peter, Lord Russell.'

'What!' I said. 'That was not Lord Russell?'

'Hardly, Edward. Lord Russell was carried off the field of honour at Calais.'

I believed him, of course, but could not accept it. 'How did you see through the disguise?' I asked. 'The Widow thought it was Lord Russell. So did his uncle, Sir Alfred.'

He shrugged. 'I see without expectations,' he said. 'May I continue?'

'Of course.'

'The events of this morning brought me to despair, Edward,' he said, 'as they did you, I think. Our strategy was defeated. When Sir Alfred testified that it was quite impossible for Lord Russell to have known that Baskerville and The Widow were followed, it was apparent to me what Sir Guthrie had done.'

'What had he done?'

'He had fed me enough rope for a noose. As The Widow gave her account, I did not believe it would be enough to save her from the noose, and I did not know what we could do.'

'"We"?' I asked, rather unpleasantly.

'Yes, we, Edward. You are still her solicitor. But as The Widow gave her statement, I looked over the drawings I had done of Mrs Lyons with great care. There were three because her initial portrait had troubled me. As I listened to The Widow, I began to see more of her. I understood the cause of her torment, and saw her in a different light.'

'What did you see?'

'When The Widow told Laura that Lord Russell had introduced her to Jack Stapleton, Mrs Lyons had refused to believe her. Why had she refused to believe? Then during the first lunch between The Widow and Rodger, The Widow told of her hope that Rodger was an impostor, and how even that was dashed. Rodger seemed to have known that The Widow had confided in someone about his true identity. I asked myself, who might that have been?'

'Those are the kinds of questions your uncle Sherlock might have asked,' I said.

'The answers were clear to me,' Jeremy said. 'Baskerville knew The Widow had confided in someone because he had been with Mrs Lyons after the incident at the British Museum, and she had questioned him about it. And Mrs Lyons could not believe The Widow had seen Stapleton, because he had not told her that he would do so. Mrs Lyons knew then that he was using her, as he had before.

'It was then that I understood what had troubled me in the drawings I had done of Mrs Lyons. I knew then of the seeds that had grown into her sense of betrayal. I understood how later, that betrayal had exploded in rage. It was obvious to me then that her freedom of that rage was the immense satisfaction she felt, in vengeance.

'And I believed that facts could be found that would support those thoughts. She had known he lived, no doubt because he had persuaded her in Dartmoor that he loved her still. Did she provide him with safe haven, and the means to escape? He would have lied to her about his true intentions, but he might well have induced her to become a close friend of The Widow, to provide him with information about her.'

I shut my eyes. I wanted to shut my ears. 'Why do you tell me so much?' I asked.

'I wish you to understand that it was not until this morning, as The Widow gave her statement, that I realized Mrs Lyons had murdered Rodger Baskerville.'

'And you knew this, I suppose, with the same certainty that you knew The Widow was a woman who could not kill?'

'Yes,' he said. 'It is a certainty you cannot accept, but I only wish I had seen it sooner. We could have talked it out, and you would have managed your attachment to Mrs Lyons.'

Would I have? I wondered. Or would I have gone to her?

'Perhaps you would have found another solicitor to look for the proofs. But today, in court, there was no time to talk to you of it. Forgive me for being dramatic, but it seemed to me that I had no more than the lunch hour to acquire some credible evidence, with which to confront the woman you love.'

'Dear me,' I said, in an effort to make light of it, as I wrestled with my emotions. 'What a dilemma.' Yet I ached for her.

'Could I trust you?' Jeremy asked. 'I did not know. Would it be better for another to investigate? Why not ask it of my uncle, Sherlock Holmes?'

'I was your instructing solicitor,' I said, lashing out at him. 'You acted dreadfully. At the very least, you should have involved me in the decision.'

He nodded. 'I should have asked you to join my uncle and me for lunch,' he said. 'But I thought only of The Widow, and the urgent need for proofs. Uncle Sherlock quite agreed with the conclusions I had drawn, and understood at once what he must do. At my request, he presented himself to Mrs Thimble as Edward Greech.'

'He could not have made himself into me.'

'Mrs Thimble had difficulty in believing him, but she still gave him the information he needed. What I represented to the jurors in court had come from her, and she will testify to as much tomorrow. There are also two witnesses from Coombe Tracey, who will arrive tonight at Charing Cross. One is a grocer, the other a young man of the village. They saw no man in her rooms, but can give evidence from which one can infer one was there.'

'You wish me to meet them, rather than the great Sherlock Holmes?' I asked.

'I do,' Jeremy said. 'When he summoned Sir Alfred from his place in the gallery in court, it was a signal to me. Circumstances had compelled him to return to the continent at once.'

'And you need me now because he is gone,' I said.

'I need you because you are the solicitor for The Widow,' he said. 'Edward, I have drawn you. I know you.' His eyes surrounded me with what could have been mistaken for love. 'I need you because I trust your heart.'

    I stood up. My flask was empty, as was my "trusted" heart. Help was near in one case, though not the other. 'What else would you have me do?' I asked.

Chapter 24

I was not in my place the following morning at ten. It hardly mattered. The witness was not there. Lord Arlington considered it a contempt of court, and--at ten-thirty--issued a warrant for the arrest of Mrs Laura Lyons. The jurors were told to return at eleven.

My business was done by eleven and from my seat alongside the jurors, I warmed my throat with a drink from my flask. While so engaged, my eye was caught by a strangely-attired older man in the section for the privileged. It was the Duke of Wendleton, in a suit that was quite out-of-fashion. He touched his cap to me and I lifted my flask to him. Jeremy was at his table, and I envisioned White Horse, pleading for the life of a bluecoat.

The cause of the Crown against Mrs Beryl Baskerville resumed. After a rather spirited discussion, Jeremy was allowed to put on evidence concerning the absence of Mrs Lyons. He called Inspector Lestrade into the witness box.

Armed with a warrant for her arrest, Lestrade had driven to her lodgings on Granville Place near Portman Square. Mrs Thimble, her landlady, informed him that she was not there. 'Rather early last evening, Mrs Lyons packed up a bag in great haste,' the inspector said. 'She told Mrs Thimble that an aunt in Edinburgh had begged her to come. The auntie was alone, and quite ill.' Efforts were on-going to verify the existence of the aunt.

Lestrade next drove to *Fashions Sabor Brazilenos*. 'A woman of Spanish extraction told me that Mrs Lyons had gone to Baring's Bank at nine, but was not back. The Spanish woman was very unsettled over it. There were customers that day, but no cash in the registers to make change.' He added that the woman had thought something was amiss, because Mrs Lyons carried a large bag.

'I drove at once to the bank, to find she had been there when the doors opened, but had finished her business and had gone. As to the nature of her business there, I would need a warrant.'

Lestrade drove back to *Fashions Sabor Brazilenos* in the hope that they had crossed paths. But Mrs Lyons had not returned. She had stayed the night there, another Spanish woman told him, in the rooms above. 'Inquiries are being made at train stations, and of taxi drivers,' he said, 'but if you was to ask me, I would say the bird has flown.'

The next witness Jeremy called was Detective Madan Asan of the Fleet Street detective agency. It hardly seemed to me that the small man stepped into the box to take the chair. As quiet as a shadow, he seemed to appear there. After reminding the jurors that Madan Asan had followed Professor Vandeleur beginning with a day in July, Jeremy asked him if Vandeleur had led him to a building on Granville Place near Portman Square. He had, the expressionless Oriental informed the jurors. I had briefed Jeremy as to what the man could say. He produced a small notebook that recorded not only when Vandeleur met with The Widow, but anything worthy of note.

On five occasions, each between the hours of midnight and three in the morning, Vandeleur had used a key to slip into the building on Granville Place, near Portman Square. The last was on Friday, September 25.

Sir Guthrie acknowledged that the lodgings of Mrs Lyons were in that building.

Mrs Elizabeth Thimble was the next witness for the defence. She had not wanted to testify that morning when I brought her to court. A man had questioned her the day before who identified himself as Edward Greech, 'but he was not you, sir. What am I to do?'

'If asked, you must tell the truth,' I had told her. 'And the truth is that you were questioned by a man who identified himself to you as Edward Greech.'

I hoped that the subject would not come up.

A primly-dressed woman with pinch-lines in her mouth, and eyes that squinted as though to shield themselves from the light, she was as plump as a Christmas goose. The fingers of her right hand caressed the small cross of gold that hung from her neck. Responding to Jeremy's questions in a small voice, she testified that she owned and lived in a building at Granville Place near Portman Square, a property her deceased husband had left her. It was divided into five flats, and Mrs Laura Lyons had one of two on the third floor.

Did she know where Mrs Lyons was employed? 'That lovely dress shop on Marylebone Lane.' Where a murder occurred? 'That awful murder. Lady Russell was charged for it but Mrs Lyons would not believe it of her.' When did you first hear of the murder? 'Why the day of it, I'm sure. It was in all the papers and my lodgers spoke of nothing else.'

Thus she affirmed that her first knowledge of the crime was Tuesday, 29 September. Had she seen Mrs Lyons that day? 'Not until past noon. Poor dear. Once I knew of the murder, of course, I understood. She was terribly upset over it, you see.... She had gone to her rooms the evening before by nine. . . . Why! It never occurred to me that such a dear person as Mrs Lyons was herself involved! Not in the least!'

Jeremy asked her if Mrs Lyons wore a black cape in the evenings when she went out. 'She has in the past, Mr Holmes.' Was she wearing one when she came in the Monday evening before Mrs Thimble learned of the murder? 'I could not swear to that.' When Mrs Thimble was asked when she'd last seen the black cape, she grew a bit secretive. 'I have it myself,' she said, after struggling perhaps with her conscience. 'It was in the trash, you see.' She found it there early in October. 'I said nothing to Mrs Lyons about it. She had given me dresses, you see, from that expensive store, and I couldn't have her think poorly of me.'

She had not brought the cape with her to court.

Sir Guthrie asked only about Professor Vanderleur. Was he ever at her building? 'Why no, sir. . . . I run a proper house and do not permit men to stay in the rooms of the women, and Mrs Lyons was never a concern. . . . He did not call on Mrs Lyons, of that I am quite certain.'

When court adjourned for lunch, I took a cab to Farrington and boarded a train for Paddington, to meet our witnesses from Coombe Tracey. We were to meet at the Great Western Terminus, and I would escort them to the Old Bailey by two. Their train from Exeter had arrived at 11:54, but I could not find them. I wired the grocer in Coombe Tracey, and in minutes, received a reply. 'Cannot attend today will arrive tomorrow thank you kind sir for your attention.'

There was nothing to do about it. I lunched alone on beer and sausage, and was in my chair at two. Jeremy only nodded at the news. When the proceedings got underway, he called Inspector Brogarth of Scotland Yard as our final witness.

Brogarth was asked if there was further information concerning the whereabouts of Mrs Lyons. 'Nothing at all, Mr Holmes,' the large man with the small voice said. 'Not a trace of the woman.'

He was asked what steps had been taken to find her. 'A warrant to search was obtained, and her lodgings have been searched, Mr Holmes.' Brogarth had looked for clues that might indicate where Mrs Lyons had gone, but found nothing. He had also searched for documents bearing the names Jack Stapleton, Christian Vandeleur, or Rodger Baskerville. 'There was an article cut out of a magazine,' he said, 'the *New Review*, of some months ago. It was written by Professor Christian Vandeleur. Nothing more.'

He had also gone to Baring's Bank, where Mrs Lyons kept an account. After producing a warrant, he was informed that Mrs Lyons had withdrawn all the funds from her account at ten that morning. She had also maintained a private box in the bank's vault, which she had emptied.

Inspector Brogarth was asked to stand down.

'Have you anything further, Mr Holmes?' Lord Arlington asked.

The Widow, with some urgency, motioned for Jeremy. 'May I talk for a moment with my client, My Lord?'

'You may.'

'My Lords,' Jeremy said, after returning to his place, 'The Widow would inform the jurors that they should attach no significance to the article, cut out of *New Review*, by Inspector Brogarth. It was she, The Widow, who gave it to Mrs Lyons.'

'Do you have anything further, Mr Holmes?'

Jeremy looked at me, and I shook my head in the negative. 'No, My Lord.'

Lord Arlington addressed the jurors. 'The evidence in this cause is before you, gentlemen,' he said. 'There will now be the summations of the evidence by the learned counsel for the defence, and for the Crown. You may proceed, Mr Holmes.'

Chapter 25

As Jeremy stood and faced the jurors, his eyes did not focus on them. They surrounded the jury with what I imagined were his visions of another time. 'All of us in the Kingdom, from the lowliest poor beggar to our gracious Queen, hunger for justice,' he said. 'Though trials in ancient times were often hideous ordeals for the accused, we believe them now to be models of fairness.'

He glanced at the dock. 'Yet they remain ordeals. Observe The Widow, on display. For two days last week and two more in this one, she has publicly endured our scrutiny. We have watched her soundless cry, seen her shrink with terror, followed her eyes when they tried to hide, and been in the presence of her radiant beauty.' He brought their attention back to him. 'No one of you--no one in this great chamber-- wants to snuff out the vibrance of her life.' His shoulders hunched inward, in the manner of one who would shield himself from a beating. 'For if she is innocent, can one imagine a more hideous end to the ordeal of The Widow, than her execution?'

The only sound in the hall were the tips of Sir Percival's fingers, drumming on the bench. Jeremy waited, and they stopped. 'I ask you, when you look at her, to see more than the loveliness which she cannot hide. Look deep into the source of her radiance. See her heart.'

The Widow blushed. Then with an honest expression, from her chair in the dock, she opened her heart to them. The jurors were in the arms of a *Madonna*. She held them, as she would a child. 'Look carefully at her, gentleman. Do you see a woman who has the capacity to kill?' One could feel their eyes examine her. 'I submit to you, and the evidence will show, that she cannot.

'The evidence has shown, however, that she can lie. For she lied to the authorities, when questioned by them on that dreadful morning.' The Widow blushed once more, and nodded her head in obvious agreement. 'That is her crime, gentlemen. Not murder. Do not condemn this woman to the gallows, for her lies.'

Two of the jurors slumped in their chairs and looked away. Others wore grim expressions, but all were quite willing to listen.

'On twenty-nine September at three in the morning, when Scotland Yard was brought in to investigate a murder, it seemed to them the most obvious of crimes. The Widow had been found an hour before, dragging the body of a man into an alleyway. She offered an explanation to Inspector Lestrade that might charitably be regarded as fanciful, and became entangled in a web of lies. Her lies made the obvious seem even more so. It was obvious to them that her fanciful account of the crime was yet another lie.'

He turned toward Sir Guthrie. 'My learned colleague will acquaint you with her lies. I would suggest to you, however, that this cause might have chartered a different course, had her fanciful account been considered objectively. Allow me to strip away the weeds of exaggeration that have grown round it, and show only the core.'

Jeremy sipped water from a cup. 'The Widow claimed to have been confronted in her office by the victim at seven that fateful evening. A short while after, her husband knocked on the front door. She opened it to him, they talked and embraced, and she went back in. She found the victim on the cutting room floor, bleeding hideously from a wound in his throat, and went to him. While so engaged, someone wearing a black cape tossed cutting room shears near her, and fled.'

He smiled. 'Could anyone be expected to believe such an incredible tale?' Jeremy asked the jurors. 'One would have to believe an unknown assailant, hidden away in the store, seized precisely the right moment to strike the lethal blow. Yet if one of the inspectors had considered the possibility that perhaps there *was* such a person, what a different shore he would have steered for.

'He would have *hunted* for evidence of the supposed unknown assailant. That was not done. There was no more than a peremptory, dismissive consideration given to that possibility. The minds of the inspectors had fastened already onto the obvious.

'Dr Mortimer told you of a curtain stained with blood, as though the shears with which the victim had been stabbed had been wiped clean. But it was not found by Scotland Yard. Rather, it came to light two days ago. Does not the finding suggest the presence of another person? If The Widow had done this, why would she go clear across the room, to a dressing room curtain, to clean them off?'

The question did not excite interest, which was clear enough. 'Perhaps you are reluctant to give credence to the finding,' Jeremy said. 'Sir Guthrie was quite off-hand over it, and admittedly, it is subject to other explanations. Yet had fresh blood been found on the curtain that morning, the finding would have been most suggestive. And *that* is what I ask you to consider.'

The vibrance in his voice had grown. 'What avenues might an inspector have gone down, before the foot-prints were gone, had the possibility of an unknown assailant been considered with the objectivity it deserved? What should an inspector have done? Certainly he would have investigated the possibility that the assailant worked for The Widow. He would have treated all the employees as potential suspects, and he would have questioned them. Ask yourselves, gentlemen. What might an inspector have learned at the beginning of this investigation, had he questioned Mrs Laura Lyons?'

I did not have the fortitude Jeremy had when faced with painful moments. I sought solace. At his mention of the woman whom he would have the jurors believe was the murderess, but to me was still a sweet perfume, I pulled forth my flask and bandaged over the pain.

He went on to suggest that Mrs Lyons might have been asked to account for her movements in the evening hours of 28 September. And *she* might have been tangled in a web of lies, for the inspector for Scotland Yard would most certainly have questioned others, to verify the account of her movements.

'What might Mrs Thimble, her landlady, have said *then*, had she been asked?' Jeremy asked the jurors. 'Might not she have remembered, if asked two months ago, whether Mrs Lyons wore a black cape when she had come in the evening before the murder was known? And after Mrs Thimble took the black cape out of the trash in early October, would she not have told the inspector that she had it? What would he have asked of Mrs Lyons *then*? "Why did you throw your cape away, Mrs Lyons? Had you read something in the news, of a person wearing a black cape?"'

Two weeks later, Jeremy continued, the Crown learned the true identity of the victim. Did they consider the possibility then, if perhaps there was truly an unknown assailant? 'Not in the least. Their minds had closed on that subject. The case was already solved. No longer did they believe that The Widow had murdered her lover, because now they had a more compelling motive. She murdered one husband, to keep his very existence from a better one. The Widow had stabbed Rodger Baskerville in the throat with cutting shears, in the belief that Peter, Lord Russell, would never know.

'Yet the cause was now a vastly different one,' Jeremy said. 'Rodger Baskerville had *lived*. He had not perished in the Grimpen Mire, as all had supposed. Why did they not look again, at the motives of others? Was The Widow the only person in all of England who might have wished that Rodger Baskerville was dead?'

The jurors agreed with the comment, judging from the manner in which they nodded their heads. 'Should not the case of the hound of the Baskervilles have been looked into again, with fresh eyes? For Rodger Baskerville had not died in the Grimpen Mire. He had escaped not only the clutches of the sand, but also from Dartmoor. Should not inquiries have been made into the manner of his escape? What might the inspectors have found *then*, had they looked? What connections might they have drawn between those who were in Dartmoor in October, 1889, and London in September, 1891?'

Jeremy paused to assess the impact of his argument on the jurors. They were listening.

'Most certainly, Baskerville would have needed assistance from someone, until it was safe enough for him to travel,' Jeremy said. 'Would he have gone to his wife for help?' The jurors close to me smiled at that. 'Then, to whom? Dr Mortimer? Sir Henry?' Each suggestion was met with dismay. 'Then where did he go? Who could the man have induced, to help him? Did any of the inspectors at Scotland Yard ask themselves that question? They did not.'

The attitudes of the jurors had become thoughtful. One could see it in the way in which chins were stroked by hands, and heads were held at an angle.

'Might an answer have been found to that question? Might not it be found even now? For only two years have passed, gentlemen. Surely someone could throw light on the subject.'

He gestured toward the empty witness box. 'Shall we ask Mrs Lyons? Unfortunately, we cannot. She packed up a bag quite hurriedly last night we were told, then withdrew all her money from the bank when it opened this morning, and has not been seen nor heard from since. Is it not obvious that she has fled from this courtroom, to avoid that very question, as well as others? She had lived in Coombe Tracey, quite close to Baskerville Hall and the Grimpen Mire. Would not Rodger Baskerville have gone to her? He knew where she lived. He had been there before, and had even proposed marriage to her. Did he go to her again? Did he work his charms upon her a second time, with false promises? Was it she who gave him safe haven?'

I thought I saw agreement, drawing the jurors together.

'Sir Guthrie will tell you that such conjecture is not worthy of your consideration,' Jeremy said. 'But on five occasions last summer, always late at night and well past the hour when the landlady would retire, a detective watched Rodger Baskerville let himself into an apartment building at Granville Place near Portman Square. Mrs Lyons had her lodgings in that building. And that is not conjecture. That is clear evidence that Mrs Lyons was with Rodger Baskerville this summer on at least five occaions, before he died. She knew he had not been devoured by the Grimpen Mire, and that is a fact, gentlemen. Not conjecture.'

The jurors were most attentive to his words.

'What are the questions Mrs Lyons would have been

asked, if she were here? Put yourself in my place, and think of what your questions would have been.'

He faced the witness box, as though addressing a person sitting there. 'When did Rodger Baskerville first visit you, Mrs Lyons, in your lodgings on Granville Place, near Portman Square? Wasn't it well before Detective Madan Asan began to follow him?'

He turned to the jurors.   'She would deny all knowledge, but you would have the opportunity to assess her credibility. A tell-tale twitch, eyes that show a dishonest heart. Watch her carefully,' Jeremy said, then faced the witness box.

'Mrs Lyons, on Friday night, twenty-five September, the evidence has shown quite clearly that Rodger Baskerville was with you many hours. Did you tell him that on the coming Monday, The Widow would stay the night in *Fashions Sabor*, then leave for Paris on the morning of the next day? Was there something in his manner that aroused your suspicion of him? Did he ask you one too many questions about her?

'Did Rodger Baskerville find refuge in your lodgings at Coombe Tracey, immediately after the horror he had inflicted on his cousin, Sir Henry Baskerville? What did he promise you, to re-gain your trust? Did he promise a second time to marry you?

'Did Baskerville get the key to *Fashions Sabor Brazilenos* from you? Were you hiding there, perhaps in a closet in the cutting room, on the evening of twenty-eight September? When he used the key and came inside, were you there too?   Did you overhear him when he spoke to The Widow? Did you see him when he tried to touch The Widow, to feel his son in her womb?'

Jeremy turned toward the jurors. 'More conjecture? Perhaps. But did any of you doubt The Widow, when she told you of Rodger Baskerville's mad plan? He would compel her to go with him to South Africa, then after a suitable time had gone by and Sir Henry Baskerville had been disposed of, he would claim Baskerville Hall as his, by right of inheritance. Had he filled the heart of Mrs Lyons with another plan? One that would bring to Mrs Lyons all that she wanted in life?'

Jeremy paused long enough to sip from a glass of water. 'Gentlemen,' he said, facing the jurors, 'I invite you to consider that The Widow's fanciful tale was true. There was indeed an "unknown assailant", and it was Mrs Lyons. She knew every corner of the store, better even than The Widow. Mrs Lyons knew where to hide. And she did so on the evening of twenty-eight September, no doubt in the hope that Rodger Baskerville would not come. But his actions had made her suspicious of him, so she waited in secret. Not even The Widow knew she was there.

'Then Baskerville boldly pushed into the store through the front door, opening the door with the key Mrs Lyons had given him. What did Mrs Lyons hear, after Baskerville had let himself in? Enough to realize he had wronged her again? That as before, he had used her?'

He turned in another direction, as though watching a stage. 'Do you see her? She is seething with rage! For he has lied to her a second time! She knows he never intended to keep his promises to her. She knows that as before, they were ruses, employed by him so that he could use her to get what he wanted. She knows that he wanted not her, but The Widow!

'Watch now, as The Widow answers the door at the knock of Lord Russell. Mrs Lyons is behind a curtain in the cutting room, consumed with hate. Baskerville slips into the cutting room, to avoid being seen by Lord Russell. Mrs Lyons peeks at him through the folds of the curtain. Baskerville listens intently to The Widow, as she talks briefly with the man she loves. Mrs Lyons silently comes out of her hiding-place and picks up a cutting-shears. She moves quietly, in stealth, toward Baskerville.

'But wait. This is a man of extraordinary physical ability, with the balance to skip through the Grimpen Mire in deep fog. Could he have been killed by Mrs Lyons if he had so much as a hint of her intent? He hears her perhaps, and turns his head toward her, but sees not the rage. Her presence is a trifling matter to him, for he knows she will do what he tells her. He cautions her to be still as he again focuses his attention on The Widow and Lord Russell--when all that bottled-up rage in Mrs Lyons is unleashed. With one vicious thrust, quite possibly with her eyes shut tight, she stabs him in the neck.

'And then she hides, in a dressing room covered by a curtain. As The Widow is confronted with the horror of the last moments of a man's life, Mrs Lyons cleans off the shears, using the curtain. Then she drops the shears near The Widow, and makes her escape.'

'Forgive me, Mr Holmes,' Sir Percival said, 'but I must interrupt. It hardly seems that you are engaged in a summation of the evidence. Confine your remarks to the evidence, if you will.'

Lord Arlington was clearly appalled at the comment. He faced Sir Percival and withered him with a frown. 'My learned colleague does not speak for this court,' he said. 'Mr Holmes, you may continue.'

'May I respectfully enquire as to whether I might ask the jurors to draw inferences, favorable to the accused, from the evidence?' Jeremy asked of Lord Arlington, knowing full well that he had that right.

'You may indeed,' Lord Arlington said. 'Please proceed.'

Jeremy turned to the jurors. 'Gentlemen, when The Widow told you of the anguish and pain she felt as the life of Rodger Baskerville left him, was that an act? I submit to you that it was not. It was evidence of her innate goodness.

'You have been with her four days now. You have felt that quality in her, and have seen it. Her innate goodness is a *fact* in this cause, gentlemen. Every witness who has touched on her essential goodness, beginning with Constable Firstson, has quite glowed with sincerity, when talking of it. And from that fact, you may infer that she cannot kill. Believe that about her,' he said, with passionate intensity. 'I submit to you that the woman who stands before you in the dock could *never* have stabbed a man in the neck with a cutting shears.

'But could a woman who had been twice betrayed by him have done so?' The heads of many of the jurors nodded up and down.

Jeremy gestured toward the table of exhibits, where the offending shears lay. 'The evidence quite clearly has shown that the victim in this case was stabbed in the throat with these shears, and it was done with enough force to sever the carotid artery. You may infer from that fact that the person who stabbed Rodger Baskerville in the throat was overwhelmed with rage.

'Would that have been The Widow, a woman of innate goodness, who grieved when the man died? Or Mrs Lyons, a woman twice betrayed?'

A weariness settled over Jeremy. He looked at The Widow, who smiled at him. You have done all you could do, her expression seemed to say. Thank you.

'I beg of you,' he said. 'Do not send The Widow to the gallows for a murder she did not commit.'

He sat down.

The Attorney-General stood before them then, at first as a man awakened from a deep sleep. Quietly, he spoke to the jurors of his deep immersion in the drama that he had just witnessed, and had enjoyed. He had been thrilled by the performance of his learned colleague, enacted and played with such brilliance. Extracting oneself from its influence was a bit like pulling oneself out of the Grimpen Mire.

But soon, Sir Guthrie had the jurors laughing. After which he spoke to them for more than an hour. It was as though he would drown the visions Jeremy had etched in their minds in an ocean of ridicule.

First, during the trial, his learned friend had singled out Peter, Lord Russell, as the murderer of Rodger Baskerville. But that ship had gone down with the weight of the facts. Now we have another suspect. What if the trial were to go on for another week? Might he then fasten the blame on one of you?

With the same sardonic tone he attacked the evidence of Madan Asan, whom learned counsel had portrayed as an assassin during the trial. Now he has elevated him to an Oriental seer. There was no real proof that Rodger Baskerville saw, or stayed, with Mrs Lyons at her lodgings. None. Who knows why the victim had been to the building on Granville Place near Portman Square? Was hers the only apartment there?

He supposes too much, Sir Guthrie insisted. 'Let us suppose that a spear was thrown in Africa,' he said. 'Let us suppose it was caught in a wind, and lifted in the ocean of air above the clouds, then dropped over London toward a store on Marylebone Lane. Let us suppose it bounded off the flooring and then, as though aimed, pierced our wretched victim in the throat, severing his carotid artery.' The layers of supposition needed by learned counsel to reach his last selection as perpetrator, 'though perhaps not quite so outlandish,' was much the same. The point of his 'parable' was simple enough. 'You have a clear duty to decide this case in its *facts*. It is *not* you duty to suppose.'

They were to consider and evaluate the evidence before them, and nothing more. As his learned colleague had suggested, the evidence at first blush was quite obvious. 'Does its obvious nature render it in some inexplicable fashion, false?' He paused, as though to give them the time to work through the question. 'Of course, it does not. The evidence is obvious for the most obvious of reasons. *Because it is obvious.*'

He showed the palms of his hands to the jurors. 'How can evidence be more *obvious*' and he stressed the oft-repeated word, 'than what the Crown has presented? The accused was caught while attempting to dispose of the body of a man at two o'clock in the morning. She offered a fairy-tale, to explain it. And can one imagine a more compelling motive for the murder of the man who had been her husband? One simply cannot.'

He reminded them of all her lies. One by one, he trotted them out and asked the jury to see each of them for what they were. They were lies. His learned friend would have you excuse all of them, because it was not in her nature to kill.

'Poppycock.'

With all due respect to his most learned friend, he suggested to the jurors that they should not be dissuaded from their duty, 'which is *obvious*. Your duty is as *obvious* as is the evidence against the accused!'

He asked them not to be dissuaded from their duty by sympathy for the accused. 'As a matter of law, you must not allow sympathy to influence your decision, and as a matter of simple decency, she does not deserve it. Her first line of defence was that Peter, Lord Russell, had done this murder.

Now she would have you believe it was her dear friend!'

Lord Arlington had little to add to the summations of the barristers. He said only that the evidence quite clearly showed that Rodger Baskerville had been deliberately stabbed in the throat, severing his carotid artery and causing his death, and that The Widow had been caught in the act of attempting to cover up the crime. But as to whether she was guilty of his murder, he would leave that in the capable hands of the jurors.

As to the charge of bigamy, however, he advised them that she was guilty as a matter of law. There was no dispute over the facts. She may well have believed that she was a widow when she entered into marriage with Lord Russell. But after learning that her first husband was alive, she knew that her marriage to Lord Russell was unlawful. Had she immediately extricated herself from that unlawful marriage, she might well have been innocent of the charge. But she did not do so. She chose to remain in that bigamous marriage, with knowledge of her deceit, for several months. To the charge of bigamy, Lord Arlington directed the jurors to return a verdict of guilt.

The jurors huddled together in their box, protected from unwanted approach or interference by the bailiff. Many spectators in Sessions House remained, but most of them filed out. After thirty minutes had elapsed, it became apparent that there was disagreement among the jurors and they wanted guidance.

Lord Arlington suggested that they select a spokesman so that he might enquire into the difficulty. A short while later, one was appointed.

All who had remained in Sessions House were still. 'Let the spokesman stand,' Lord Arlington said.

A large man in the middle of the box rose to his feet.

'As to the charge of murder, have you reached a verdict?'

'We have, Your Lordship,' the man said.

'Then what can possibly be your difficulty?' Lord Arlington asked.

The man hesitated, and looked to his fellows. They seemed to urge him on. 'It's--you see,' he said, with an absence of bravado, 'that other charge, My Lord, that we cannot agree on. The charge of bigamy.'

'You've been directed to find a verdict of guilty on that count, my good man.'

'Some of us can't do that, Your Lordship,' the fellow said. 'And none of us think it's right.'

Lord Arlington smiled at Jeremy, as though to congratulate him. Sir Percival did not. 'To the charge of murder then, my good man,' Lord Arlington said. 'The one you agree on. What is your verdict?'

'We don't believe it was her who done this, Your Lordship,' he said. 'Not guilty.'

Chapter 26

Spring had come to Trafalgar Square, and with it, hundreds and perhaps thousands of pigeons. Societies have grown round the flea-infested pests, to protect them and feed them. Their excrement was not yet a thing of wonder, however. Not even the most strident of pigeon lovers would choose to sit in it.

I cleared a bench of the stuff and sat down. In front of me stood Nelson's Column, upon which a squadron of pigeons were perched and squirting their juices on the people below. Such was my mood that it amused me.

In my hand I held a letter which I had not yet read. It had come to me from Angers, in France, though the name of the sender was not appended. However, I recognized the handwriting on the envelope. It was that of Laura Lyons.

After the jurors could not agree on the count of bigamy, Sir Guthrie--to the applause of all--requested the Court to dismiss the charge. Soon, The Widow was back in her store. Once again it was a place of high fashion, though it was rumoured that she would not stay. Sir Henry Baskerville was quite attentive, but she was not drawn to him. Lord Russell had also made overtures, but she wanted nothing to do with him. An explorer, just back from the jungles of Africa, held her interest, however. He intended to conquer the huge cap of ice that covered the North Pole.

Since the trial, my breathing had descended into sighs. But as I opened the letter, the fragrant scent of my dear Laura invaded me once again, and I breathed it in. Yet I knew she cared nothing for me. 'You are a tool to her, Edward,' Jeremy had said.

My dear Edward

Before you read another word, I have a request of you. Please pull your flask from your coat, and open it up, and lift it toward me in Angers. It is quite beautiful here. The city is aptly called The City of Flowers.

I did as she directed, of course.

You must come to visit me, dear man. I should so enjoy a drop of Irish whiskey with you! My address is as shown, above.

You cannot know the joy I felt, on reading of the outcome of the trial. The Bastard is indeed a magician, and I was delighted to learn that Beryl did not face the prospect of the gallows! Let me add what I am sure you must know of me. Beryl was never in danger of hanging. Had The Bastard not succeeded in gaining her acquittal (which I never doubted he would do!) then I would have fled from London and sent a letter to the Attorney-General with convincing proofs of her innocence. Jack wrote to me from South Africa on three occasions, and I had the presence of mind to keep those letters. I would have enclosed one of them in my letter to Sir Guthrie, along with my confession. Needless to say, I am delighted that it did not come to that!

Should you see Beryl, will you please let her know that I think of her often, and love her still?

Edward, I would like to engage your services. I have inherited the estate of my father, James Frankland, which-- though it will not make me rich--should be sufficient to provide for my needs until such time as I can re-establish myself in business. But there are details of a legal nature to attend to, before it is of any use to me. May I turn them over to your capable hands? I should like to liquidate the estate, which consists of his residence in Dartmoor, and some securities.

However, there are problems. I applied for letters testamentary last summer, but have not been to the court in

Exeter to obtain them. And as you know, my father had a somewhat litigious turn of mind. There are seven liens against the property which must be resolved. Your fees, if any, will be paid by the estate.

Can you also make some inquiries for me? I understand from the news of the trial that a warrant was issued for my arrest, in that I did not appear in court to testify. Of course, I only followed your advice, but that probably does not constitute a sufficient legal excuse. Be that as it may. Can you determine if the warrant is still active? I should like to return to England, but not if it means that I should lose my freedom!

There is also the question of Jack. Perhaps I am merely grasping after straws, but isn't there a doctrine of law that would prevent another trial for his murder? After one person is charged and tried, can the Crown charge another? All I know of the law, after having lived many years with my father, is that the law is a peculiar animal, filled with odd little twists and bits, known as doctrines. Is there one of that kind?

If that is mere wishful thinking on my part, then I must assume the worst: that the Crown has the right to bring me to trial. But though they have the right, do they intend to pursue the matter? I should dearly like to know if Scotland Yard has re-opened an investigation into his death, and if they have, whether or not I have been targetted by them. Would you be so kind as to give me the benefit of your thoughts on these questions?

Do come see me, dear man. There is a wine bar near my lodging with an extraordinary selection of ports. I would love to expand your tastes in fine beverages!

With love and affection,   Laura

I returned the letter to its envelope, put it away in a pocket, and pulled out my flask. After lifting it in the general direction of Angers, I enjoyed another long and delicious toast to my former drinking companion, then got up and began the walk to the club.

Since the trial, I had dragged about London, not caring whether I lived or died. How could I maintain my affections for a woman whom I knew was a murderess? But the letter from Laura was medicine to me, and there was buoyancy in my step. I smiled at the pretty girls, and touched my cap to them..

Jeremy was not in our corner when I arrived. Had he been there, I would have gone up to my rooms. He would not see the letter from Laura, or know about it. Nor would he know of my response. I began writing on a legal tablet.

My dear Laura

Thank you so much for your letter. It was a comfort to find that you are safe, and to learn of your address in Angers.

I would cherish your words forever and hold the letter next to my heart, but cannot. I have given it to Inspector Lestrade, of Scotland Yard.

Let me hasten to add that your fears are not groundless. There remains an active warrant out for your arrest, and Scotland Yard has indeed re-opened its investigation into the murder of Rodger Baskerville. And you, my dear, are the prime suspect.

Incidentally, their case against you would have been quite circumstantial and rather weak. But that is no longer the case. You have confessed the crime to me, and that should make it immeasurably stronger. They know now too of letters to you, from the man you murdered, after he was presumed to have died. The French police may, at this moment, be on your doorstep.

You suggest in your letter that your reason for departing in such haste was my doing, as though to threaten me over it. I

shall let the Yarders make of it what they will. You also would
have me believe that you would have intervened to prevent the
execution of The Widow. My dear Laura, I do not believe you.
What of those lines on your face, seen by Jeremy as lines of
torment? Would you have suffered them, had you intended to do
as you say?

Jeremy knows, incidentally, that he should never have
interrupted his examination of you. It was his duty to crucify
you, not give you an opportunity to escape. But that is his
nature. He has no love for you, but cannot abide the death
penalty, even when inflicted on those who are deserving of it.

Dear one, I feel a delicious joy at this moment, not unlike
the joy you felt when you drove cutting shears into the throat of
Rodger Baskerville. I am free of you. I am no longer your tool.
Most sincerely, Edward

I sealed the letter in an envelope, addressed it to her, and later that day, posted it.

That night, I enjoyed the inane conversation of my fellow Bastriches, in the hall, by the fire. 'What is that in your hand, Edward?' one of them asked me. He sniffed the air. 'A scented letter? From a woman then. Is it a love letter?'

'Impossible,' another Bastriche said. 'Who could love him? Not even his mother.'

'You would be surprised,' I said, holding the letter to my nose. 'She is a woman of passion. As a gentleman, I can say no more.'

I tossed the letter from my dear Laura into the fire.

Also from MX Publishing

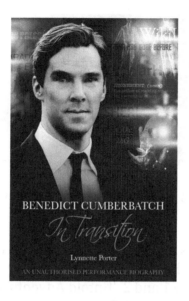

MX Publishing is the world's largest specialist Sherlock Holmes publisher, with over a hundred titles and fifty authors creating the latest in Sherlock Holmes fiction and non-fiction. From traditional short stories and novels to travel guides and quiz books, MX Publishing cater for all Holmes fans. The collection includes leading titles such as *Benedict Cumberbatch In Transition* and *The Norwood Author* the winner of the 2011 Howlett Award (Sherlock Holmes Book of the Year). MX Publishing also has one of the largest communities of Holmes fans on Facebook with regular contributions from dozens of authors.

www.mxpublishing.com

  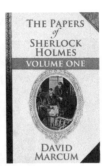

London, 1920: Boston-bred Enoch Hale, working as a reporter for the Central News Syndicate, arrives on the scene shortly after a music hall escape artist is found hanging from the ceiling in his dressing room. What at first appears to be a suicide turns out to be murder.

Also coming in 2014 the second in the Enoch Hale series – 'The Poisoned Penman'.

Also from MX Pubilishing

"Phil Growick's, 'The Secret Journal of Dr Watson', is an adventure which takes place in the latter part of Holmes and Watson's lives. They are entrusted by HM Government (although not officially) and the King no less to undertake a rescue mission to save the Romanovs, Russia's Royal family from a grisly end at the hand of the Bolsheviks. There is a wealth of detail in the story but not so much as would detract us from the enjoyment of the story. Espionage, counter-espionage, the ace of spies himself, double-agents, double-crossers...all these flit across the pages in a realistic and exciting way. All the characters are extremely well-drawn and Mr Growick, most importantly, does not falter with a very good ear for Holmesian dialogue indeed. Highly recommended. A five-star effort."

The Baker Street Society

Also published in Italian, Russian, and audio versions and the sequel 'The Revenge of Sherlock Holmes' is released in spring 2014.

www.mxpublishing.com

Links

MX Publishing are proud to support the Save Undershaw campaign – the campaign to save and restore Sir Arthur Conan Doyle's former home. Undershaw is where he brought Sherlock Holmes back to life, and should be preserved for future generations of Holmes fans.

SaveUndershaw
www.saveundershaw.com

Sherlockology
www.sherlockology.com

MX Publishing
www.mxpublishing.com

You can read more about Sir Arthur Conan Doyle and Undershaw in Alistair Duncan's book (share of royalties to the Undershaw Preservation Trust) – *An Entirely New Country* and in the amazing compilation *Sherlock's Home – The Empty House* (all royalties to the Trust).

CPSIA information can be obtained at www.ICGtesting.com
Printed in the USA
LVOW01s1353270714

396236LV00001B/132/P